A SUMMER OF SMOKE AND SIN

TJ NICHOLS

A SUMMER OF SMOKE AND SIN

To stop a serial killer a detective will need to explore his own vices...

Nathanial Bayard wants nothing more than to find the nobleman creating snuff pornography. If he fails, his career in the recently formed Nobility Task Force will be over and as the youngest son he'll be forced to obey his father and join the church. But a life of celibacy doesn't appeal. Nathanial has never even kissed another man, fearing for his soul and his reputation.

Jericho Fulbright has never lived a wholesome life. After behavior unbecoming he was discharged from the army and sent home in disgrace. His inventor and nouveau riche father refused to have anything to do with him, so Jericho turned to what he knew best: opium, gambling and sex.

As the owner of the Jericho Rose, a club for gentlemen who like men, he enjoys a certain notoriety. Some would say he has a golden tongue, but the truth is a succubus lives within him feeding on souls. Once he needed her help, now she is a burden that keeps him from getting close to anyone.

After the unfortunate death of a young noble man in Jericho's bed, Nathanial is sent to investigate. He is scandalized and intrigued by Jericho, but soon realizes that Jericho could be exactly who he needs to help break the snuff case. Together they are drawn into a web of lies that will result in Jericho facing prison unless Nathanial can unmask the real creator of the snuff, a man with rank and privileges that reaches almost to the King.

HONG KONG, 1904

Sergeant Jericho Fulbright is an irredeemable rogue who takes great pleasure in corrupting the other men of his platoon. He gambles and smokes and his debauchery knows no bounds. He lives only to develop new vices. It is my recommendation that he be discharged from His Majesty's Army and sent home before he brings all Englishmen into disrepute.

— COLONEL RICHARD HESSBOTTEM

1

LONDON 1907

Jericho Fulbright's body was heavy as though he'd taken one too many mouthfuls from the pipe when he knew he had barely taken one. There were parts of his body that ached that most definitely shouldn't be aching. It took two goes to open his eyes, but already the sharp edge of panic was pressing against his throat.

It wasn't just opium that made it hard to wake in the morning.

Jericho glanced across the pillow to see who was in bed with him. Blond hair and smooth skin and not a piece of night wear to be seen. He swallowed and checked his own attire. There was none. With a groan he closed his eyes, suspecting what had happened but having no recollection. His companion didn't stir.

With a hesitant hand he reached out and touched his friend's back. Doxley's skin was cool. Jericho jerked his hand back, even though he'd stopped fearing death several years ago; he'd had to as it happened all too frequently.

"Damn you, Eulalia. Why him?" Guilt twisted and writhed as it always did after killing, even if this had been out of his control.

Stephan Doxley had been young and beautiful with a smile that could raise the most shipwrecked spirits. He shouldn't be cold and dead. He should never have been in Jericho's bed. Jericho remembered inviting the young lord-in-waiting for a private drink. There had been no coyness about what either of them had wanted. Jericho knew how to be careful, how to take some pleasure without it being fatal for his lover. However sometime after the first brandy his memory of the evening vanished.

Eulalia had taken over and stolen her supper.

He squeezed his eyes closed tighter. It was his fault Doxley was dead. He'd known Eulalia needed feeding; the fever had started two days prior and last night every man who'd smiled at him had felt like a possible conquest. Lust had conquered his body and then wrecked vengeance on the unfortunate man now lying next to him. Today it left him defeated and to deal with the aftermath.

Inside him Eulalia purred with satisfaction.

He was too reliant on her gift, but without her golden tongue he'd be in the poor house or prison. Probably prison. He could still end up in prison if someone found him sleeping next to a corpse; they would assume it was far worse than it was. Though what it had been was still a two-year prison sentence.

And wouldn't the scandal sheets have a delightful time with this bit of gossip?

Jericho untangled himself from the sheets and pulled on his neatly folded, obviously unworn pajamas. They were a scandalously bright, but he was no lord who needed an air of dignity. He'd left his dignity in Hong Kong the day he was discharged; not even Eulalia's gift could save him that day. His father has disowned him shortly after, around the time he returned to London.

He pushed aside thoughts of his father to finish dressing and start planning. Suitably attired in yellow pajamas and a blue floral robe he turned his attention to the man...barely a man. Doxley was all of twenty. Even in death, he was pretty. Regret at his folly pinched hard and for a moment Jericho couldn't draw breath. He should've fed Eulalia sooner, then Doxley would've been alive and they'd be waking up reminiscing about last night.

Usually when he needed to feed Eulalia, he scoured the streets for the kind of man that wouldn't be missed. The kind who brutalized others for sport. If he had to feed the demon inside of him, he could at least do the citizens of London a service. Not that they would thank him if they knew.

It wouldn't take long for someone to wonder where Doxley was, less time for them to know he was here. There was no point in hiding that. He closed his eyes and pinched the bridge of his nose. His head pounded like a dozen horses were using his skull as a racetrack. Just how much had he drunk last night while Eulalia was in control?

"If I finally get to have sex, and commit a dozen crimes in the process, it would be nice to remember the good bits," he muttered. But he never did. When she was in control, he had no memory of what she did with his body. Which was disconcerting at the best of times.

While male-marriage had been brought into law at the turn of the century, even if the man were still alive, this was still a crime as what they did was out of wedlock. While few among the nobility were prosecuted for slipping and landing on a stiff prick, people like Jericho would feel the full force of the boot of the law. Too many would delight in seeing him get strung up for murder.

He tried to stay out of the scandal sheets, but somehow his name was always there. His stepsister's debut had been sullied by the mention of her irredeemable brother, and he'd never even met her. His stepmother had made sure he'd been shipped off to the best school his father could afford and from there, to the military, before her daughter was born.

He looked too much like his mother for his father to tolerate looking at him.

He brushed a lock of Doxley's hair off his face and let the knife of guilt twist deeper. This was not the first death to occur in the Jericho Rose, though the first he had been responsible for. Last winter a man had smoked too much opium and had fallen into a slumber he'd never awoken from. There was no reason to assume this young man hadn't suffered a similar fate.

Although he couldn't remain in Jericho's bed—that would lead to far too many awkward questions. Nor could Doxley be found naked. Jericho needed to dress him. He was sure it had been more fun removing the clothes.

Wrestling the young man's undershorts and trousers on was not the best way to start the morning, but it was quite the workout accompanied with many muttered apologies to Doxley even though his soul was long gone. Quietly Jericho crept out of his room, hoping the housekeeper was still asleep. He slunk through his house like a thief then unlocked the door between his private rooms and the club. A cursory check of the premises revealed no one had been in to clean up yet. Perfect.

He went back to his room and hefted Stephan over his shoulder. Dead men weighed so much more than the living—or was that the weight of guilt?

"A little help, Eulalia, since you caused this problem," he mumbled. He was sure he heard the succubus's laughter in his mind. But he wasn't Bedlam bound; he was just occasionally thoroughly possessed.

The demon's strength flowed through him and he managed to get to the club and deposit Stephan in a quiet corner where it was likely that he could've been overlooked at closing time. Jericho hadn't been around for the closing. How many people had seen Stephan leave with him for that private drink?

He shoved the thought aside and draped the man against the sofa in the smaller room as though he had been sitting on the floor and had nodded off, then he walked back to the door to make sure none of the body could be seen. Excellent work, considering he'd had no tea and his head felt decidedly tender.

"Up early, Mr. Fulbright."

Jericho flinched as though the housekeeper had slapped him on the arse. How much had she seen? "Just opening up the curtains."

He walked in and did just that. When he turned, Doxley was visible. He stepped back, hand to his throat as though deeply shocked. He'd honed his acting skills out of need.

"Whatever is the matter?" Edwina bustled over and stopped. "Oh, dear Lord. My Jeremy said they was all gone when he locked up."

"Clearly not." The lie burned his tongue. He hated doing this to his staff; Jeremy would blame himself for days. "Best send for the coppers." There went any hope he had of enjoying a quiet breakfast. Now he'd have to play the devastated owner instead of gutted lover. Looking too comfortable with death was a sure way to attract suspicion. "Make sure they send the Nobility Task Force. I think that one has blue blood."

A MESSENGER BIRD rang the bell announcing its arrival. Nathanial Bayard glanced up from his tea and toast—he'd never been one to tolerate a large breakfast. A message arriving this early never brought good news.

His butler came in holding the metal bird. "A message, Sir."

"Thank you, Godfrey." Nathanial took the bird and saw it bore the crest of the Nobility Task Force. He winced. What party had turned sour last night? Was it an illegal duel? A jewel theft? Perhaps a slighted husband? Or a gaming debt long overdue? He turned the dials to his pin code and the bird's belly opened. He unfurled the message.

Death at Jericho Rose. Arrive at your earliest convenience.

Death…murder or natural? At the Jericho Rose it could be either. While the place wasn't known for violence it made a regular appearance in the scandal sheets for other activities, which of course only increased its popularity among the young lordlings and nouveau riche who liked to rub shoulder with their betters. It was said membership was full and could take a year or more to acquire.

But it wasn't just gambling that went on there. It was a gentlemen's club for men who didn't want to behave like gentlemen. Vices could be dabbled in. Most men grew out of such things when they realized life would slip past them if they remained in an opium infused stupor.

Most.

Some spent every pound they had and wound up in the less respectable dens until death claimed them.

Nathanial folded the paper and slipped it into the pocket of his morning coat. He sipped his cooling tea but left the cold toast.

That the Nobility Task Force had been requested meant that the case involved a nobleman. No noble wanted a commoner poking around their affairs. He smiled. Most nobles didn't want one of their own poking around, until they needed his help. Of course, then they pretended how much they appreciated the work he did, while at the same time wondering why he worked at all.

There wasn't much of anything for the youngest son, and the church was the last place he wanted to spend his days. He shivered and blamed the cool tea. While he could take his automated bicycle to the Jericho Rose, the summer had been unsettled and rainy so it would be better to hail a cab. It was early enough that the streets wouldn't be bustling, yet.

He gathered his satchel and hat. "Don't bother with lunch. I won't be making it home."

Godfrey nodded. "Would you like me to send the bird back?"

Nathanial handed the empty device to Godfrey then stepped outside to another overcast day. A mix of smog and cloud gave the city a grayness that even the sun couldn't break apart. Though perhaps the somber day was appropriate. A man was dead, and someone would have to break it to his family where he'd died.

Nathanial fixed a pleasant smile on his face and shored up his defenses against vice and temptation. He didn't frequent places like the Rose because it was all too easy to slip and fall. While he'd turned down the church as a career, he wasn't ready to cast his soul to hell for temporary pleasure.

Nor would his boss approve of one of his officers succumbing. The men of the Nobility Task Force were supposed to be examples of virtue. But virtue was tedious and gave little earthy reward. His life was so impossibly dull that going to the Jericho Rose for a possible murder investigation was the highlight of his week.

If it was murder, he'd better find the killer. His boss would be none too happy if he failed to close yet another case. He drew in a breath… maybe it wouldn't be murder.

2

*J*ericho didn't bother dressing for the police. He didn't want to appear calm and collected with a dead body in his establishment. However, he was dressed entirely inappropriately to be receiving visitors, so maybe they wouldn't stay long. He walked through the parlor that hadn't been cleaned yet. While he didn't care about a few sticky tables or abandoned card games he did care that there were a few porno pamphlets left around the place.

Gentlemen could acquire their favorite from him; several had standing orders. Otherwise they could be purchased discretely. For those that didn't care to take their pleasure home, there were old editions that Jericho kept on one of the bookcases.

He scooped up two that featured spanking, one with a male and female couple, and the other with two men. From a sofa he rescued another that displayed a rather well-formed man either putting on his clothes or getting out of them. Jericho's lips curved. He didn't have time to stop and reread the story that went with the picture, but his eyes skimmed down the page anyway.

Heat washed through his body and he lifted his gaze before the words could stir him. He was not going to talk to the copper semi aroused. With brisk actions he returned the pamphlets to their place then picked up the display case. Another sheet fell out.

With his arm full of leather-bound display case he bent and paused. The sheet on the floor wasn't the usual material he kept. Had it been included in his last order by accident or had someone brought it in?

He picked up the paper and hoped his first impression had been wrong. On closer inspection, he'd been too kind. A masked man had his hands around the throat of pretty blond woman. She wasn't fighting back...she wasn't doing anything. Her eyes were unfocused, and her hands were limp as though she were dead. If she were dead that made the man even more deplorable.

Jericho shuddered and scrunched up the paper, wanting nothing more to do with death. He'd speak with his supplier and ensure nothing like that came here again. He didn't want any kind of snuff porno, even the faked kind, in his business. He ran a respectable gentleman's club—the kind where men could indulge their other needs if they desired. Which put him at the very fringes of respectability, but also made his business very popular among those with similar tastes.

If other men could run spanking clubs why could he not run his club the way he chose?

There was a knock on the front door and then the rapid footsteps of Edwina as she went to answer the door. And Jericho was still clutching the porno.

He tossed the crumpled sheet into the unlit fire, then stowed the rest in the cupboard where the cards, dice, and other games were stored. There was a secret drawer that just happened to fit the leather-bound display book; getting the cupboard modified had been a very good investment. He shoved it in and closed the drawer and the cupboard then took a seat to play the devastated owner.

His heart was beating fast and he could do with a cup of tea or a brandy. Was it too early for brandy? It was too early for all of this.

Damn you, Eulalia. I would've fed you today and then we wouldn't be in this mess. If I go to prison, you are coming with me.

While she didn't respond her smirk of self-satisfaction reverberated through him.

He should've fed her yesterday the way he'd planned to, but he hated going trawling for her meal. The whole process of dressing rough and going to the docks or the slums and finding someone to kill made him feel less than human. Even though he didn't do the actual killing, he was an accomplice, and no one would believe his demon-based defense. He shuddered. He much preferred to choose the victims than let Eulalia take over. He didn't like her taking over at all, but sometimes it was necessary.

She'd made it necessary this morning. Without her, Jericho wouldn't be able to talk his way out of this trouble. He was sure she'd done it deliberately. She was bored of him and wanted a new host. And while there were times that he was done with carrying a demon around and killing to keep her alive, he needed her. With Eulalia, Jericho could talk his way out of any trouble. He was someone worth knowing and a club worth visiting. Without her he was a no one, a pauper whose father wouldn't even speak to him and certainly wouldn't save him. That was the trade; Eulalia made him someone and he'd gotten used to being notorious. He didn't want to vanish into obscurity and die in a gutter.

The door to the parlor opened and a rather severe elderly gentleman dressed in black from head to toe stood in the doorway. If this man was a crow, Jericho was a peacock.

"Doctor Tallingworth, sir." Edwina gave a little curtsey.

The doctor gave a sniff as though being here was an affront to his senses. That or he was enjoying the lingering scent of opium. Maybe both. The air in the room was still sweet. The windows would usually be open by now to let some fresh air in. "I've come to examine the young man."

Not the body. Did the doctor think that Jericho didn't know death when he saw it?

"He's in the smoking room." Jericho stood.

"Did you try smelling salts?"

"Yes." He'd gone through the motions of trying to revive Doxley while Edwina had sent a mechanical bird to the police station. He couldn't bring himself to use the bird's proper name. He'd also apologized repeatedly to Doxley even though he knew it was foolish. His soul had been devoured hours previously. No heaven or hell for him. Just nothing.

After all these years with Eulalia he wasn't sure he believed that there was anything after death even if one died naturally. Eulalia had never answered his questions about what happened to the souls she took. So, while he believed in demons—that or his mind had broken that night in Hong Kong, and for several weeks he thought that had been the case—he didn't believe in God.

Jericho showed the doctor to the body and the doctor searched for a pulse.

If Doxley had consumed too much opium, his heart could've weakened to the point where it stopped beating. That was a much more believable cause of death than having his soul sucked out of him when he reached completion. Dying in the throes of pleasure wasn't a bad way to die.

A flicker of a memory formed. Of Stephen mounting him, riding him hard. *A thousand curses on you, Eulalia.* He much preferred to do the riding. She responded by letting him feel how much he'd enjoyed it. Ribbons of heat threaded through his veins. His skin flushed and he was ever so glad he took after his mother and lacked the fair complexion of most Englishmen.

The doctor finished his examination of Doxley, or rather the flesh that had once been Doxley. "It appears that his heart failed."

Jericho nodded solemnly while Eulalia taunted him with delectable memories of last night's sinning. It would be nice to sin without the consequences.

Release me and you can.

Release her and he was damned to a life of poverty and inconsequence. He was nothing without her golden tongue.

"Mr. Fulbright?" Edwina said from the door. "Detective Bayard is here."

Jericho turned. The detective was far too young for the job, as well as far too pretty and delightfully flustered. His cheeks were colored, and his eyes didn't know where to settle. Did the Detective not appreciate the art on the walls or the small nude statues in the corners? Or perhaps he didn't know what to do with a man in pajamas.

Maybe he did know and that was his problem.

Jericho's lips curved. "Detective." He closed the distance and offered his hand.

Bayard glanced down then seemed to remember his manners, unlike the doctor who glared down his thin nose like he wanted to order Jericho to be scraped from his shoe. Bayard's grip was firm even if his gaze wasn't steady.

"Is the young man recoverable?" Bayard said to the doctor.

"He is gone. Too much opium." The doctor stood. "If that will be all?"

"Can I have that in writing?" Bayard asked as though he knew exactly what he was doing.

"I will send it to you." The doctor swept past like he couldn't get out fast enough.

Bayard walked around to look at the body. "How well did you know the man?"

They had kissed on the cheek once, but Jericho couldn't be intimate with anyone unless he wanted them to die. He couldn't touch them as they spilled, but they could get him to spill, and Doxley had done that the last time he was here. He'd sucked Jericho dry and it had been glorious. "He's been here a few times. His name was Stephan, I think. And from his clothes I thought he might be noble."

Many men here used only their given name, so they weren't too easily recognized.

Bayard nodded. "He is. His parents will be most distraught as his sister died not two months ago."

Jericho bit his lip and turned away. He didn't have to feign regret. "His heart had been made weak by loss."

The excuse fell from his tongue while bile rose in the back of his throat.

This was exactly the reason he preferred to choose the victims, instead of letting Eulalia. She liked the wounded ones. He chose men who were rough bastards. With the demon in him, it was easy to sense who was kind and who was vicious. Eulalia had seen something in him that had made her want to jump into him that night. Since then she'd seen others, but he'd never let her jump, bribing her with souls.

Keeping her fed.

Needing her voice.

This is what she'd wrought. She'd killed an innocent man, a man with a good heart and soul, who'd recently lost his sister and was seeking to bury that grief in opium and warm flesh.

He was delicious. So delicate. Not like the dregs you force me to dine on.

Jericho ignored her. He wouldn't draw on her voice unless the detective arrested him.

You don't need me. The detective does. He has a burn in him. A hunger that needs to be sated.

Jericho glanced at the detective. A blond lock of hair had come free and hung over his forehead. His dark blue eyes were troubled even though he'd declared this wasn't murder. What could a man of noble birth possibly need a demon for?

NATHANIAL SCANNED THE ROOM. Everywhere he looked there was artwork or statues of naked men. On the small tables were smoking implements, and opium residue stained the glass. He'd never been in such a place before, but it was obvious what happened here.

The owner, Jericho Fulbright, stood in the middle of the room in his garish blue floral robe. The robe didn't hide his yellow pajamas. He was as extravagant and lacking in morals as the scandal sheets declared. Who wore yellow pajamas? Sensible men wore night-robes. "Would you like to dress appropriately before I interview you?"

Jericho smiled. "Would you prefer me to dress?"

Nathanial glanced at his notebook. Yes, he would. Because all he could think about was the two thin layers of fabric that covered Jericho's body. He'd heard of Jericho Fulbright—who hadn't?—but the sketches had done him no justice and the cartoon of his flamboyant dress had made him appear to be quite devilish in appearance. He was no devil, though. Just a man.

"I do not care either way." He was sure he could see the word liar on Jericho's lips, as though he knew exactly what Nathanial kept hidden.

"Very well then, let's sit. I'll call for tea." Before Nathanial could agree or disagree Jericho rang a small bell, then sat on one of the chaises.

Nathanial perched on the edge of an armchair. "What exactly is this place?"

"Is this part of the interview?"

Nathanial considered Jericho for a moment. His dark hair hadn't been combed and he hadn't been shaved. His moustache was unkempt, and he had the general appearance of someone who'd just gotten out of bed. What kind of gentleman went wandering through the house in such a state? "Yes."

"It is a gentleman's club."

Nathanial pointed to a painting of two naked men wrestling, and then a statue of a naked man on his own in what seemed to be either the final throws of death or pleasure; his back was arched, and his mouth was open. "With very specific art."

Most clubs were much more subdued with art depicting scenes of hunting.

"For gentlemen who appreciate the male form." Jericho's voice was as smooth as silk and in that moment, he seemed impossibly pretty and extraordinarily predatory. "Are you suggesting something illegal happens here?"

That had been what he'd been suggesting.

"Perhaps behind the curtain? Or maybe in the parlor over the chess board?" Jericho purred.

The idea when spoken aloud seemed ridiculous. But the notion had been firmly planted in his head. "No private rooms?"

"My private living quarters are upstairs. There is a locked door between them. Would you like to see?"

For a heartbeat Nathanial wanted to say yes. "No. And in the club?"

"The smoking room, the parlor. There is another room for more..." Jericho licked his lip. "Discerning men."

"You mean those with higher status who don't want to accidentally rub shoulders with the nouveau riche." That the Jericho Rose let in those kinds of people had been a scandal on its own, though it hadn't harmed business.

"Exactly. Judges and dukes like privacy. I give them that."

Meaning that if they were committing sodomy out of wedlock, Jericho didn't care or want to know. Nathanial knew there were other things men could do together, but he only knew that from the porno pamphlets. He'd paid a female prostitute to do the same to him but closed his eyes and imagined it had been a man's mouth around him. It had only been the once and he'd felt terrible afterwards.

The tea arrived and Jericho leaned back to sip his. His gaze never left Nathanial, though it had softened, and the edge had faded. Nathanial took a seat and prepared his tea. "Tell me about this morning. Is it your custom to drift around the house in a state of undress?"

"Yes, though I put the robe on so I would be decent."

"You don't care that the servants will see you in your night wear? Your maid?" Nathanial balanced the tea while he made notes.

"Edwina and her husband have worked for me for years. I can assure they have seen all there is to see, and me in pajamas isn't half as shocking as finding a body."

"Yes...you found the young man." Nathanial knew Stephan Doxley though only as acquaintances.

Jericho leaned forward, the glint of danger back in his eyes. "I did."

"Explain that to me."

"I came downstairs and unlocked the door. Then started opening up the curtains; I like to open the windows to let the clean air in."

The windows were closed but the curtains were open. He noted that down, too. "Is that your normal habit?"

Jericho tilted his head a little, his features suddenly sharp. "Detective, are you insinuating that I had something to do with the young man's death? If I killed someone wouldn't it make more sense for me to remove the body from my place of business and not call the police at all?"

Well, that did make sense. If one were guilty, calling the police would be foolish. Nathanial blinked and stared at his notes. Unless one were deliberately trying to not look guilty. "Do you monitor your patrons' usage?"

"Excuse me?"

"How much they smoke."

Jericho shook his head. "No. I am not a nursemaid."

"Can you give me a list of men who were here last night?"

Jericho got up. He walked over, took the pencil and note pad out of Nathanial's hand, and sat on the arm of the chair where Nathanial had first rested. "I can go one better." He wrote something down. "Come and see for yourself, Detective Bayard. Is that the Bayards of Emmaly Estate?"

Nathanial nodded. Jericho handed back the notepad.

Detective Bayard, you are cordially invited to one free night of entertainment at the Jericho Rose.

Jericho Fulbright.

The signature was a piece of art in its own right.

"Is there anything else I can help you with, Detective? Or can I bathe and get dressed while you arrange for the removal of the body?"

Jericho was too close; Nathanial had to look up to meet his gaze. Which was a mistake as up close his eyes were gorgeous. Dark brown and framed by impossibly thick long lashes. He'd thought Jericho's eyes were blue, not brown, but that must have been a trick of the light. "Jericho is an unusual name."

"It's where my parents met. I'm sure enough has been written about me over the years for you to know the rest." He stood and walked across the room to open the window.

Nathanial put down his almost empty teacup. He didn't know what kind of tea it was, but it wasn't what he was used to drinking and it wasn't unpleasant. "I'm asking you as part of the interview."

Jericho didn't turn. "My mother died a month after my birth. That my father had married her in the first place was a scandal I'm told. I was raised by my nurse and then sent to boarding school. My father remarried."

"And you aren't close to your family?"

He turned and fixed Nathanial with a glare. "How does this aid your investigation?"

"I'm assessing your character. The scandal sheets have a dash of the truth and the rest is a delicate confection of outright lies and tidbits of salaciousness." He was also very curious about the kind of man who'd run a place like this that was so clearly dancing along the knife edge of legal.

"My family prefers to forget I exist. I am either an embarrassment or a painful reminder."

"You chose this."

"I need to make a living, and this seemed like a good idea. It wasn't the business that drove the final wedge. It was getting kicked out of the army."

Nathanial's eyebrows lifted before he could get them under control. That had never been mentioned. "Should I ask why?"

"I got into a fight with another noncommissioned officer."

"What were you fighting about?"

Jericho was silent for several heartbeats. "He killed my lover."

3

Nathanial reread his notes as he sat at his desk. The Nobility Task Force had a nice set of offices above the police station. There were three detectives, all of them younger sons. Between the three of them they travelled from London as far north as Scotland and west to Wales. His boss was the man who'd set up the task force after discussions with the King, when he'd taken the throne after the assassination of his mother twenty-five years ago.

Across his desk were the files of open investigations, and behind him were the cases that he'd failed to close. The ones where he'd gotten close, had almost everything, but then the case had fallen apart at the last moment. It had happened several times and his boss was none too happy.

This case was simple. With fresh paper and pen he wrote up his findings and his impression of Jericho Fulbright. Well, not his full impression; there were some things that didn't need to go on file. The doctor's report had arrived and all that needed to be done was for his boss to contact the family.

They would be devastated to lose another child, and while the location of Doxley's death was less than savory, it was not as traumatic as his sister's. She'd been at a cousin's estate and they hadn't been able to wake her in the morning. It was only when the collar and cuffs of her night gown were drawn back that everyone realized something ghastly had happened to her. Then the pictures had appeared.

Nathanial flicked open a file and thumbed through several reports until he reached what he was after. The picture had been paired with an awful story. Someone had killed her and photographed himself in the act.

That wasn't the worst part.

Nathanial had a collection of similar photos. Different women, different poses. Same man. He pulled out his magnifying glass and examined the man more closely, the way he had so many times before.

The now familiar scar on his ribs, the smug grin on his masked face, the dark hair. But his jaw line was wrong, his lips were too thin. It wasn't Jericho. Plus, there'd been no marks on Doxley's body. He'd asked the doctor to check and confirm.

"Staring at porno again."

Nathanial startled at his boss's voice. Lord Francis Amberton was the kind of man that expected everyone to follow the strict moral code that he exemplified. He didn't go to clubs and his name was never near a scandal. Except for when Nathanial couldn't close a case, or it fell over just before it went to court. Amberton despised it when that happened. Nathanial was the worst cop on the force.

"Making sure the masked man wasn't Mr. Fulbright." He put the magnifying glass down, glad that he hadn't dropped it.

"I take it he's not the snuff killer."

Nathanial shook his head. "The death this morning was from too much opium and a weak heart."

"And now I have to tell the parents." Amberton blew out a breath. "Nothing else at the Rose that you can get Mr. Fulbright on?"

Nathanial shook his head. Amberton would love a reason to shut down the Jericho Rose and all the other places like it. He blamed the clubs for gentlemen's poor behavior. Nathanial blamed the men. If the clubs and brothels weren't there, they would find some other outlet.

The only reason he still had a job was because Amberton thought Nathanial was morally shiny clean.

But he still needed to find the killer. He tapped the photo. "He's one of us. I'm sure of it."

"He may not be, but the person who owns the camera is."

"We find the man with the scar and we can bring down this whole thing." Three dead women all of noble birth, though the first one was born to a mistress.

"Well you can't go around asking everyman to unbutton his shirt." Amberton huffed as if the very idea was appalling. He'd be horrified if he knew that Nathanial had interviewed a pajama clad Jericho.

Nathanial glanced back at his notepad. He hadn't planned to accept Jericho's invitation no matter how tempting and terrifying. "I was given an invitation to go back to the Rose."

"Why on earth would you want to go back? I thought you hated places like that?" From the curl of Amberton's lip under his well-developed moustache, it was clear he couldn't imagine a worse place.

"I do loathe them. It was most unsettling even in daylight. But it's a club where men discuss things…"

"What kinds of things?"

"Their proclivities." While Nathanial hadn't seen any, he was sure that there would be porno pamphlets, and that Jericho would know where to purchase them. He tapped the pamphlet. "He might have a supplier."

Amberton grunted. "That family needs closure."

"We need to catch the people involved before they do it again." Nathanial needed to catch the men involved and close his most high-profile case. Everyone knew about it from the king to the women who laundered clothes. No doubt the masked man was laughing over his brandy.

"*You* need to catch him before he kills again." Amberton pointed a finger.

"It might take another death. We have nothing." If he'd been able to determine anything more from the photos, he'd have been interviewing suspects already.

"Find something."

"Then I have permission to return to the Rose?" Nathanial hoped he didn't sound too eager. He wasn't. It was a den of temptation. Of sin.

Amberton nodded. "Convince Mr. Fulbright that it would be in his best interest to help the police."

Nathanial knew he didn't stand a chance of convincing Jericho to do anything, but he nodded dutifully and prayed for his luck to turn.

NATHANIAL DIDN'T KNOW if the butler who opened the door was going to let him in even though he had the handwritten invitation. The butler stared at him and the note for several moments before deciding that Nathanial would be allowed into the club. Perhaps the butler had recognized him from the morning, or perhaps he knew Nathanial didn't belong.

His clothing was appropriate for the evening. His waistcoat revealed just the right amount of white shirt and his cravat was neatly tied and in a suitably subdued dark plum. While no one would've called him bold in his fashion choices they wouldn't have called him dull either. He wasn't like the staid men of his father's generation who believed men should wear black suits and white shirts and no other color, except maybe charcoal if they were feeling lively.

His mouth dried as he walked down the hallway following the butler. He didn't know anyone, but it wasn't the kind of place he would invite his friends. Plus, he was still investigating. This was work not pleasure.

Male laughter drifted through the walls. When the butler opened the door, it was clear why. Someone was standing on a chair reading a particularly rowdy piece of poetry complete with hip thrust.

The room had been so quiet this morning, so innocent in sunlight despite the recent death. Now it was littered with men, their coats discarded and their faces bright from wine and brandy. Nathanial was overdressed and quite the dull peahen when compared to these peacocks. He scanned the room looking for a familiar face, both hopeful and terrified of finding one. His gaze settled on Jericho.

Jericho lounged on a sofa, his waistcoat completely undone, as were the top few buttons of his shirt. While his trousers were gray his shirt was a soft shade of blue that complemented his violently turquoise waistcoat. The effect was startling against his golden skin. Was he dressing or undressing or happy to recline in the other man's arms? There was something intimate about this gathering. When Jericho laughed at another line of poetry, his Adam's apple bounced. The man he was leaning on murmured something and Jericho looked over.

His gaze sharpened as he got up and made his way over like a cat on the prowl.

Nathanial looked away, but everywhere he glanced was another show of intimacy, a kiss or caress though there was nothing lewd about it. Not even the artwork was safe to stare at, for everything celebrated the male body. This was not how he'd imagined the club this morning.

He wasn't sure what he'd hoped to find.

A tide of heat spread over him. His cravat was choking him, and his coat was too tight, too heavy.

"Well, I didn't actually think you'd come." Jericho's hand slid to the top button of Nathanial's coat. There was something about the way he said the last word that suggested something much more.

The poet finished to applause. He took a bow and accepted the drink that was offered and the kiss on the lips that lasted for rather longer that propriety dictated.

Nathanial dragged his attention back to Jericho. "I didn't want to waste the invitation."

Jericho's smile was all knowing, as though he could read the desires flitting through Nathanial's brain and body. What would it be like to be kissing like the poet?

Jericho's hand slid to the next button and Nathanial did nothing to stop him from popping it open. His overheated blood filled his member. That such a simple touch could be having such an effect on his body was horrifying.

"Since you are here, you had best take your coat off." Jericho flicked open the last button. "You are far too overdressed in case you hadn't noticed."

He wanted to keep the coat on to hide what was happening, and as armor against temptation, but he let Jericho ease it off his shoulders as though he were a manservant. The coat was handed to the butler who then shut the door and disappeared.

Without the poet to distract the men, all eyes turned to him.

"Let's take a turn about the room." Jericho offered his arm as though he were about to escort a lady. For a heartbeat Nathanial wanted to refuse, but this is what he'd wanted for so long. He wanted to be able to link arms and take a stroll, though he'd never been brave enough.

There were still preachers who railed against these kinds of relations. But there was nothing illegal here. Just men enjoying the company of men. The kind of intimate company that would ruin a lady. No lady would sit in a man's lap or allow such lingering touches the way men did here.

Nathanial accepted the offered arm and tried to ignore the thrill that chased through him. They walked around and Jericho introduced him by first name only to the other men also by first name. He recognized the name of an artist and an author and thought he might know Eustace…had they met at a garden party a few years ago? Some of the men had very finely made clothes, nobility of some kind, but they were here rubbing shoulders with men whose families worked for a living. Though it was clear there was some kind of entrance requirement that he barely met.

"A drink? You appear quite flushed." Jericho's lips seemed to be in a permanent half smile. He was a different man than the one Nathanial met this morning. His hair was carefully parted, the curls tamed. His moustache sharp and thin, no doubt styled to draw attention to his lips. While he affected carelessness this evening with his dress it was clear it was just for show. This morning had been genuine carelessness, a man who'd woken up and wandered around his house and who hadn't planned on guests.

Unless that too was just another costume.

"Please." Nathanial accepted the glass of wine and took a rather large drink. The alcohol did nothing to dampen the burn in his body. "So, this is what it's like at night."

"This is the more boisterous of the rooms. Would you like to see the smoking room?" Jericho leaned closer. "As part of your investigation, of course."

Yes, of course. He was here for work. He needed to stop goggling at everything. He nodded. "Thank you." The smoking room was where Doxley had been found.

***

JERICHO LED Nathanial through to the next room. The air was laced with smoke and while there was conversation it was muted. The embraces were more intimate, hands inside shirts...inside trousers. It was an intimacy that he longed for but that had been out of reach since the night he'd accepted the kiss and the demon.

The sweet smell reminded him too much of Liang and the nights they'd spent together. At times it made his sick to remember; tonight, it was pleasant. A time he wouldn't trade. He only wished he'd killed the prick who'd beaten Liang to death for nothing. There had been no theft, only the wounded ego of a man who felt slighted by Jericho's disinterest.

Nathanial drew in a breath and Jericho felt his body tense. Was it too much for the young policeman? Had he never pulled another's clothes off in a fit of desperate lust?

"How could he have been forgotten?" Nathanial whispered.

It took Jericho a moment to work out what Nathanial meant. Damn it all, that was the hole in his tale. "The curtains are already drawn for privacy; a cursory check would've been done at closing. Perhaps a more thorough check should be done each night, but who would expect someone to hide? For what purpose would he remain?"

The way Nathanial glanced at him it was clear that he knew exactly why a man might linger.

Jericho shook his head. "Not here. This is not a brothel, nor do I encourage illegal activities."

There were guest rooms and if a gentleman enquired discretely, they could be opened so that a man who so wished could stay the night. He only ever let close friends stay. Friends who wouldn't speak about what went on.

"Did you wish to have a taste?" His fingers brushed the inside of Nathanial's wrist, and his pulse quickened beneath Jericho's fingertips.

Blond, pretty, and too honest, too good. Nathanial was exactly the kind Eulalia liked to devour. She wouldn't get her claws into Nathanial, but that meant Jericho couldn't enjoy his company either.

"No. Not tonight." Nathanial mumbled, his gaze darting to the man whose eyes were half closed as another stroked him heedless of who was watching. Being watched was that gentleman's desire. He liked people's attention and regularly gave himself over to display. Many enjoyed the watching. It was usually all he allowed himself. After the latest incident, he wouldn't risk anything more. No matter how tempting.

But he could still have fun.

Jericho glanced at Nathanial and smiled. "I think you'd like to stay for just a little longer." His hand slid away to glide down Nathanial's back, over his buttock and to his hip. "He likes an audience."

Nathanial swallowed. Like the others in the room his attention became fixed on the man.

The man's trousers were unbuttoned by another and the head of his ruddy prick was exposed. A napkin was thoughtfully laid in his lap. It was a scene Jericho had seen many times before, but even so this time he was transfixed. Not by the man as much as by Nathanial. The way his lips parted, and his lashes lowered before he found the courage to look again.

All Jericho wanted to do was kiss him and slide his hand over the hard length of flesh he knew he'd find pressing against Nathanial's very proper black trousers.

The man on display lifted his hips as the hand worked over him, then he erupted in a spill of white. Nathanial made a small sound that could've been shock or longing. What was clear was that he'd been mesmerized. The hunger in his blue eyes was heartbreaking. Had he never enjoyed another's touch?

"Um." Nathanial drank the rest of his wine in a hurry drowning himself to hide what Jericho could see written on his face. He turned as if to leave then stopped. "They weren't there this morning."

Jericho glanced over his shoulder. The porno pamphlets were on display and there were several on a table. "They are put away at the end of the night."

"May I?"

"Of course." But he wanted to drag the copper from the room. There were some explicit photos that would be classified as an affront to decorum and land the subjects in jail or at the very least heftily fined.

Nathanial picked up the display book and leafed through the pages as though he was searching for something very specific. Jericho had gone through the book and the ones he had for sale. He'd found three more duplicates of the limp woman getting choked. That was far more offensive than any picture of a man buggering another.

The copper turned to a page and glanced at Jericho…guess he'd reached that page. It was a popular one. Jericho joined him, then took the book off him. He'd better do this the right way and give Nathanial something, so it looked as though he cared about legalities—which he did but only when it suited his purpose.

Having someone creating that kind of material would only bring unwanted attention to everyone. For the moment keeping Nathanial on side could be useful.

"I have something that might interest you, officially." Jericho put the book back on the shelf. "It was a disturbing find in my regular delivery."

That got Nathanial's attention. "Where is it?"

"In my study."

"Not in the club." The lust that had made his eyes shimmer had been replaced with wariness.

"Don't worry; I won't try to corrupt you." Though that would be most excellent fun. He offered Nathanial his arm again and he took it without hesitation. "I will extend you an invitation if you'd like to return on an unofficial capacity, if you think the club suits your tastes." Which it clearly did.

"How can you be sure I meet the membership requirements? Don't you need someone to vouch for me?"

"Usually, yes. But you are of noble birth and I saw your reaction..." He glanced at Nathanial as his cheeks darkened. "So, I will vouch for you." He paused at the door that separated club from house. "Though if you bring my place of business down, I will hunt you to the ends of the Earth."

Eulalia's excitement at the imagined revenge made his heart beat faster.

"I'm not here to bring you down."

Jericho considered the copper for a moment. "Then you are welcome. I will supply you with a card and make sure the butler knows to let you in." He unlocked the door, led Nathanial upstairs, and then unlocked another door.

"I'm not sure I can afford to join." Nathanial hesitated, as though unwilling to venture deeper into Jericho's lair.

"You can't afford not to." His study was stacked with paperwork, and on his desk were the pamphlets. He picked them up and handed them to Nathanial. "I get a selection; these were in it. I think they should be investigated."

Nathanial glanced at the pictures. "They're already under investigation." But he took the pages, grimness thinning his lips. "This is the dead man's sister."

Oh...curse you, Eulalia. This was far worse than he'd thought. Doxley's sister had been murdered.

He wanted to forget. I released him.

"Is that how she died?"

Nathanial considered him for a moment. "Yes. And she isn't the only one."

Jericho rocked back, sickened. He'd seen many things both in London and Hong Kong that would make a man question the darkness of some souls—hell, he'd became one of those things. Could the man in the picture be another?

Was there more than one demon in the world? He'd never seen another, but it didn't strike him as impossible. Eulalia mixed death with pleasure the way most men mixed tea and sugar. For an instant he was struck with the urge to meet another who harbored a demon to ask questions that no one else could answer, but at the same time he wanted nothing to do with another demon.

No one should have their death exploited in this way. Demon, or not, the killer needed to be stopped. And if the man was completely consumed by his demon and had no memory of the events? Was he guilty? Yes. Jericho wore the stain of every death even if he wasn't in control at the time. The courts would only see his guilt and if he spoke of demons and he'd be sent to Bedlam which would be worse.

"Where did you get these?" Nathanial asked as he slipped them into his pocket.

Jericho swallowed and refocused on the detective. For the moment they wanted the same thing: the man stopped, though for very different reasons. "I'm not revealing my supplier."

"And the opium? That is meant to be sold only through pharmacies." Gone was the cautious young man who wanted to explore his attraction, the copper was back. His voice was sure, and the uncertainty was gone from his features. This was a man Jericho couldn't trust.

But Jericho was just as untrustworthy.

"What is it that you want, Nathanial?" His voice lowered and took on a resonance as Eulalia surged to the surface. He shouldn't be drawing on her dark gift, but he was not going to let the detective shut him down because he had his morality compass shoved up his arse instead of what he'd prefer. Jericho took a step closer.

Nathanial didn't move, but his lips parted. It was a mouth that was made for sin, not for honesty and the law. Getting the honorable detective on his knees would be a delight. Eulalia wanted more.

Release me so that he may get his heart's desire.

Revenge, justice, or whatever it was called was not something the heart truly desired. He'd learned that the hard way. Nothing could bring the dead back or make up for their passing. Nathanial, for all his good work, could not raise the dead and put things right.

That didn't mean that the guilty shouldn't be punished, but their guilt had the power to consume the innocent's lives so their damage spread.

"To catch the killer."

Jericho smiled. Nathanial was looking right at one and didn't realize. How would he be able to catch the masked man? Jericho might be able to. If he were to see the man he'd know. He knew too much about most people. Their wishes and wants called to him and made Eulalia hungry. She wanted Nathanial, though not in the same way Jericho did.

"That's not why people come here." Jericho reached out and ran his fingertips down Nathanial's cheek, his jaw and then to the well tied but dull cravat. "Next time dress more appropriately."

"You mean be more undressed."

Jericho undid the dull cravat and tossed it to the floor. "If you wish. I will not stop you from stripping to your undershorts and nor would anyone else. I'm sure there would be some who would be quite taken with the idea." He was taken with the idea of continuing to undress the detective until he said no. He toyed with the top button of the starched collar. It was attached to the shirt; a wealthy man like Nathanial wouldn't wear detachable collars and cuffs. The button came undone.

Nathanial drew in a breath and leaned closer. "I want the name of your porno supplier."

"Hmm." Eulalia was in every word he spoke. It would be easy to let her take full control and seduce the detective. Hell, he could probably do it without her help. Heat and desire clouded around Nathanial like smoke. "Come back tomorrow."

"This isn't pleasure." But his eyes closed as Jericho's hand brushed his inner thigh.

"Of course not." His hand slipped higher, caressing the soft balls then the hard length through the fabric of Nathanial's trousers. For a heartbeat he let his fingers linger on the button as though he planned on undressing him further. Then he let his hand fall away.

He wanted Nathanial too much. One kiss and Eulalia would slip free to a new host, and he'd be free of her demands. But he'd also lose what little power he had. The life he'd built for himself would crumble and he'd be on the streets. He wasn't ready to give her up, and he had no backup plan. He needed to come up with one so that he could escape her clutches. She growled and cursed him. But this was not the first time he'd resisted the urge to kiss and set her free.

"But I think I have what you are looking for." Jericho stepped back. He pulled out a different pamphlet. This one showed three men. One sucking, one fucking, and the one in the middle having all the fun. He handed it to Nathanial. Nathanial blushed as though he'd never seen anything so scandalous. Maybe he hadn't.

"It's one of the best sellers."

"You sell them here?"

"If you know where to look, you can find almost anything." How hard did the detective want to look? It was one thing to want something, but to actually chase it down without thought to the consequences? Not every man had the gumption for that. He wasn't sure Nathanial did.

Jericho drew in a breath and made sure he was back in control. "Come back tomorrow and we can talk some more about my supplier." If Nathanial was willing to come back, perhaps he did have the courage.

"Here?" He folded the pamphlet and placed it in his pocket.

Jericho couldn't help but smile. "Maybe not this room. I'm the host; I need to be out there. As you said. This is business."

Nathanial nodded. He picked up his cravat and turned to leave. "Are the games and cards for show?"

"No, but I doubt you'd approve of the stakes." But by God Jericho would love to see Nathanial on a losing streak.

———

NATHANIAL SAT in his night-robe with the pamphlet folded in his hand. The house was silent and the servants asleep. A single candle burned. He could've turned on the light—electric lights had been installed two years ago—but it was too harsh for what he was going to do.

Even the candle was too bright, but he wanted to read the story and stare at the picture. He forced himself to unfold the paper and look again at the scene. As before heat bloomed on his cheeks and spread down his neck. His heartbeat quickened and he hardened. The memory of Jericho's casual caress had kept him hard the whole way home.

The erotic scene in the smoking room had haunted his thoughts as he'd gotten changed. No one there had given a damn or been the least bit uncomfortable.

Only him.

Only because he heard the preacher at his father's church and his father railing about how male marriage and women's suffrage would damn them all to hell. He was already in purgatory. Unable to accept the salvation that he needed when it was right in front of him. If he'd asked, Nathanial was sure Jericho would've been more than happy to continue undressing him and more.

What did he want? Who was he in the photo? The sucker or the suckee? The man all too happy to be filled or the one with his cock buried in the other's arse?

He wanted all of it.

He wanted Jericho even though he shouldn't. He was the wrong class, the wrong everything. He was virtually a criminal. But when Jericho smiled there was something there that made it hard to look away. He shouldn't have let the man undo his cravat or his collar. He wished Jericho had done more. He wouldn't have stopped him.

Nathanial put his hand under his night-robe and stroked himself. Jericho would finish unbuttoning him, slid the suspenders off his shoulders, then undo his pants. He glanced at the picture, not needing the story when his imagination was already aflame. Each stroke stoked a fire that had been lit years ago and never went out despite never being tended.

His palm became slick as he imagined Jericho pulling down his trousers and shorts to expose his arse. Then Nathanial would turn and put his hands on Jericho's desk. His body jerked as he spilled over his hand and on his night-robe. His breathing was hard as pleasure tumbled through him.

It wasn't wrong to want pleasure.

He crumbled the paper as old guilt rose to smother simple joy. He shouldn't have done that. He should've gone to a brothel and done what gentlemen usually did with a woman. But he hated that. He didn't like to pay, and he didn't like the women whose job it was to pretend they wanted him. Once had been enough. Maybe there were places where men like him could go and pay, but he didn't know where they were, and he didn't think he'd like them either.

At the Jericho Rose it had been pleasure for pleasures sake. As debauched as that idea was, it held an appeal. Or maybe it just was the owner that appealed.

Nathanial Bayard is a dedicated detective. He applies himself fully to the job, interviewing witnesses and suspects and gathering clues, but he cannot put a case together that holds up in court. Aside from a few early convictions, he has failed. While he desires justice, he lacks the desire to submerse himself fully in the work. I do wonder if he would be better suited to some other kind of work; perhaps he should reconsider the priesthood. He has the moral backbone that is required.

— LORD FRANCIS AMBERTON

4

____

"Lady Featherington is here to see you, Sir." Godfrey stood in the door of Nathanial's study.

Nathanial put the pamphlet he'd been looking at down. He didn't want his staff thinking that he enjoyed the kind of thing he was investigating. "Show her to the parlor."

"Don't be silly. I'm more than happy to sit in here." Lady Featherington peered around the butler.

Nathanial winced, and forced a smile. He didn't want his sister in here at all. "That is impossible. I have sensitive work-related information in here." He stood and greeted his sister with a kiss on the cheek.

"Don't be so dull." She grinned and tried to peek around him, but Nathanial steered her toward the parlor with a hand on the small of her back. "I wouldn't tell anyone."

Maybe she wouldn't but it would not be worth the humiliation if she knew what he was investigating. It wasn't just murder; it was the way it was done. He hastily buttoned his waistcoat, his mind full of the way Jericho had happily lounged with his spread open. There was a certain liberation in being less buttoned up—except for when visitors came by unexpectedly. "I thought you were in Bath."

"Bertie still is, but I missed London. So, I decided I would visit his sister. She's just had her third baby."

"Which explains why you're here visiting me." He wasn't dressed for guests. His shirt sleeves were still rolled up and she'd notice more if he fiddled with his clothes.

"Well I couldn't be in London and not visit. It's like you don't want to see me." She frowned. They weren't close in age, but they'd been close while growing up. She'd treated him like a doll, and he'd been happy to tag along in all her games. Their older brother had no patience for a baby brother fifteen years his junior.

"I do. I am just busy. Forgive me."

"You must take a break and come to Bath. Bertie has bought himself one of those new automatic cameras."

Nathanial shook his head. He didn't have time to go to Bath and he didn't really want to listen to Bertie talk about his cameras, but his sister was excited. "Why is it automatic?"

"You set it up and then it will take a series of photos without you doing anything." Her cheeks flushed. "It is an amazing thing and Bertie is quite taken, though the novelty has worn off for me as he spends all his time with it."

Bertie was also a keen bird watcher. Nathanial had sat through several talks on birds and seen many of Bertie's photos. He had no interest in seeing more. "When this case is done, perhaps."

The maid brought a tray of tea in and then slipped out of the room.

"Your work consumes you."

He nodded and sipped his tea. He didn't want to admit how close he was to failing. He had no idea what he'd do if he did. He'd have to find some other job. The idea of living on a paltry allowance from the family estate was something he abhorred. His father would control his life until it was unbearable, and Nathanial caved to all his demands. That was how Father worked.

"Papa would like you to attend his next party." She retrieved the invitation. "You are getting advance notice so you can make sure you are there."

Ah, the real reason for her visit.

"He just wants to talk me out of police work. Does he want to convince me to quit my job and go to the church? Or will there be a parade of young ladies from wealthy families for me to pick from?"

"You are twenty-five. You should be thinking about marriage." She paused and gave him a look that he couldn't discern. "Unless...would you prefer a parade of eligible young gentlemen?"

Nathanial sipped his tea and didn't answer. He was not going to admit a thing.

His sister wouldn't be dissuaded. "You were very excited when the Male Marriage Act was passed."

"It was logical."

"Why is there no female marriage act then?"

"What sin do women commit?"

His sister raised one eyebrow. "Do you really think Aunt Bethany and her companion were chaste?"

They had been close and quite affectionate when surrounded only by family. "You aren't suggesting..."

She sipped her tea. "Don't be naïve, Nathanial. And if you tell me you don't think women deserve a say in government, I will have to box your ears."

His lips curved. When they were younger, she'd been able to that; these days he doubted it, but he wasn't willing to risk it. "I think women should vote. If they are to marry each other, then one will need to work."

It was a complex issue. When men married, they both worked. The people who argued against female marriage claimed it was unnatural for a woman to assume the role of a man and be head of the household. Priests had said similar about the Male Marriage Act, but others had fully supported it. It had passed but only by a slim margin. A couple of artists had been the first to wed in public. Many had treated it as a joke, but they were still together.

"Thus why we need suffrage. But you clearly need a husband."

He laughed. "Father was apoplectic when the Act passed. I don't think he has changed his mind."

"Ah, that's why you haven't been home in so long." She sighed. "Papa still hopes you'll commit yourself to the church."

Some things didn't change. His father would have a fit if he knew where Nathanial had been last night. He couldn't go back home. He needed to accept his father's invitation; avoiding this summons home would only make things worse. But if his father thought Nathanial had come to his senses and was ready to do the 'right thing' by the family instead of pursing this silly notion—as Father called the Nobility Task Force—he was wrong. Silence consumed the parlor as they drank their tea and nibbled cake.

"There is something else wrong. Are you already with someone on the sly?"

"No. I wouldn't." The shame that would bring to the family…he shook his head. "There is something I need to do for work, but I don't know if I can do it." And he wanted to do it too much. Jericho's world was…it was perfect. Like living in a dream.

"That sounds awfully serious."

"It is. I am investigating a murder. Several actually." Perhaps his sister could give him an extra insight.

She put her teacup down. "Oh. How terrible. You must find the killer."

What did she think he was trying to do? His sister had probably known the victims at least in passing, but he couldn't show her the photos. They would scandalize her. "Did you know the Doxley lass?"

She paled. "Those murders?"

"What do you know of them?" He was stunned that a lady like his sister would know such things.

"That no young lady will step outside a ballroom without her guardian, not even if she is being courted. To have such a death captured forever…"

Nathanial almost dropped his tea in his lap. He put the cup down with a rattle. "You've seen the photos?"

"No, but I read the scandal sheets. Why, do you have them here? In your study?" His sister was already getting up.

He stood ready to stop her. "No, you cannot see them."

"Nathanial, I have birthed five children and buried two. I am sure that a few pictures will not harm me. Besides I might be able to help you." She held out her hand as though he were a wary five-year-old and they were about to do something that would get them into trouble. He was sure he was going to regret this, though he wasn't sure how in that moment.

He took her hand and she led him back to his study. She'd never liked hearing no.

"Are you certain? They are quite traumatic."

"I'm certain." She fixed him with a look. "We must all do our part to make sure it doesn't happen again."

Nathanial pulled out the four porno pamphlets with the masked man and handed them over.

"Oh…" His sister looked more saddened than horrified.

"Do not read the story. It is not related to the picture." His skin heated and he wanted to blame the warmth of the house, but there was no fire as it was summer. And not even a warm summer.

She turned away and blinked a few times. "I can confirm that all those young ladies are indeed dead and that they weren't staged."

"I already know that. I do investigate these things for a living." He was sure his sister had just wanted the inside track on this gossip.

Her lips were pressed together. "What is it you need to do?"

"What?"

"You said you had to do something for work, to catch him I'm guessing."

"I need to join a club…but it is not the kind of place one talks about."

"A club of ill repute?" He could see her brain churning through a catalogue of names. For a lady, his sister knew a lot about everyone. "A club for a gentleman with specific tastes? Not a flagellation club?"

"No!" He put the papers away. "You aren't helping me at all. You're just being nosy."

"Don't be like that." She put her hand on his arm. "Do you think the man is a noble?"

"Yes. How else would he get the girls alone?"

His sister frowned then reached around him to grab the file.

"That is police property. Give them back!" He tried to grab the papers, but she turned away. Given that they were no longer children, it wasn't appropriate that he tackle her to the ground and make her eat a ladybird. She'd put a dead mouse in his bed in retaliation, and then they had both been given a hiding.

"They are porno pamphlets. I could buy them myself if I knew where." She examined each of the images in much the way he had.

"That is half the problem," he muttered.

"You don't know where to buy them?" She lifted an eyebrow as though surprised. "I know where Bertie keeps his."

"I don't want to know. But no. The run of the mill ones can be purchased at various locations." That he wasn't going to divulge. Usually brothels. Some clubs. "The more specific, the more one needs to be in that club."

"You need to join."

"I do. But word will get around. It always does. Father will be mortified. You will be."

"I doubt that. Did you know Bertie's cousin recently married? It was a lovely wedding. The grooms wore matching monte carlos—quite the scandal when clearly they should've been wearing frock coats." She held up the papers. "All taken in different bedrooms."

"I know. I have gone over the photos in great detail."

"It's a good quality camera. The detail is astounding even though it's a print. The person or persons definitely has money. What a pity he wears a mask."

"If he wasn't, he'd have been arrested already." Did she think him that hopeless?

"Were the girls already dead in these photos?" She handed back the folder.

"I don't know. They were only found the next day. Asleep in their beds, but unable to be woken." Nathanial wasn't sure which was worse, if the pictures were taken as they died or if the man was being intimate with a corpse. "At first they were treated as a natural death as there were no other signs." Some of the girls had bruising but his sister didn't need the grim details. "Then the pictures came out."

"You must stop him. I'll deal with father. I'll even persuade him that you have no intention of marrying or going to the church because you are so dedicated. Oh, that would work—you are saving mortal lives instead of souls. Surely, he wouldn't be able to argue with that? We can deal with the other issue later."

"Thank you for dealing with Father." Though he doubted Father would listen to her. Nathanial managed a smile. "There might be something else you can do for me."

"This is becoming a long list," she said with a smile, her eyes bright with mischief. She would keep his father from grasping his coat tails and bringing him to heel at least for a little while. That he still needed his sister's interference rubbed, but for this he would swallow his pride.

"Ask Bertie about his camera and where he buys the good quality ones from. Perhaps I need to take up photography."

She put her hand to her temple. "Not you, too. That is a step too far." Then she grinned. "Bertie will be delighted to bore me for hours. You could come to Bath and ask him yourself."

"No, I'll tackle things from this end."

She put her arms around him. "Do be careful. Scandals fade, but death is rather permanent."

JERICHO RAN through the accounts of the business and checked the liquor and opium supply. Both were fine. He never put out much opium, just enough to add an air of danger for those who liked to think they were reckless and take the edge off those who were unsure.

Nathanial could do with a dose.

The copper had been on his mind all morning and for all the wrong reasons. Eulalia had made sure his dreams had been haunted too, the demon making the attraction a hundred times worse and harder to ignore. She'd found a new host that she wanted to inhabit and would torment him until he either gave in and kissed Nathanial or Jericho stopped seeing him, forcing her to wait and find another.

He needed the demon. How else was he supposed to talk his way out of danger?

But he'd had his vengeance years ago. The brawl that had gotten him sent home had been the start. He'd gotten drunk that night and gotten himself a demon by accident. The man who'd killed Liang had fallen to his death just before Jericho shipped out—not on one of the new dirigibles that made the journey faster, but on a creaky old ship that was bound for the junkyard.

Eulalia had proclaimed his innocence even though he was the first suspect and all who heard her words on his tongue had believed them. It was then he'd realized the power of what he had with in him. And the first time he'd had sex upon returning to London, the horror.

It was a tempting thought to hand her off, but he couldn't do it to someone so innocent and unsuspecting as Nathanial. And he knew exactly how innocent the copper was. That was another of her gifts. Souls were as readable as a book.

Jericho was not the corrupter of innocents, as he was so commonly portrayed in the scandal sheets. Well, not unless they wanted to be corrupted. And Nathanial was still making up his mind.

Jericho drew in a breath half hoping the copper wouldn't show tonight. He really shouldn't have given him an invitation to return. If people found out a member of the Nobility Task Force was here it would be bad for business. With luck, Nathanial wouldn't show.

Eulalia's laughter echoed in his mind. It would be nice to have full control over his body again, but it would also be lonely without her in his head.

As it drew closer to opening time, Jericho bathed and took his time to dress in a mock careless fashion, when really every detail was considered down to how many buttons he should do up on his waistcoat. Two today, and he'd leave his cravat on, but untied as though he'd been interrupted. He smiled at his reflection, though he saw not just his face, but hers. She gave him blue eyes and sharper cheekbones and skin like a ghost.

Only he knew she was there. Everyone else blamed the light or their own eyes.

From his room, he could hear the staff talking. There were serving men who poured the drinks…and sometimes they did a little more. A woman in the kitchen who made the sandwiches or treats that were served up. Then there was his maid and butler.

All were discreet. All had previously worked in less reputable places and he'd made it very clear that if they chattered, they would be gone without character, making it impossible for them to gain good employment. After three years of working together, he trusted his staff completely.

Jericho made his way downstairs, locking his study and then the connecting door. He liked to maintain the illusion that he had a life separate to the club. He'd tried very hard at first to do that. But in the end, it was easier to be here most nights. He was sure the club could run without him. Almost sure at any rate. He'd never tested it. He was always here to greet patrons and to make sure everything was just so.

He was worried that if he went away for even one night the thin veil of legality would be shredded, and he'd come back to a charge sheet and a criminal case that not even Eulalia could save him from.

NATHANIAL'S COAT hid his state of undress. Leaving the house with his waistcoat undone was wrong. He had left his collar undone but had tied his cravat. He was not going anywhere without his necktie, though he had bought a new one in a rather garish rose.

The carriage stopped down the block; if the driver suspected, he said nothing. Nathanial waited until he'd driven off before making his way to the house. And it was just a house. From the outside it looked very ordinary. The curtains were drawn and while there must be comings and goings all night, there was nothing that suggested anything of interest went on here.

What did the neighbors think? Or did they not care because they frequented the place or rented the houses while they lived on their country estate?

Nathanial glanced up to the dark sky and the darker outline of the roof. More to the point how had Jericho Fulbright, a disgraced sergeant in His Majesty's Army, afford such a place? Perhaps the father had given Jericho something, though from the distain in Jericho's voice when talking about his family Nathanial doubted it.

He drew in a breath and marched up the four steps. He needed to know where Jericho got his pamphlets. He was here for work.

And he was going to enjoy every moment of it.

5

The butler let Nathanial into the Jericho Rose and took his coat without a sideways glance. If the butler judged the men who came here, he didn't show it at all. A lesser man would have, and plenty of greater men did.

It still took Nathanial a moment to fortify his resolve before he walked down the hallway to the parlor. That feeling that he didn't truly belong was an insidious vine that crept around him and strangled each breath. Worse, what if he did belong? What if this was what he'd been looking for all these years? He spoke of waiting for marriage but while his father was alive, he doubted very much that he'd ever have the blessing for that to happen. Did he want to wait another decade, or more, to truly live?

Not that wished his father dead either. His older brother was no less sanctimonious. With fifteen years between them he barely knew his brother.

He put a slight smile on his lips as though he were comfortable being here and let the butler show him into the room. There were less people tonight, though he had arrived unfashionably early. There was indeed a game of chess in progress. Both men had their waist-coats off and were frowning intently as though it were a matter of life or death. Maybe it was. Jericho had implied that the stakes were high.

As though thinking of him had summoned him, Jericho appeared at his side. "You took my advice."

Nathanial inclined his head. He didn't want to come here and stand out because he was dressed too drab. Dressing in his normal manner drew attention he didn't want. "What do they play for?"

Jericho chuckled. "Who will suckle the other."

Nathanial flinched and Jericho grinned. Was he telling the truth or having a jest? It was impossible to tell. But Nathanial liked the way his mouth curved, the hard, thin line of his moustache a contrast to his lips. Nathanial looked away. There had to be better men here for him to admire than a disgraced sergeant. No part of Jericho was respectable. But that was part of his allure. He lived and didn't let anything, or anyone, stop him. He made his own rules.

"Have a drink. I have instructed the staff to put it on your tab. Your month of membership is due on the first of July. I'll gift you the rest of June."

"And in return?"

Jericho lifted one eyebrow, his eyes shimmered blue and his features sharpened with some trick of the light. "Don't tempt me." He leaned in close, so his lips brushed Nathanial's ear. "When you are ready, you will give me what I want."

The way his hand slid down Nathanial's spine left no doubt as to what that was. He could step away or say he wasn't interest, but he'd be lying, and he'd never been much of a liar. He had abused himself upon waking, unable to get the thoughts of Jericho and the pamphlet and what went on here out of his mind.

Would another put himself up on display?

Would he watch?

He'd have liked to say no, but now he was here his resolve was lacking and his morals had abandoned him. He pushed aside the thoughts as much as he could. He needed Jericho's help, though he was beginning to think that the price would be far too enjoyable. But if his own hand caused him so much guilt how could he ever do more?

Before he'd agreed or disagreed Jericho had moved on, talking to another patron.

Nathanial got a brandy and made short work of it before ordering a second. The game of chess was almost over. Already the winner was clear; the man in the lilac shirt was the victor. Money changed hands between the watchers. Nathanial waited to see what would happen. After a few more heartbeats it was clear no debt would be settled here. He was disappointed, and then equally horrified that he'd been so eager for more than just a game.

The man Jericho had been talking to came over and introduced himself as Robert. From the cut of his clothes he was noble born, but neither of them asked about their families or estates. Instead they talked about the King's 25th jubilee, the latest scandal, and court cases. Eventually one of the writers got up to read something that could never be published without breaking the obscenity laws.

Nathanial glanced around the room, but there were no pamphlets in here. Robert put a hand on Nathanial's leg, a gesture that was casual yet intimate. Nathanial's breath caught. He wasn't here to find a lover. He was here for work.

Yet he was enjoying himself. There was none of the pretense that some clubs had. There were no ladies trying to find a husband like there were at parties or the fashionable salons. He could just be, and no one would give him odd looks.

Another brandy and another hour slipped by and he laughed and smiled more in Robert's company than he'd ever thought possible in a social gathering. Jericho reappeared. Had he been attending guests in the other rooms? Their gazes locked and a frission of something slipped through Nathanial's body.

Jericho's lips turned up at the corners. He lifted his glass and took a sip never breaking the spell. This place held some kind of witchery, entrancing him into making him forget what he needed to do. He drew in a breath and excused himself to find the privy. He needed air.

The backyard was cool and dark. Laughter drifted out from the smoking room along with the sickly scent of opium. He made his way to the small outbuilding, where a lantern hung in the corner casting a pale-yellow glow. Unlike the rest of the house this room wasn't wired. But who needed to see the details? When he was done, he lingered in the yard, hands shoved deep into his pockets, completely ruining the line of his clothes. He needed to go back in, but he couldn't be drawn under again. He needed to keep his wits.

How many brandies had he drunk?

His skin was tight, and irritation buzzed through his blood. He should ignore it and let it fade. But after last night he didn't know if he could. He needed...wanted...he shook his head. What he needed was to go back or he would be missed.

A smothered moan by the side of the house made him pause. His head turned even though he already suspected why there was moaning. The chess players were up against the side of the house. One was squatting with the other in his mouth. The man in the lilac shirt leaned against the wall, head back, eyes closed, a hand pressed to his lips.

Nathanial's heartbeat quickened but he kept walking. They would notice him if he paused. Had they not seen him walk past the first time? Maybe they didn't care because they were so caught up.

He tore his eyes away jealous, and frustrated, and at the same time hating that they could. He was waiting. He was being respectable. He was doing the right thing; not like these men. But he wanted to be like them and comfortable in his own skin.

After the cool of the yard the house was stuffy, and the walls were too close. All he wanted was to get home. This had been a mistake. He was weak and the temptation to sin was too great. But then Nathanial remembered why he was here; not for himself, but to find a killer. This pleasurable torture was nothing, a passing discomfort that the finality of death couldn't compare to.

He fixed a smile and swept back into the parlor. Jericho hadn't moved from the armchair he was lounging in. At some point during the night his shirt had become unbuttoned revealing the line of his throat. His waistcoat hung fully open. He was the perfect picture of a disheveled gentleman, though he was no true gentleman.

Nathanial perched on the arm of the chair, needing to talk to

Jericho but not willing to discuss business here. Jericho reached out and put his hand on Nathanial's knee as though to keep him in place. The heat of his palm sunk through the thin fabric of Nathanial's trousers. He was too close, and he wanted to be closer.

"You've ruined the sketch!" someone shrieked.

Nathanial glanced over to see a man with paper and charcoal. "I'm sorry."

He went to rise, but instead was tugged back, so he landed on Jericho's lap.

"How's that?" Jericho asked. His hand was now on Nathanial's thigh. Nathanial's head rested on Jericho's other arm. It was a position that would ruin a lady's reputation.

"Perfect." A new sheet of paper was flipped over.

Nathanial realized he was now trapped and about to be immortalized. Mortification paralyzed him. Too many eyes were on him. He was an ungainly lump with none of Jericho's ease and he hated being the center of attention.

"I really should get up." He made a few small movements of protest that couldn't have been called trying.

"Relax." Jericho ruffled Nathanial's hair. "This will hardly make the National Gallery. Though it may hang in my room." That smile was just for him, not the gathering. Jericho's hand inched a little higher.

Nathanial needed to stay focused. They were trapped for the moment so he could put it to use. "We need to talk."

"Just talk?"

Nathanial swallowed and nodded. He would not get sucked in. But there was a heat and hardness now pressing into his hip. He knew what it was. He moved but only ended up rubbing himself against Jericho's erection.

"Stay still or you'll ruin another sketch and we'll have to stay here longer." His arm moved higher to rest over Nathanial's hips. "What did you want to talk about?"

"Here?"

"Why not? Everyone else is absorbed in other things. Besides do you trust yourself to be alone with me?" Jericho's fingers moved slightly, and Nathanial's desire was no longer a secret.

He lowered his gaze. "This place...it has a way of breaking my resolve."

"And what resolve would that be? To live in denial?"

"To be virtuous and wait for marriage." The words were wooden on his tongue. Ridiculous to be spoken here, like a priest claiming to be chaste while balls deep in a bawd. He expected laughter or mockery but got none.

"Not all of us have the luxury of respectability."

It was no luxury, but a weight around Nathanial's neck that must be dragged to every social event. If he mucked up his father would be quick to cancel his funds and the Nobility Task Force didn't pay well, on account of the staff being nobles and having independent incomes.

"So, what is it you want to discuss while you are safe in my embrace and with an audience to keep me honest?"

Nathanial did his best not to squirm. Every movement he made pressed him to Jericho and he was already feeling more than he ever had of a man. "It's work related."

Jericho considered him for a moment. "I don't know how I can be of any use."

"I need to know where you get your—"

"No. I will not give up the name of my porno supplier."

He'd known it wouldn't be easy, but Nathanial was determined. If he could track the photos from supplier to delivery and then to creator... "The King would be most appreciative in bringing the man to justice."

"The King doesn't know I exist. Why is it so important?"

"Someone must deliver the photos for printing."

The smile faded from Jericho's lips. "I will speak to my people. You will not. But first you must do something for me."

"What?" He'd do anything. Almost anything. He glanced around the room. Maybe not anything, because in this place anything was rather broad and likely to wind him in scalding water.

Jericho shifted so he was closer as though they were having an intimate conversation.

"That's good. Nathanial, put your hand on his neck," the artist called.

"How do they know my name?"

Jericho lifted Nathanial's hand to comply with the request. "They all know you. If you take us down…"

The threat lingered in the air. He would be ruined socially and financially.

"I will not do that." With his hand on Jericho's neck and the way they were sitting their conversation had become more intimate as if it were just the two of them curled in the chair. The room was too hot, his face was burning.

Jericho trailed his knuckles down Nathanial's cheek. "Anyone would think you're an innocent." Nathanial didn't respond. Jericho tipped his chin as though to kiss him. "That is the price for my help. Tell me, are you truly a virgin?"

POLLINGTON'S POPULAR NEWS

When a gentleman visits establishments of pleasure he must be sure to keep his wits about him lest the ladies take more than their worth. That was the predicament that one Lord F found himself in on Saturday night.

The wallet in question was lifted from the lord's trousers while he was otherwise occupied. Upon discovering it missing he flew into a rage, destroying the bed chamber and scaring the woman near to death.

Once the wallet and its contents had been returned, he departed without paying for damages. It is said he's been banned from returning even though he was a regular visitor.

A gentleman should always cover any damage. But then a gentleman would also be more careful about where he places his personal items.

6

Nathanial stiffened in Jericho's arms. If he tried to break free Jericho wouldn't stop him; he wasn't that cruel. But if Jericho was going to be helping the police—which he didn't really want to do even if there was another demon involved—he wanted Nathanial to pay for his help.

He didn't need money. He didn't lack for male attention; he could've had a different lover every night of the week. But it had been a long time since he'd wanted so desperately that his sleep had been disturbed.

He blamed Eulalia for some of that, but he couldn't blame the lust invading his bones, his flesh, and soul on her. There was something about Nathanial that had drawn his gaze. Maybe it was that he was too innocent.

If you will not let me help him, let me devour him. His soul is perfect. You would enjoy it. Eulalia was the devil in his ear, promising him the world at dusk but leaving him holding nothing but a cold lump of coal come daylight.

"I don't see why my personal life has any bearing on what I've asked you to do."

"It doesn't," he whispered, his lips so close to Nathanial's cheek.

"But that is my price. You want me to dig for information for you, thus I am entitled to dig in return."

Nathanial sighed. "That depends on your definition."

"Or maybe it depends on yours. It's a yes or no answer." What had Nathanial done? Whatever it was hadn't left him feeling good about desire or sex. Which was a pity. He could have made some very close friends here…not that Jericho wanted to share.

"Then yes," Nathanial murmured without looking at him.

"Change position. I shall paint this in oils and call it a gentleman undone." Francis, the artist, was determined to make the most of this moment and Jericho had to agree that it was a moment to savor.

"You will do no such thing. The art critics would savage you," Robert said.

"But a collector would appreciate its worth," Francis replied as he flipped the page to make another sketch

It was fun to play along, and it was an excuse to keep Nathanial close. "One more?"

Nathanial rolled his eyes and gave a dramatic sigh. "Very well, but I want to ask you a question."

"You will owe me another answer, too."

"Agreed."

Jericho's eyebrows lifted; he'd expected more reluctance from the copper. "Face me, straddle me." *And give me a thousand dreams.*

Nathanial moved, as though uncertain. Jericho sat up instead of slouching, and gripped Nathanial's thighs drawing him closer, then his hands slid to Nathanial's buttocks. Oh, to have his trousers unbuttoned right now.

Nathanial looked dawn as if realizing the intimacy of the moment, his eyes wide as their gazes locked.

"What was your question?"

Nathanial cheeks were red as though he was sun burned. "Do you have many lovers?"

"No. But it is not the number that matters, but the quality." His fingers slid along Nathanial's inner thigh. Nathanial quivered and gripped the arm of the chair. Christ, Jericho was hard, aching as though it had been months not days. "I know a good many tricks. Want me to teach you some?"

There was a pause where Nathanial seemed to stop breathing, where he stared down into Jericho's eyes and for an awful moment Jericho thought Nathanial was going to agree. For all his teasing, Jericho couldn't play the lover. He wouldn't let Eulalia take Nathanial's soul or inhabit him.

Francis moved to the side intent on capturing the moment.

Nathanial shook his head. "I will wait."

"And what was it that made you take a vow of chastity like a maid worried about her reputation?"

"I do have a reputation. My family has standing."

Jericho's finger caressed the inner seam of Nathanial trousers. They were tight around his groin, where he was straining to be free. "That's not it."

Nathanial rocked back and Jericho let him ease away, but he didn't leap from his lap and put respectable distance between them. He remained there, close but not close enough. "When I first moved to London I went with friend to a brothel."

"You tupped a woman?"

He shook his head. "It felt wrong even being there. Dirty. But I let her…suckle." The last word was whispered. "I vowed never again after that."

While the artist and his friends were chattering with excitement. Jericho could only focus on the man on his lap. "Loving someone with your body is never dirty or wrong."

"I didn't love her. I didn't even want her."

"And now you deny yourself every pleasure. What a waste of youth."

Nathanial closed his eyes. "I'm here."

"That you are." He put a finger under Nathanial's chin and drew close as if to kiss him. The urge was strong and threatened to overwhelm him. But he would not surrender his demon. Not yet. He'd forgotten what it was like to not have to share his body and mind. His lips brushed the copper's cheek. Eulalia screamed with frustration and so did he. "And where will I find you when I have information?"

"Come to the Nobility Task Force office."

Not his personal address, but had he really thought that Nathanial would extend that invitation? He'd hoped. He shouldn't have. Hope had a way of getting destroyed.

NATHANIAL GRIPPED the latest scandal sheet in his fist as he pushed through the door. He stopped at the desk of the regular police.

"Are you investigating this?" Or was it going to land on his desk?

The man read through the page. "No. The woman didn't want nothin' to do with us or the man. Seems no one wanted to risk him coming back. She should've kept her fingers out of his wallet. Lucky he isn't the one pressing charges and getting her shipped off."

"Do you know who he was?" Lord F could be several men. If it was Lord Featherington, his sister would be horrified. Nathanial would be horrified that his sister was married to such a brute. Though he couldn't imagine Bertie even walking into a brothel and he was supposed to be in Bath.

The man leaned closer. "I heard from one of the other women that he was real regular, but not real popular. Seems he had a peculiar way about him." He leaned back. "There are some things a respectable lady would never do. Not that I know any ladies like that, Sir."

"I don't care what he liked, when a man pays, he can get what he wants." Did they not care that the emotion was faked? The memory of Jericho's hands on him from two days ago was still enough to make Nathanial's blood heat, but he still couldn't believe that he'd shared his deepest shame. That he'd struggled to do anything with that woman. At the time he'd thought he was broken; it had been another six months before he'd let himself believe the truth about his preferences. "I want to know his name."

"You didn't hear it from me. No one is saying because he wants to keep his reputation clean." The policeman gave Nathanial a knowing look as if the first concern for all nobles was their reputation followed by their wealth. For many it was.

Was he any different?

"I won't tell a soul." He placed his hand over his heart.

"'Tis Foxhall."

Nathanial let out a relieved sigh. Not his sister's husband. Though he knew the name from around the place. "If he changes his mind, at least I'll be prepared."

"That's good thinking."

Nathanial smiled and went upstairs to his own office. He shut the door and leaned against it. There was a mechanical bird waiting on his desk. He picked it up, but it wasn't a secured bird, nor was it marked with any crest. Just plain bronze.

Curious he popped open its belly. A piece of paper was neatly rolled inside. The ends were a little crushed from where it had been forced to fit, and he struggled to pull it out for several seconds. Then it sprung free and unfurled on his desk.

There was a charcoal sketch of him in Jericho's lap. It wasn't clearly him, the lines were too rough to tell, but he knew his own face and the memory of that night was burned into his mind. Both men were smiling in the sketch. He didn't remember smiling. Or looking at Jericho like that. He touched the lines of Jericho's hand as it rested on his thigh. They looked comfortable as if they knew each other well and were…happy.

He rolled up the picture and shoved it into his desk.

It was only then he noticed the tag around the metal bird's neck. It was addressed to him which was how it had ended up on his desk. He turned the creature over to reset it to return home, even though he knew where it had come from, then stopped as the makers mark caught his eye. Fulbright Delivery Birds. Not that anyone called them that; he didn't even think of them by their proper name.

But they were *Fulbright* Delivery Birds.

He hadn't made the connection before. The idea that Jericho Fulbright could be related to those Fulbrights… He had talked about his father cutting him off but little else that would give Nathanial a clue about the connection. Nathanial dashed off a letter to his sister and grabbed one of his own birds, using her London address in the alpha numeric code the bird accepted. Then he opened the window and sent it on its way.

Instead of sending Jericho's bird home empty he added a small thank you note. He was glad to have the picture, and he would take it home so he could enjoy it at his leisure. He didn't sign the note, nor had Jericho. If someone intercepted an unsecure bird, then all kinds of secrets could be revealed. Jericho really should upgrade; if he was related, he should have a flock of secure birds.

Nathanial slipped the tag with his name on it from the bird's neck and sent it home.

He stood by the window watching it fly until it was nothing but a speck. Was anyone ever truly free or were they all birds with programmed orders they had to follow?

There once was a place no gentlemen goes
Unless he is inclined to debaucheries woes
Many carnal delights,
Male flesh in full flight
All wanting a taste of the Jericho Rose

— ROBERT PENNYWORTH-
TRICKETT

7

Jericho dressed respectably and somberly for the occasion. Today he did want to get lost in the crowd of black morning suited, hat wearing men. He caught a cab to where the printer was located. Given that it published scandal sheets, humorous digs at the nobility, the law, and just about anything else as well as poetry just this side of not obscene and porno pamphlets on the other side it was not in the best part of town.

Some people just wanted a cheap bit of entertainment and they didn't care about the quality of the paper or ink. Today's laugh was tomorrow's kindling.

He side stepped some refuse, dropped a few coins in the hands of a child that needed schooling and feeding, and then slipped inside the non-descript building. The scent of ink and the sound of the press assailed him the moment he entered.

He didn't come here often, preferring to have what he needed delivered to the Rose and send messages by bird if required. He rang the bell on the counter and waited for what felt like the best part of an hour, not five minutes. The noise and the smell made his skin crawl and his head thump.

"How can I help you, Sir?"

"By not calling me sir." He might dress as though he was part of the upper class, but he wasn't by any stretch. Even though his father had married a noble woman, he had still not earned a place among the nobility; Jericho heard enough gossip from the parties to know that it ate his father up. He quite enjoyed knowing that piece of gossip. His father had cast him off and yet it had made no difference to his social standing. "Mr. Fulbright will be fine."

The printer's eyes lit up. "Come to my office. It's quieter in there."

Jericho doubted that but followed. The office was a small cramped space that appeared to double as a storage closet. There was a table and two chairs, both of which had boxes stacked on them. Would the printer be able to help him? If he couldn't, then at least Jericho had played his part and could brush Nathanial off.

Though without Nathanial, he'd never be able to find the killer and determine if he did have a demon doing the killing or if he were just an awful human. He wasn't ready to ask the copper what he thought about demons.

If he had no information for Nathanial after this, then he wouldn't stop by just for a few drinks and conversation. Although, he was a bit too tightly wound for that at the moment. It would be safer for both of them if Nathanial didn't visit, as the copper was a splinter he couldn't pick free of his skin. Nathanial consumed far too many waking moments and all of Jericho's sleeping ones. And Eulalia was making the lust ten times worse than it needed to be, he was sure.

"How can I assist you, Mr. Fulbright?"

"I'm here to talk about my order." He forced a polite smile.

"Is there a problem with your order?" The printer pulled out a file and thumbed through the pages until he found what he was looking for. "Ah, I see you are one of our more discreet clients."

That wouldn't have been how Jericho would've phrased it, but he wasn't about to argue when he was the one needing the favor. "I received some material that gave me pause."

The man raised his eyebrow, and Jericho knew why. Most of the material Jericho received would give respectable people pause. "How so?"

Jericho pulled out the pamphlet with the woman being choked and passed it across the table. "This did come from here, did it not?"

There was a slim chance it had been slipped into the file by someone in his club, but that didn't bear thinking about. It would be untraceable if that were the source.

The man nodded. "Yes. That is a more specialized taste."

Clearly the man didn't know the woman was dead or dying, and not merely acting—though that was also disturbing if some men found that alluring. He suppressed a shudder and the urge to tell the man never send such filth again. Instead, he loosened his grip on Eulalia so she could blossom on his tongue. She purred in his skull and took over his mouth with a whispered, *I'm hungry.*

"One of my patrons would really like to acquire more."

"A special order?"

"Yes. Do you know who took the photos?" Someone had to get paid. The lies kept falling from his lips. "Perhaps even a meeting could be arranged. My client is willing to pay, and you would not be forgotten."

The man nodded in Eulalia's thrall. He went through his papers. "The photos are delivered by a Mr. Harrison Smith. He only accepts cash; many of the photographers don't like any paperwork." He wrote down something. "This is his address." Greed flared in his eyes. "My compensation?"

Jericho slid a pouch of money over the table, and regained control of his tongue. Eulalia hissed her displeasure, and her hunger heated his skin. The fever was beginning because he'd used her too frequently. He'd have to act swiftly this time. Another body in his place of business would not be seemly.

The printer blinked and looked at the money, and then at the address and name he'd written down as though surprised that he'd been so forth coming.

Jericho smiled, his voice his own. "You have been most helpful."

THE NOBILITY TASK FORCE was situated above the offices of the regular police. Jericho knew where the station was because he'd been dragged in there more than once and had only walked free because Eulalia was able to work her magic. If not for the demon, he'd have been locked up or shipped out to Australia for hard labor, neither of which appealed.

No one stopped him as he walked up the stairs. He was dressed the part of a nobleman, a boring individual who was probably the victim not the criminal in the eyes the regular police. Perhaps they thought he was here to report the theft of a silk handkerchief.

Upstairs, there was a man on the desk guarding the entrance to the offices. He stood. "Who are you here to see?"

Apparently not just anyone could go through. "Detective Bayard."

"Let me see if he's in. And you are?"

"Mr. Fulbright." Let the man make of that what he would. Men tended to either know of his notorious club or they knew of the family fortune that he would never get his hands on. That no longer burned; he hoped his father choked on a penny.

The man glanced at him again and his eyebrows drew together as though not sure which side of the family Jericho belonged on. It would be better for Nathanial if they assumed that he belonged to the respectable inventor side. Jericho widened his smile and let Eulalia shimmer closer to the surface. The man blinked and hurried through the door. In only a few moments, he was back and showing Jericho to Nathanial's office.

The office had a walnut desk and leather chairs. A microscope and magnifying glass were set up on the sideboard along with a collection of note pads. A map of London covered one wall. On another wall, blank paper had been pinned up and written on. In the center were three names. One of which was Miss Doxley's.

The two other names were the other two victims then?

Nathanial stood and Jericho let his gaze land on him. His dark blond hair was carefully slicked down, making Jericho want to mess it up. His clothing was as dull as Jericho's and just as buttoned up, but that didn't stop his imagination from lingering on the unbuttoning. It would be a thrill to get the copper out of his clothes.

"I didn't expect you so soon." Nathanial held out his hand as though they were colleagues.

Jericho shook it and kept up the pretense, though from the color on Nathanial's cheeks, he was thinking of more than a handshake. "I wasn't in the area, but I thought I'd update you on my findings." He pulled out the piece of paper and placed it on the table. "Do not expect much to come of it. False names and cash payments abound."

"With good reason."

Jericho inclined his head in agreement, then turned to face the sheets of paper. A web of names that made no sense. "What is this?"

"People they knew. The underlined ones were also at the parties."

"And the list to the side?"

"Is a full guest list. There is substantial overlap."

"And here I was thinking you spent your days searching for lost jewels and pilfered handkerchiefs." He gave Nathanial a grin; he was only half serious.

"And preventing duels or prosecuting those who go through with them. But also, any crime that a common born man commits, a noble does as well. They just don't want everyone to know."

"So, you cover it up?" That would not surprise Jericho one bit.

"No. But prison isn't always the answer. Loss of money and status for some is worse."

That, Jericho didn't believe. He couldn't imagine a noble born person getting charged with the crime of loitering, or of failing to show good moral virtue, even though they had affairs a plenty. And he had yet to hear of a noble born man being charged with sodomy out of wedlock, and he could think of a dozen who did without breaking a sweat.

"Men with particular tastes start small. They dip their toes to see how far they can go." He glanced at Nathanial. A man with a demon would be cautious at first, testing the power. It would be tempting to give in and revel, and perhaps if one had enough money there would be no consequence.

How did the deaths not weigh on the man's mind? Jericho hated feeding Eulalia and regretted the deaths even though he was selective. Doxley's death still pained him.

"What do you mean?"

Jericho wanted to reach out and run his fingers along Nathanial's jaw. "Like an opium addict. It starts as a taste then becomes more." He returned his gaze to the board. "Your masked man has been doing this for a while. Probably without the camera. He may not have even killed the first few times. But now he needs the sharper edge. The thrill of letting people know what he's doing."

"And how do you know this?"

"I study people. I have for a very long time. It was a way to survive boarding school and then the army. I tried to fit in. but I also saw what people were up to when they thought no one was looking."

"Perhaps you should have been a policeman."

Jericho laughed. "I like people, not the law." He pointed to a name on the list. "Robert Pennyworth-Trickett. You were speaking to him last night. What did you think of him?"

"Polite, well read. Well versed in politics and art."

"He is also a writer of obscene poetry and what some would call a kept man."

Nathanial frowned. "What on earth do you mean?"

"He is a by-blow with few prospects, so he took it upon himself to find a wealthy benefactor. Well, two actually. One pays for the house the other his clothing. It's a better life than where he started. You would've turned your nose up at him three years ago and called him a whore." Jericho lowered his voice further in case the walls were thin. "Maybe you still would as he loves neither but is happy to trade his body for his lifestyle."

"He seemed so charming."

"He is. It's why he is so well positioned." Jericho had envied Robert for a time and the ease with which he got his way without a demon riding in his skull.

"Why share this?"

"Because the people at these parties are sharing only the face they want you to see. You will need to dig deeper and see beneath their pretty masks of proprietary." The killer wouldn't flaunt his tastes at balls, even if they were his hunting grounds. Before killing noble women, he'd probably started with maids. People who could vanish.

It would be too easy to assume every killer had a demon, a reason to be vile. Jericho knew human nature could be just as rough. Liang's killer was human and with no excuse beyond simple hatred. The snuff porno wasn't about hate. It was about power.

Nathanial wasn't looking at the papers or the names; he was studying Jericho. Jericho wanted to turn away or fidget, but he made himself hold still.

"You came here dressed the part of a respectable man."

Jericho smiled. "I didn't think you appreciate my bright pink cravat or rose patterned silk waistcoat."

"You wear a mask depending on where you are."

He leaned closer. "As do you, good Detective. Lucky is the man who can cast it off and live his own life. For if there is no heaven and no hell, no amount of self-discipline or denial will amount to anything more than a wasted life."

"You believe in nothing?"

"I don't know what I believe. But I know I will not waste these precious breaths. What are you holding your breath for? What reward do you hope to claim?" He tore his gaze away and studied the papers. No other names leapt out at him even though he was familiar with many from gossip or scandal sheets. One of them was the killer or had held the camera. "You masked man won't stop. He will be thinking of his next victim and working out how to do it."

He knew that because that was how he hunted his prey to feed Eulalia.

Nathanial didn't see a killer when one was in his office; he was never going to be able to find one on his own. "Let me know if I can be of any further assistance. You know where to find me." He tipped his hat and didn't wait for Nathanial to bid him farewell. If this was the end of their dealings, he didn't want to hear goodbye.

8

It was barely dusk when Jericho slipped from the Rose and onto the streets. He wasn't dressed in quality clothing now; instead, he wore the course trousers and linen shirt worn by common laborers. If one was going to Leicester Square or other rougher areas of London it didn't pay to be overdressed or flash about too much coin.

While he'd have rather stayed in the Rose, he needed to get out and ease the fever before Eulalia took control and killed another of his patrons—that would be incredibly bad for business and his reputation. The fever weakened him and strengthened her.

While the summer night was cool, his skin was hot and sticky. He needed to find someone. He thought about going into the park where cheap flesh could be found and enjoyed in the shadowed corners, but they were just making a living and trying to exist in a world that told them to vanish. He wanted a different soul. One that…he couldn't say deserved to die because who was he to make that judgment…but one that was dishonest.

He followed the sidewalk to where restaurants of dubious quality doled out food to half-drunk men who'd soon be spilling out into the night to look for someone to complete their evening. Some would want a woman, others a man. From experience, Jericho knew soldiers were often the first to bend over at night and the first to lash out in daylight if anyone made even the coyest suggestion.

Jericho lingered, waiting, listening not with his ears but with Eulalia's senses. In this they could work together. A man with a genuine interest in an encounter passed by and Jericho let him go. That wasn't what he wanted. He wanted to take an angry man, one who couldn't face himself in the mirror, off the streets. Maybe if he killed enough of them, Liang would forgive him. And he'd forgive himself for not doing anything at the time.

His fingers curled as though this time he was ready to fight. This time he'd change the past. He exhaled and relaxed his fingers. Impossible. And if he had stepped in three years ago, then he'd have been swallowed into the fight and killed. He'd reported the assault, the murder, and had been laughed at by the brass. With anger in his veins instead of blood, he'd picked a fight with the killer. They'd both been disciplined, but someone had stepped forward with the truth and he'd been the one discharged. Love was a worse crime than murder.

Eulalia's excitement vibrated through him. Coming down the street was a man who had clearly had too much to drink, but he pulsed with a hunger that he didn't want to admit to. Jericho would relieve him of that burden.

The man looked at Jericho and smiled that slippery smile. Jericho had seen it a hundred times over, yet it still made his skin want to slide off his bones. For a heartbeat he wanted to turn away. To find someone else. A woman who beat her children and let them starve, a man who hit his wife. But they weren't easy targets that could be lured into the alley with the promise of sex. They took time.

He didn't have that time tonight, nor did he want to dig that deep into someone's mind. So, he fell into step with the man who wanted him now, but who was already making excuses for in the morning. The man hated that others could live the life he wanted but wasn't brave enough to grasp. Nathanial, while not brave, didn't hate. That was the difference, and it was important to Jericho. This man would, in daylight, use his fists to make sure Jericho didn't look at him that way again.

Without a word, Jericho was steering them into the closest ally. The man produced a coin and Jericho accepted without argument. This wasn't about the price.

The man licked his lips and revulsion tossed Jericho's stomach about like a ship in a storm. He was actually going to have to get this man to spill so Eulalia could take his soul. He loathed this bit. The intimate act twisted into something callous and dark.

With a sigh, he let Eulalia swim to the surface, but not take over as she wasn't above using his body in ways he didn't enjoy or approve of. This oaf wasn't getting any part of him.

"You're a pretty one," the man slurred.

Jericho's lips curved into a smile. He was still there, aware and awake, but his body was something else. A tool to be used. He could snatch it back, but he let Eulalia have her way. It was better that he kept her on his side. Their relationship was already frayed because he hadn't passed her onto another host. She liked the kill; he didn't.

His hands touched the man, reached for his trousers, and tugged them open. His semi-erect cock fell out. This wouldn't take long. There would be no need for Jericho to perform as the man expected.

Eulalia laughed.

He vowed to snatch back control and walk away if she though that Jericho was either going to get on his knees or bend this man over. His hand worked over the man's flesh and he wanted to slink further away into his mind, so he didn't have to be part of this at all, but he needed to be there to make sure Eulalia behaved. Not like last time. He could've had fun with Stephan without it resulting in death if Eulalia hadn't taken over.

The man's cock stood proud and Eulalia's voice dripped off his tongue like honey. The man drawn in by every word. His eyes lost their focus and his breathing quickened as Eulalia whispered one erotic thought after another. Did she convince the man that he was getting what he wanted? Or was she able to control the man's desire so that it didn't matter.

Jericho stepped back as the fountain erupted and the man's seed and soul slipped free. He gagged as Eulalia swallowed the soul. Thick and alive it squirmed in his throat as though fighting its fate.

Then the moment was over.

The man was dead and slumped against the wall with his penis poking out of his trousers like a dead worm. Eulalia purred and the fever was gone. He stumbled out of the ally and made it a whole block before he stepped to the side and threw up in the refuse-filled gutter. People laughed and called him a drunkard. He didn't care. Better they think him that than what he truly was.

He wiped his mouth. The soul was gone, consumed, but the sensation of having that living, coiling darkness inside of him lingered. Eulalia was right; the nice people did taste better. Nathanial would be like a sugared confection.

IT WAS PROBABLY a bad idea to return to the Jericho Rose, but the idea of going to one of the staid clubs where Nathanial's friends liked to start their evening before they went looking for more daring adventures didn't appeal—not that Nathanial was going to let his membership lapse because that would raise eyebrows and create gossip.

When he entered, the building the tension that had hounded him all day melted like the last of winter's snow. He went into the parlor and got a drink and seat. Robert was reciting something lewd, but all Nathanial could do was smile at the clever rhyme instead of being shocked.

He tried to see Robert as the kept man with two different lovers paying for his way, but nothing about him suggested that he was anything but happy and carefree. He did enjoy life and the benefits he had and if anyone knew of the arrangement he didn't seem to care. Many a mistress didn't care as she traded her looks and affections for security instead of the demands of marriage.

Nathanial still aspired to marriage even though he would have to wait until his father turned up his toes. But Jericho's words had worked their poison. What if there was nothing after this and he was waiting, living his life bound to some arbitrary moral code that had been in place for generations, for no good reason? If this was all he had, was he wasting it? More to the point, if there was a God—and he was convinced there was, even if Jericho didn't believe—was it an affront to God to waste the days he'd been given on this Earth?

They were questions best debated by more agile minds than his.

With the poetry finished and Robert taking his bow, Nathanial slipped into the smoking room, but Jericho wasn't in there either. As before in this room the embraces were more intimate. Kissing and fondling. An openness he'd only dreamed of.

A blond man smiled and offered him the pipe. Nathanial was about to refuse, but he couldn't find a good excuse. One taste. Why not?

He drew the smoke into his lungs and coughed, his eyes watering as he handed it back. The man moved closer, but Nathanial wasn't here to play. To watch, maybe. He shook his head which seemed strangely disconnected. A hand slid around his neck, a soft caress that was soothing and alarming. He glanced up as the owner of the hand leaned over the back of the chair and whispered in his ear.

"Come. This room is not for you." Jericho helped Nathanial up and he let himself be led away.

Nathanial glanced back, but the man had moved on. He was already forgotten. Were they there just to make plans for later in the evening?

Jericho sat him down in a small room, that in another house might have been a dining room. There was a grand table in here, but Nathanial doubted many dinner parties were hosted. A glass of brandy was placed in front of him. He drank it without asking why.

"Don't go there in there unless you are prepared to offer yourself up for their games."

"I wanted to watch again."

Jericho smiled, but tonight it held an edge as though he'd swallowed glass. "No...if you watch you must play eventually. I don't think that's why you're here. Though if I am wrong please remove your waistcoat and your scruples and return to the smoking room. I shall enjoy the show."

"You watch."

"I own the club. I supervise." Jericho turned a chair and sat so he faced Nathanial.

"But never join in?"

Jericho swallowed. His dark eyes, merciless pits. "My life is separate to the club."

Nathanial propped his head up on his hand to consider Jericho. "And yet you live upstairs. How did you come to own this house? Did your father buy it?"

He laughed, but it lacked humor. "No. I made an arrangement with the owner. He had no children or wife, and I suggested this club. He died a year after it opened. I inherited it."

"He gifted you a house?"

"I was his…companion…when I returned to London."

Oh. No wonder he knew so much about what it was to be a kept man. "And what services did you perform as *companion?*"

Anger flickered across Jericho's face, something cold and hard surfaced, and was gone as his eyes flashed blue. "Reading and taking him to the opera mostly. He was going blind, but still enjoyed company. So, you can drag your thoughts out of my trousers."

Nathanial couldn't seem to drag his gaze or his mind up. Slowly, he stood. Still not entirely sure of his body or the way the room seemed to move, he took two steps and sat on Jericho's lap, facing him, with his arms around his neck. "What if I don't want to?"

For several breaths Jericho didn't move. His face seemed to morph and shift as though he were not real. Was he thinking up ways to reject him? If Jericho tossed him off, it would be easy to never return. But Jericho put his hands on Nathanial's hips and drew him closer. "This?"

The heat and hardness were there. A temptation he didn't have the will to resist. He would do whatever Jericho asked. He leaned closer, wanting a taste of his lips, but Jericho turned so Nathanial's lips grazed his cheek instead.

"I'm not good company tonight." Jericho's words were little more than a whisper.

"I don't want company." He wanted…he wanted to know what he was missing. To be with another. There were other things that didn't require breaking the law and he wanted to sample them. He wanted Jericho.

Jericho's fingers pressed into his hips, rocking him close so a delicious burn spread through him. He'd had men make suggestions at parties, but he'd always declined out of fear that somehow his reputation would be smeared, or worse it would get back to his father. He was safe here. Nothing could touch him.

Jericho's eyes were blue when he looked at him. His cheek bones were sharp, and his skin had a sheen as though he were bathed in moonlight. The opium was playing tricks with Nathanial. Jericho's eyes were brown, and his skin was dark like honey. What he was seeing was something far more angelic. Too pretty. He leaned closer as though to kiss Nathanial, but Nathanial leaned back.

Something wasn't right.

Desire had changed into something more predatory. The way Jericho looked at him was wrong somehow. He struggled to get free, but Jericho wouldn't release him. They ground together as they struggled, and the throb in Nathanial's cock was unbearable. Jericho growled like a beast and Nathanial went still. His heart hammered. His hands were on Jericho's shoulder's, holding him at bay even though Jericho's hands kept their hips pressed together.

After a while, Jericho looked up. His eyes were brown, and his lips turned down as though he were the most miserable person in London. "Do not give up your dreams on my account. I envy you your morals."

"My morals bind me tight and do not warm me."

"Casual encounters will not sate your hunger either. They are like boiled lollies. Delicious while in the mouth but gone too fast leaving only a craving for more." He released Nathanial.

"I already crave." Being here was like watching people feast but not being able to take a bite or taste the wine. "But you do not." He pulled away and stood, the carpet rocking beneath his feet as though it were a river. He steadied himself on the table. He was never tasting opium again.

Jericho steadied him and cupped his face. "I do. I just know what I cannot have."

Nathanial brushed Jericho aside and stumbled. "Then you are blind if you cannot see it on offer."

Why could Jericho not be the kind of rogue that would take full advantage?

"You would hate me, and yourself, for giving in so easily come dawn." He drew Nathanial close, into a tight embrace.

Nathanial struggled at first, then let himself be held. He felt the press of Jericho's erection. The body didn't lie, and Jericho had admitted to wanting him. "I hate you for being so honorable."

Jericho's breath brushed Nathanial ear. "The feeling is mutual."

Dearest Nathanial,

I have two pieces of news for you, both of which you'll find delightful!

Bertie was most excited at your interest in photography (I didn't tell
him why and he doesn't need to know). He is keen to introduce you to
members of the photography club and by happy chance most of them
will be at Father's party. This means you will be attending.

I have taken the liberty of telling Father that you are looking forward
to it and that you should be able to get away from work for the weekend. I am doing this to help you though I know you will be cursing me
as you read this. Bertie said he'd lend you one of his old cameras and I
had to agree even though we know this is a sham. I'm sure you won't
mind going along with it though I struggle to belief that one of the
club members could be behind the atrocity.

With regards to your other question. The Fulbright family that
married into the Swinson clan is the maker of the Fulbright Bird. The
father married an Israeli woman, but she died soon after giving birth
to a son. A few years later, he made his fortune and married the

impoverished Swinson daughter. Bertie's mother (who is here to help with his sister's new baby, no I won't bore you with the details except to say he does wail a lot and I had quite forgotten how tedious newborns could be) was quite chatty about it all. Apparently, the bird design was hers, and when she died Fulbright took it as his own. Given that most men think women too dull to come up with such an invention, no one gave credit to the idea that it was hers, but her name is on all the plans.

Any way to cut a long running scandal short, the son is that notorious club owner. I think you know the one I mean since you were asking. The father cut him off, though I don't know why…perhaps because of the foreign mother. Apparently, that was a terrible blow up at the time.
In closing, I am most desperate to hear what happens next and how this all marries together!

Madly curious,
Your sister M

9

 $\mathscr{N}$ athanial screwed up his sister's letter but stopped short of tossing it into the fireplace. He should've known there would be a price for her help. Joining Bertie's photography club was close to the last thing he wanted to do. The other was go to work.

His head was quite at sea.

And he'd had the most awful nightmares. He was sure they were just misshapen dreams, though he remembered seeing odd things too. Odd things that had grown and become something monstrous, a monster trying to break free of human skin. Skin that belonged to Jericho.

His stomach rolled at the memory of the dream. He was never touching the opium pipe again. Part of him wanted to vow never to return to the Jericho Rose, but he couldn't make that promise. The way Jericho's hands had been on him...and the way they had been pressed together...

He shivered with a heat that started low in his belly.

Jericho was clearly a better man than Nathanial was. Nathanial had offered it all after a few brandies and a puff of opium. And Jericho had politely knocked him on his ass and called him a cab so he could get home safely. Last night's anger at being brushed off had faded to embarrassment.

He couldn't show his face there. He'd never be able to look Jericho in the eye.

Nathanial smoothed out his sister's letter and re-read it. He was going to have to find a way to ask Amberton for next weekend off so he could attend. He'd rather go back to the Rose and apologize for being such a love-sick dimwit.

No, not love-sick. He didn't love Jericho. He admired him, the way he'd rebuilt after several hardships and the way he did the right thing even when Nathanial had been hoping Jericho was a terrible rogue the way the scandal sheets claimed. He must be lust-sick; that was illness wasn't it? If not, it should have been.

Lust-sick: the illness that afflicts virgins, nuns, and priests so they craved for a release that cannot be imagined. Symptoms included longing of the loins and temporary madness where the sufferer was willing to throw all cares and morals away.

But he hadn't, because Jericho had stopped him. So aside from a headache and private humiliation he was fine. Except he wasn't, because he wasn't sure what he wanted anymore.

Why was he waiting?

Who was he hoping to please?

It certainly wasn't himself.

THE OFFICE WAS MERCIFULLY quiet when Nathanial got there. Maybe there had been some drama overnight that had called them all away. When he'd first started this job, he would have been burning with curiosity to find out what had happened. Now he had enough of his own work to worry about that he didn't let other people's cases trouble him.

On the back of her letter his sister had listed some of the people in Bertie's photography club. He put a mark next to each of the names on his papers. Several of them were at each of the balls. That was to be expected.

He took a cab to the address Jericho had given him regarding the supplier of the photographs and bought lunch in the area but didn't see anyone of interest. It was late afternoon when returned and began the effort to find who owned the property and under what name it was rented under. He was expecting it to be a different name, if not a different person, to the one the printer paid.

A shadow darkened his doorway as he made some more notes on the case. Nathanial glanced up at Amberton and put down his pen.

"You missed a duel this morning. Had to arrest both young men," Amberton said with a huff as though indignant at the idea of making arrests.

"What were they fighting about?" Not that he cared, but he didn't want to launch into his request without at least attempting small talk.

"A card debt of all things." Amberton shook his head and sat. "How is your case going?"

"I have several leads. I'm trying to track down the person who sells the photographs, as well as the man taking them. To that end I will be joining a photography club."

"Your social life is really going places."

"Contrived amusements for the case." Nathanial gave his boss a thin-lipped smile. He didn't want Amberton thinking that he enjoyed his time at the Rose. Men of his boss's age tended not to be forward thinkers. They tended to be like Nathanial's father, remembering the good old days of the queen's reign.

"And it is working. I'm impressed."

Nathanial nodded. "My father is hosting a party this weekend. I would like to attend as several of the photography club members will be there."

"You cannot go in there and lift their shirts."

"That is not what I was planning," Nathanial said dryly. "I have to draw the line somewhere."

Amberton chuckled. "Maybe not you. That Fulbright fellow though…"

Whatever Amberton was thinking the answer was no. "I'm not sure what you mean?"

"Take that Fulbright fellow with you and see what he can discover. He probably knows several of them intimately."

"He's not noble and he doesn't have an invitation." There was no way he was taking Jericho to his father's party. Although the idea did hold some appeal; hopeful mothers wouldn't shove their daughters at him and maybe his father would stop trying to push him into the cold arms of the church.

"Take him as your partner."

"Pardon?" He was sure he'd misheard what his boss had said.

"His father will most likely be at the party—or so I heard, as Miss Fulbright has a rather large dowry and many young men would like to wed her. So take him as your partner."

"That would suggest to everyone that I have a relationship with him." Respectable men didn't pay visits to men like Jericho unless it was by the hour. Though he'd gotten the impression last night, or from what he could remember of last night, that Jericho had never done that kind of business. "Not only that, but Mr. Fulbright being there would damage her standing. Scandal follows him like a hungry puppy."

Amberton stared at him as though he could pull Nathanial apart and read how he was put together. "I'm aware of all of that. But I do not care about the marriage prospects of a social climber. I care about catching a killer."

"As do I, but I don't need Jericho at my father's party." He knew he'd made a mistake as the words fell from his lips.

Amberton smiled as though he had Nathanial right where he wanted him. "You are already working with him. Tell your father that he is assisting in a police matter and if he takes issue with that, send him to my door."

Nathanial hesitated. Amberton was right; Jericho could do things that he couldn't. More to the point Jericho had a way with words. People listened to him and liked him. "My father doesn't approve of the Male Marriage Act."

"But nothing is happening between the two of you, so you have nothing to worry about."

"It will appear as though something is going on."

And Nathanial's biggest issue with this plan was that he wasn't sure how he felt about that. Not only was there Jericho's reputation, there was also the class difference. Jericho's family was known for trying to climb into bed with the nobility, and the people there would see Jericho no differently. Or they would view Nathanial as the kind of man who didn't care about his reputation and the gossips would do their damnedest to blacken it further.

Amberton was waiting for his agreement.

If he agreed and this all went badly—which it probably would— then he would be dismissed. The Nobility Task Force couldn't be filled with men who didn't take their rank seriously. With all his recent case failures, Amberton was looking for ways to get rid of him. He drew in a breath. "What will I tell Fulbright?"

"Whatever you want. Suggest that it's in his best interest to assist. He is one whisper away from arrest at the best of times."

That was all true. Would Jericho agree, though? Or would he see it as a horrible intrusion and disruption to his business. He wasn't looking forward to asking. "My father will probably ban me at the door for arriving with a man. Would it not be best for me to pursue the photography angle and leave Mr. Fulbright out of police matters now that I have the details of the photo seller?"

"You are taking Mr. Fulbright so he can get undershirts. I want this bastard stopped before he kills again. Am I clear? That, or will you hand your resignation to me before you leave tonight."

"You have made yourself clear." One way or another Amberton was pushing him out of the nest. Unlike the mechanical birds, Nathanial had no home to return to. "I will solve this case."

"I hope so. For both our sakes."

<hr>

"ARE YOU OUT OF YOUR MIND?" Jericho paced the dining room floor.

He poured himself a brandy and drank it just as fast. He should've taken Nathanial to his study, where privacy could be assured, but after the death of Stephan and the way Eulalia had tried to take over last time Nathanial got close, he didn't trust himself to be alone with Nathanial. "I am not going to some country party."

He had nothing to wear for a start. His wardrobe was for evening events, not picnics. There would be picnics at some point, he was sure of it.

"It's not a big thing, just dinner and dancing. A ball."

That was worse. Polite conversation with puffed up men whose biggest source of pride was how much they'd inherited from their father, and women who knew how to assess a man's funds and his character with a single glance. "I don't dance."

"I don't believe you."

Jericho smiled. Few ever said that to him. Most nodded their head and believed any lie he told. "Fine, I can dance." The man he'd once been a companion to had liked to put on his gramophone and dance when his gout allowed it. He had been most thrilled about the idea of a place where men could associate more freely; he'd loved the club in its earlier incarnation. "But I don't want to go. My life is here. I have a business to run in case you haven't noticed."

Nathanial had stayed well away from the smoking room this time, to Jericho's relief. He didn't want Nathanial to surrender what he held onto as dearly as a maid with good marriage prospects. He might be the youngest son, but Nathanial could still marry well.

"One night. We don't even have to spend the night." Nathanial held up one finger to reinforce the point. "Your father and step-mother will be there."

Jericho rocked back onto his heels. He hadn't seen his father in many years and even then, it had only been in passing. Jericho had been in uniform before leaving for Hong Kong and his father hadn't recognized him. At the time, it had hurt. What kind of father doesn't know his own son?

His father wouldn't know him now. Only once a clever gossip realized there were two Mr. Fulbright's in the room would his father look in his direction and then there would be a kerfuffle. "That is not a feature the changes my mind to the positive."

"The killer will probably be there, too."

Nathanial had lulled him into a polite conversation with an update on the case, so Jericho knew all about the photography club. Half the gentlemen in it had probably taken nude photos of their mistresses for their own viewing pleasure. Not everyone would stoop to buying porno pamphlets.

"You can't be sure of that."

"No. But wouldn't it be grand if he was and we were able to identify him?"

While Jericho would be able to do that in a very short conversation —no one could bury that kind of darkness completely no matter how hard they tried—how did he explain that to Nathanial? And if it was another demon, what then? They both killed, but where Jericho kept it secret, that man made it public as though he reveled in it. Perhaps the demon had full control.

"And without evidence, how do you get a conviction? A scar will not matter in a court."

"Search his house and estates. If we know who it is, we can close the net around him."

Jericho had seen too many criminals slip away. Money bought a presumption of innocence. He ran his hand over Nathanial's hair, then kissed his forehead. "For all that you were raised with the foxes you do not behave like them, so you fail to see them as the predators they are."

Kiss his mouth, you fool. I can help him. Let me find the man he wants, Eulalia hissed. *I can stop the murderer from killing again.*

The desire to kiss Nathanial on the lips was part his own and part hers. Jericho pressed his lips together, but that didn't stop the hunger. Eulalia was right. It would be better for the case if he passed her on, but that would mean corrupting Nathanial and he couldn't do that. He doubted Nathanial would want a demon, and he'd want Jericho less if he knew about Eulalia and the price of keeping her fed.

Nathanial brushed Jericho's hand away, breaking the moment

where Jericho might have given in. Anger blazed in his blue eyes. "I am not some naïve fool who doesn't understand the world."

"I never claimed that you were. There is a difference between naivety and good natured." He took a couple of steps away then turned back to the copper. "What do you plan on doing? Going there and interviewing each man in the photography club until they confess their deviant nature?"

"I am joining the club."

"And they all know you are a copper, even if you are one of them." Nathanial's social set was too small and too claustrophobic for him to succeed. Eulalia was right; if Nathanial had her then he'd be able to find the killer and put this revolting business to bed. "Men like him, they like using their power over others. And they will do anything to hold onto that power."

"Then why the photos? Why kill women who will be missed?"

"Because it's a game and he thinks he is so much smarter than everyone else." Jericho sighed and sat.

It was only a matter of time before he was caught with a body in his own hands. Without Eulalia he'd be a no one, but he'd be taking less risks. The club would fall, the cops would shut him down, and he wouldn't survive two weeks in prison. No, he'd have to help Nathanial.

I am not yours to keep. Her anger vibrated through his body as heady as lust but as rough as cheap gin.

He drew in a sharp breath. Nathanial needed to realize the dangers they were heedlessly rushing towards. It wasn't as easy as just go to the ball. Nothing was ever that simple. "If I go with you, your reputation will be done. The scandal sheets will be awash with the news of your relationship with me even though there is nothing going on."

He would love to make fire if they were going to be blowing smoke. There was no point in letting the sheets have all the fun and ruin reputations on a whim. If Nathanial was sunk, he should at least get some pleasure out of it. Jericho smiled as he reassessed the copper.

They could work around his demon problem.

Problem? If you don't like my interference, hand me over and we can both be free.

Jericho hadn't known what he was getting into three years ago. He wouldn't give Nathanial the same burden. He would tell him the truth first. Maybe if he understood Jericho's limitation when it came to bed sport, he'd be willing to have some fun.

Nathanial stared at his hands as though completely defeated. "If I do not take you, then I will lose my job."

Jericho stood, fury on Nathanial's behalf shooting through him. Even Eulalia seethed at the injustice. "What? How is that possible?"

Nathanial lifted his gaze and Jericho had never seen a more morose man in his life. "Amberton has been wanting to get rid of me for a year. Now he's found a way."

"Why does he want rid of you?"

"Because I cannot close a case. I get so far…then it all falls apart. It happens all the time."

Nathanial didn't strike him as the careless type. He seemed like an adequate copper. "What goes wrong?"

He shrugged. "Evidence goes missing, or witnesses refuse to testify."

"Money buys power if not justice." Jericho was sure that with enough money all manner of charges and evidence could be made to vanish.

"That is the problem; the victims want the case solved. They want justice, yet somehow the noose always unravels. And Amberton blames me."

"So, you lose your job. Your family has money."

Nathanial shook his head. "This job is all that was keeping me from the priesthood."

"You don't strike me as a very pious man, even though you have professed your faith as a reason to stay virginal." Jericho really didn't understand the nobility at times. They made so many rules for themselves when it came to behavior and all because they wanted to appear to be a better kind of person than everyone else. From his observations they were exactly the same. And at the end of the day they would all be worm fodder. Death and lust were great equalizers of men and women. He saw no reason why women shouldn't vote or wed each other. Though he could see why some men feared that—they were worried no one would wed them—those men were usually the kind that made terrible husbands.

"I am the youngest son. My brother is fifteen years older and has heirs. My father is a devout man and he wanted me to go to the church as proof of his faith. I got a job instead."

"And if you lose it, he expects you to give up living for his aspiration of a place in a non-existent heaven?" Anger eddied through Jericho. "Take off to the continent."

"I will have no funds. He swore there would be nothing for me if I didn't obey."

What kind of a man didn't care for his child's happiness? Jericho knew too well. His father had sent him away to boarding school to wash his hands of the lingering scandal. A part of him liked the way his name made the scandal sheets so regularly. He hoped his father squirmed. "So let him keep his precious money."

"And what am I to do with no coins to my name?"

"Live like the rest of us."

"Like you?"

"There is nothing wrong with my life. Most of what they say about me is lies. If we go to this party, you will see firsthand how a glance, or a dance, can become a fiction fit for consumption in Pollington's." Jericho ran his fingers through his hair. If they lingered for much longer in the dining room, people would assume what was going on anyway. "You need to think about how you, and your father, will deal with the ensuing scandal."

"Does that mean you will come?"

Jericho smiled; he hoped he would. "You will owe me a favor."

Nathanial narrowed his eyes. "What kind of favor?"

Jericho widened his smile. "If they are going to gossip anyway, you might as well enjoy it."

He'd expected a refusal, or shock. Instead, Nathanial considered him for a moment and nodded. "If you help me identify the man, then I will...um..."

"Frigging?" Mutual masturbation was something Jericho hadn't done in a bloody long time. He couldn't do mutual anything. "Sucking?" Red bloomed on Nathanial's cheeks. "I'll let you think about it."

"You're very confident that you will find him."

"If he is there, I will, but you must introduce me. I think I am looking for some photos of a particular nature. Something for my patrons to enjoy. I'm sure the photographers there have taken nudes before."

"I doubt that."

"I do not."

"Very well. We have an agreement." Nathanial offered his hand and Jericho shook it. He didn't want to let go. He was drawn to Nathanial. Maybe it was his innocence. It had been a long time since Jericho had been so pure, yet they were close in age if not in status or life experience. "Visit my tailor so he can make sure you are suitably attired."

"That was not part of the agreement. And what makes you so sure I don't own the suitable clothing?"

Still holding Jericho's hand Nathanial stepped closer. "It's a suspicion I have."

"What other suspicions do you have about me?"

"I think you value fairness and dislike deceit. That is why you don't hold the nobility in esteem. Here everyone is equal, united in conversation."

"Is that what you call it?" He laughed, but Nathanial was right. While the trappings of lust and sex were here, there was no sex for sale. That could be bought on Fleet Street in one of the male brothels. His club had always been about bringing like-minded men together. His smile faltered; no one had ever read him so easily and it was disturbing to be so bare.

"I also think you are honorable. Another man would have taken advantage the other night. Thank you for seeing me as the fool I am."

Jericho drew Nathanial into an embrace. "You aren't a fool. What kind of person would I be if I used you, knowing full well that wasn't what you truly desired?"

"Ah, but I do desire. Maybe if I have no reputation to save, I will stop caring."

"I shall be the model of respectability. No one shall think there is anything more than a shared appreciation of the male form between us." It was going to kill him to be like the over starched shirts in the room, but he'd do it for Nathanial. And to find out what kind of man killed for pleasure.

"I will send a message regarding the details, via Fulbright Bird."

Jericho's eyes widened. So, Nathanial had researched him and his family. He shouldn't have been surprised. How on Earth did Nathanial fail to close a case?

Dearest Margaret,
you will be thrilled to know I am coming to father's party (where I
will meet with Bertie's photography friends).

I will also be bringing a friend. Yes, he is just a friend, though one who
has been assisting. There will be gossip and I will need your help to
keep a lid on it, though I have no idea how to even try I am sure you
will.

Amberton is going to talk to father so at least he will not assume the
worst from me. Though that will do little good with the rest of the
guests. I fear my reputation will be in tatters, yet I must go through
with it.

I know you are only reading on because you want to know who I will
be bringing, so I will not keep you guessing for any longer as that
would be cruel (and if you know in advance you can help me form a
plan to save myself). I will be bringing Jericho Fulbright with me. If
you don't know who that is then you may ask Bertie as I'm sure he
knows.

As you can read, my life has become quite the mess since you visited.

I dearly hope you will still associate with me after this.

Your loving brother,
Nathanial

10

The idea that Nathanial was not only sending him to his tailor but also paying for the new clothes rubbed like an ill-fitting, overly starched collar. Jericho's suits weren't shabby or cheap by any stretch of the imagination, but they weren't to this level of refinement. Nathanial had already picked out the fabrics and there wasn't a hint of color anywhere. He was going to be as black and white as the other men at the ball. He'd blend in. He'd be bland.

Which was probably for the best. Nathanial wouldn't want to be drawing attention to who he was bringing. Though Jericho suspected that news would travel faster than one of his father's birds.

He lifted his arms for the tailor to continue taking his measurements. If the tailor knew who he was, he was doing a very good job of keeping his feelings about dressing him very well hidden. He didn't want to think about how much Nathanial, and by default his father, was paying for the clothing or the manners.

If he didn't find the killer, or the photographer, he was going to be in Nathanial's debt. If he was unsuccessful, he might have to pass Eulalia on—after he warned Nathanial about the hazards of housing a demon and given him a choice, which was more than he'd had.

Though at the time he'd have taken any chance for revenge. The anger had been too hot and hungry.

At the moment the recent meal and the promise of a hunt was keeping her happy. She delighted in revenge, and while that wasn't his need anymore, the hunt was enough. For the moment. But he'd have to relinquish her sooner rather than later.

He knew he couldn't go on like this, but he didn't know how to break free and be himself anymore. He'd need to live more respectably...

Something he didn't know how to do at all.

And he had to close the club for a night. He was sure it could operate without him there, but he didn't want to chance it. Did he need a manager so he could take a night off, or even step away? Word had gotten around the club that he was going to a ball—he hadn't been able to keep the reason it would be closed a total secret—and some astute fellows would have worked out which one. No doubt Lord Emmaly, Nathanial's father, was getting a rush of late acceptances because they didn't want to miss out on what was sure to be the most exciting party of the summer.

He would do his best to make sure that it wasn't exciting because of anything he did. He'd feed Eulalia before he went. There could be no mishaps. He didn't want to embarrass Nathanial, so Jericho would have to do his very best.

His best had never been good enough.

THE CARRIAGE ARRIVED at Jericho's house five minutes early, the Featherington crest decorated the side. Nathanial hadn't mentioned that detail, yet it was definitely for him. Jericho fiddled with his collar and cravat in the hallway mirror one more time then put his hat on. He looked the part of a staid gentleman. But he knew too well what could lurk beneath even the most severe clothing.

He left the too quiet house and shut the door, then strode down the stairs as if he went to balls every other weekend. The footman opened the carriage door for him and all he saw was a confection of lilac skirts. This could not be right. He glanced up.

A woman with the same golden hair as Nathanial was staring at him. "Hurry up, we don't have all day." Her gaze swung away. "Did you not tell him we were all travelling together?"

Nathanial was seated across from the woman There was another man also in the carriage. This was most definitely not right, and it felt like some kind of set up, though Jericho wasn't sure what he was being set up for. He had nowhere to fall to, and one generally didn't trip upwards and land in respectable society.

"It was a last-minute arrangement." Nathanial gave a strained smile. "Get in and I'll do the introductions."

It was too late to back out, so Jericho got in, sure he'd bought himself more trouble than he could afford. The door was shut, and the carriage started rolling. This could be the longest two hours of his life —there were already several contenders for the *worst* two hours of his life.

"Mr. Fulbright, may I introduce Lord and Lady Featherington. Lady Featherington is my sister."

Jericho tipped his hat. Lord Featherington did the same as he considered Jericho very carefully, but without the malice Jericho had expected. Perhaps Nathanial's sister hadn't wanted to leave her brother alone with him and thought a chaperone was in order.

Good grief, that is exactly what this was. The carriage was uncomfortably warm, and he was so tempted to loosen his cravat, but didn't. He didn't want to shock a very proper lady. But Nathanial and he were arriving at a ball with a chaperone…if there wasn't going to be gossip before, there would most certainly be some now.

He glanced at Nathanial, but Nathanial simply shrugged. "My sister gets her way in the end."

"Ha. Never a truer word was spoken," Featherington agreed.

"You don't begrudge me a thing, dear. When Nathanial told me that you would be attending, I had to meet you beforehand." She beamed at him. "With Bertie travelling up from Bath for the event, I thought why not all go together?"

Jericho could list a handful of reasons without thinking too hard. The carriage was definitely too warm, or he was too overdressed. This whole event was a mistake, but he had to go, and it was too late to stop the carriage and run. "You don't fear for your reputation?"

"Mine? Heavens no. Nathanial's?" She tilted her head and scrutinized Jericho like he was a bug on a pin, and she hadn't decided if he was worthy of being added to her collection.

"What my wife is trying to say is we want to make sure nothing goes awry." Featherington put his hand over his wife's. "Nathanial told us you are helping him with a case. It must be quite unusual."

"And we are not at liberty to say how unusual," Nathanial interjected. "Only that it is worth the condemnation."

Would it be? Jericho shot Nathanial a glance. His lips were pressed together, and he looked anything but happy to be there.

"It will be grand. Father is looking forward to seeing you. He has a new toy to show off apparently, and he has decided to join the twentieth century and is going to do a gentleman's waltz."

Jericho kept his smile fixed in place. He was going to be expected to dance with Nathanial. This was getting worse and they hadn't even arrived yet.

"He didn't have to go to that trouble for me," Nathanial said through gritted teeth.

"Blame your sister for that." Featherington patted his wife's hand and she pulled it away. "I'm sure you will get plenty of offers to dance," he said to Nathanial, before giving Jericho an uneasy glance.

Jericho wasn't expecting anyone to dance with him and he was fine with that.

"I will dance with you, Mr. Fulbright. I don't care what they say. I bet you are charming…you've certainly charmed my baby brother.

Nathanial looked as though he wanted to slide into the crack of the seat. It would be improper for Jericho to join him but leaping out the window of the moving carriage was still an option.

Featherington's eyebrows disappeared into his hat. "You will not dance with him. He is unmarried."

She leaned closer to her husband. "Are you volunteering, dear?"

And that was how Lady Featherington managed to get her way, and it was decided Jericho's first dance would be with the well respected and keen photographer Lord Featherington.

***

THE JOURNEY WAS two hours and while his sister did her best with conversation there were pauses where it was clear that not even her wit could keep the atmosphere from being choking.

Nathanial loved his sister, but he had hoped to have a couple of quiet hours with Jericho where they could talk about the case and what they'd do. This wasn't a party; it was work. And he had reminded Margaret of that, but she didn't appear to be inclined to listen. Or rather, she didn't care. She was too giddy that he was bringing someone to their father's party.

Given that she wasn't one to fake enthusiastic friendship, Nathanial had to assume that she genuinely did find Jericho fascinating. He'd been far less chatty than usual though no less charming and he hadn't let the conversation wander to sex or murder once—even though Margaret had tried to pry details of the case from both of them. Bertie had no idea Jericho and he were investigating his photography club. As it was Bertie wasn't as warm toward Jericho as Margaret, but that was to be expected. Featherington was slumming it by associating with Jericho, and he'd been tricked into a dance, which he could've refused. From the look on Jericho's face, he wouldn't have cared.

The carriage rolled to stop out the front of Emmaly manor. Nathanial had spent most of his childhood here, but now he rarely visited. In part because of father and his archaic views, but also because the threat of poverty if he failed to obey the man. He didn't like to be reminded of the axe over his neck—which was looming closer with each failed case.

Bertie helped Margaret out of the carriage.

Nathanial glanced at Jericho. How did they do this?

"Did you want me to hand you out?" Jericho quipped without a grin.

"I was about to ask you the same."

"You go first. You have the rank. Shall we agree to act as associates not lovers?"

"We aren't lovers," Nathanial hissed, well aware his sister was watching and waiting for them. She had insisted that she act as chaperone to forestall any extra gossip. The downside to that was that it would appear that there was indeed more between them, so acting as merely friends would do nothing but raise more questions.

"I know, but people will assume we are romantically linked."

And Nathanial could yell that they were wrong until he passed out, but it wouldn't matter. If he was going to be socially crucified, he could at least have some fun in the process. Given how stiff Jericho's upper lip had been in the carriage, he didn't know if Jericho would be willing. The heat that usually existed between them was gone; Jericho was playing the perfect gentleman and it was quite dull.

Nathanial got out of the carriage and Jericho followed.

The manor hadn't change since his last visit. It was still massive and gray with extremely formal gardens. He was sure that his father would have the plants all growing in perfect symmetry if he could.

With other people arriving they couldn't dally outside. They needed to go in and be announced. Heat then cold washed over him and for a moment Nathanial thought he was going to be ill. He had to do this. No matter what was required of him he was not going to lose his job because some rich bastard thought he could kill with impunity. That was infinitely worse than Nathanial's choice of partner for the evening.

His father greeted Margaret and Bertie warmly, as did Mother.

"Mr. Bayard and Mr. Fulbright, Junior," the butler announced with a voice that could slice through crystal.

He didn't need to look at Jericho to know he was bristling. The junior added to his name was a reminder that his father would be there or was already. People would assume he was a social climber like his father, when in truth it was Nathanial's fault he was here at all.

Lord Emmaly shook Nathanial's hand. "Good to see you here for a change." His attention switched to Jericho and Nathanial held his breath. What had Amberton said to his father about Jericho? After a pause his father held out his hand and shook Jericho's. There was no other greeting, no welcome. He'd been forced to let Jericho attend, but he didn't have to like it and Nathanial had the feeling there would be hell to pay later.

Jericho simply smiled and kept as silent as Emmaly.

Nathanial followed his sister into the ballroom. As much as he resented her offer of the carriage, he was infinitely glad to have her presence near him as he walked in, trying to keep his head high as if he did this all the time and wasn't the estranged youngest son. The glances became more curious stares. No mama would be shoving their daughter toward him now as they would assume he was after their sons—which would be correct, but he hadn't planned on coming out in quite this way. He'd always put that issue aside for later when he was free of his father's reach.

His sister greeted her friends and introduced him and Jericho, and if there were questions that the polite ladies wanted to ask, they bit their tongues—for the moment at least. While Nathanial felt as awkward as if he were wearing ill-fitting shoes, Jericho was grinning and gracious and it was impossible to believe that he didn't have some blue blood in him somewhere. That innate charm he had worked on everyone apparently, even those who narrowed their eyes at his name as though they were sure they knew exactly how disreputable he was.

Jericho's eyes flashed blue in the light and his skin seemed to glimmer as though he were angelic, not sin incarnate. It was a good thing the respectable ladies couldn't read Nathanial's mind, or it would have been him being shown the door. What he wanted to do with Jericho was not the kind thing that was ever discussed—even at the Jericho Rose.

"That wasn't so bad was it?" Margaret whispered to him.

"There is still the rest of the evening to get through, including dinner." He wasn't going to make it. He didn't have his sister's devil-may-care attitude, or Jericho's charm. This had never been his scene. He would have much rather sat in the library and read a book.

Already the whispers were starting. Were they engaged? Planning to wed or was this some folly, a youthful rebellion before he settled down?

If Jericho heard the gossip, he didn't show it. He moved closer to Nathanial, but not close enough for it to be ill construed. "I am going to have to dance with your brother-in-law very shortly and I don't think he likes me."

"He doesn't dislike you…he just isn't sure what to do with you. It would be easier for him to be able to put you in a neat box. He'd probably prefer it if we were courting. It would be tidier."

"Where is the fun in tidy?" There was nothing innocent about the grin Jericho gave him. "I believe that after this dance is out of the way he will introduce us to his friends?"

"Hopefully, though my sister has already told me I'm dancing with her widowed friend. You might be as well. You won't have to do a thing. My sister will make sure you don't have a free moment all night."

Jericho's grin became strained at the edges. "You do realize I haven't done this kind of thing before."

"You were a companion."

"He didn't go to many parties and if he did, I was there only to help him get around and fetch him drinks."

"Well then I guess this is your debut. You should enjoy." It was reassuring to see that behind the smile and polite conversation Jericho was nervous and hating this as much as him.

"Right, let's get this out of the way. The band is all warmed up." Lord Featherington offered his arm to Jericho.

"You don't have to go through with this," Jericho said in a soft voice.

"I am the one who has to go home with her. So, we are doing this." Featherington put Jericho's hand in position. "I'm leading."

"Never doubted it."

"Then everything will be fine." Featherington gave Nathanial a nod before claiming a spot on the floor with the other couples.

Margaret hooked her arm through Nathanial's. "I don't care what everyone else says. I think you are lucky to have found him. He's a delight."

"You know what he does, right?"

"He runs a business. A gentleman's club for a certain type of gentleman. Your kind of gentleman."

"We are working together. That's all." Nathanial didn't believe his own lies. He wanted more, just once.

Jericho was as fluid as a cat on the dance floor. He followed Featherington's lead perfectly. They weren't the only male couple dancing; two older men were also giving it a go.

"You say that, but your eyes betray you."

Nathanial couldn't look away from the dance floor. He wanted to be the one dancing with Jericho, feeling his hands on him. "Father would skin me."

His father would never accept him marrying a man. And certainly not one who lacked the breeding that father, and so many here, considered essential.

"I will work on father. You concentrate on what you must, and do not let the gossip of fools get in the way." She leaned in. "I will keep my ear out for pertinent gossip. It's so much more fun coming to these things when there is something afoot."

"You didn't tell Bertie?"

"No! What would be the fun in that?"

He bit his tongue. While his sister thought his life was an amusing game to be arranged, she wasn't the one who was going to have to pick up the pieces after the board had been flipped.

11

Jericho turned with Featherington, managed not to step on his toes, and kept a very polite distance. He hated every second of it, knowing that people were looking at him and wondering why someone like him was here and dancing with someone like Featherington.

"You dance well," Featherington said with only the smallest amount of surprise.

"It was part of my schooling." There was no need for him to give the details of his life. He glimpsed Nathanial talking to his sister. He'd rather be dancing with him...but that would lead to gossip, more gossip.

"I have deduced you are here for official reasons." Featherington kept his voice low, but he kept the respectable distance between them.

"Then you know I am not at liberty to discuss." Jericho kept his face fixed in a polite smile.

Featherington's gaze bored into him. "Your involvement with Bayard isn't just professional."

Jericho wanted to deny it, but he couldn't quite find the words. They hadn't done anything, but he wanted to do things he hadn't been able to do for so long because of the demon. He could barely remember what it was like to kiss, or to share the moment of completion with another.

Featherington's grip tightened for a moment. "If you hurt him, I will skewer you and make sure you don't recover from it."

His usual retort was that he did the skewering. But Featherington cared about Nathanial. And so did Jericho. "That is not my intention. I will open my collar so the strike can be clean."

If Featherington was as smart as he appeared, then he'd take that to mean that nothing was happening.

They turned again and Featherington continued to study him like he was some rare bug. "Good God, beneath that glib smile you have feelings."

Was it that obvious? "Don't say that too loud or you will ruin my reputation."

"You will ruin his. His father—"

"I know. I am not the right class. I'm not right." He should push Nathanial away and refuse to have anything to do with him after this case. But when Nathanial looked at him, he didn't see the club owner or the scoundrel. He saw him. And Jericho liked that.

He didn't want to be this person forever. It was a cloak he'd put on to survive. Now it was heavy and hot and scratchy and he wanted to throw it off, but he'd become so entangled in the cloth he didn't know where to start.

"That isn't what I was going to say. The sooner you marry him the sooner he will be free from his father."

"He would be disowned." And the scandal sheets would be filled with tales. Though Nathanial wouldn't be the first noble to fall in love and marry beneath their standing.

"Possibly. But Margaret would smother me in my sleep if I left him penniless."

"Does he know that?"

Featherington nodded. "He wants to carve his own way. He will not lean on others."

"Then he will not accept my help."

"And yet here you are." Featherington lifted an eyebrow.

The music wound to a stop and they bowed, Jericho making sure to bow deeper. He couldn't afford to be seen as anything but a supplicant here as they all knew he didn't belong.

"Let's get some drinks and then I'll introduce you and Nathanial to some of my club. I do not believe for a minute that Nathanial has a sudden interest in photography."

"Perhaps I do. Maybe I'd like some specific pictures for my club."

Featherington nodded. "Perhaps you do. In which case I can tell you that Dotherwell is not worth talking to. He likes to take photos of his horses and hunting."

They gathered cups of punch for Nathanial and Margaret who were having an animated conversation with two other ladies.

Margaret's attention snapped to Featherington and Jericho as they drew closer. "Tell me gentlemen do you agree if there is a gentlemen's waltz then there should be a ladies' waltz?"

The gentlemen's waltz had been created to celebrate the Male Marriage Act and it had become the thing for fashionable people to include to prove how modern they were. Some of the older people still made their opinions clear, and some of the younger gentlemen thought it was a bit of fun and treated it as such with one of them acting overly effeminate.

Featherington took a large drink of his punch and gave Jericho a nudge so he had to step into the trap Margaret had set. "Certainly."

The ladies nodded and the one in the blue gown spoke. "So, you also agree with women's suffrage?"

"Why should men shoulder all the responsibility of running the country?" Women ran households while men gambled and drank themselves into debt, often taking their families to the gutter with them. Perhaps the country would be better in the sure hands of a woman.

"So, you agree out of laziness?" Margaret said with a smile as the trap tightened

"I agree because I believe that all souls are the same, they simply wear different flesh." Jericho sipped his punch. Eulalia had taught him that and he'd helped her devour enough souls to know it to be true.

"One of those Scandinavian countries has just given women the right to vote and to be elected to parliament. And yet here we are, chattel to be married off to the highest bidder." Margaret flicked her hand; clearly this was one of her favorite topics. But instead of telling her to hush or walking away, Featherington watched his wife with admiration in his eyes.

"It is not so different for me, sister. Parents push their aspirations on their children." Nathanial stared at his punch and Jericho noted he hadn't drunk a thing.

"And what about you, Mr. Fulbright. What aspirations did you successfully throw off?" the blue dressed woman asked.

Nathanial's eyes widened, and even the Featherington's became frozen.

He had no idea what hopes his father had had for him while he'd still been in the womb or newly born. His mother had died within a few weeks of his birth. All of his early memories were about his nanny. He remembered his father's second wedding then the pain of being sent away to school. The birchings for no good reason except to remind him he was an outsider. At school he'd insisted on being called Jerry. The same for his time in the army. It was only upon returning to London he'd reclaimed his name. It was because of his love for his first wife that his father had cursed him with a name that would forever mark him as other.

Eulalia took over his tongue. "A career in the army." He drank the rest of his punch in a couple of impolite swallows as though he could shut her up, but he never could. She was always there ready to help when he was drowning, and he had forgotten how to swim in her presence. "I found I didn't care for uniforms or the men wearing them."

The ladies gave polite giggles. The tension that had formed broke.

This was the kind of dancing that he hated.

NATHANIAL FOLLOWED Bertie to the drinks table where several of the photography club members were deep in conversation. Jericho walked next to him, with that rigid posture that was completely unnatural on him. Nathanial much preferred the languid, fluid moves, the unbuttoned waistcoat and missing cravat. While Jericho looked the part of a gentleman, he seemed to have cut off a part of himself to fit the suit.

Three lords were gathered at the table. One was an older gentleman with a large white moustache and no hair. The two others were about the same age as Featherington.

"Nice footwork, Featherington," the older one laughed. His gaze slid to Jericho and lingered too long. Nathanial wanted to wipe the smug smile off his face.

"A gentleman should be able to dance with anyone," Featherington said.

"Quiet," said the redhead who raised his cup to drink to himself.

Nathanial remembered why he avoided these things. It wasn't just that his father was here, it was all the other starched shirts with their equally stiff opinions of themselves.

"Let me introduce my brother-in-law Bayard and his associate Fulbright." Featherington indicated to each of them. "Bayard is thinking about taking up photography and Fulbright is looking to add to his collection."

Featherington ran through the lord's names. Nathanial knew of them all and he was sure he'd met the redhead before but couldn't place him. While he asked about cameras and equipment, Jericho made polite enquires about their favorite subjects and they made almost lewd suggestions about what he collected. He never quite answered but smiled as though they were all in on the secret.

He glanced at Nathanial and gave a small shake of his head.

Nathanial had listened to the conversation and had thought the redhead might have been a possibility. He certainly liked to talk about taking pictures of people undressing.

The conversation started to stumble. And the lord's eyes began to take on gleam as they flicked between Nathanial and Jericho. It wouldn't be long, maybe a few more drinks, before someone started to ask the pertinent questions.

Why is Fulbright here?

What is between you?

Is there a church date?

They would want details and gossip and if Nathanial didn't offer any then some would be made up.

A tall man strode toward the group. He looked as though a snake had bitten him on the ass. His face was blotch with rage. "You have some nerve."

Jericho turned and smiled, but it was a peculiar thing that made his face sharper and almost unhuman. "Gentlemen, may I introduce my father, Simon Fulbright."

JERICHO HELD his father's furious stare. He'd known this moment would come as soon as he'd agreed to attend, though he had expected his father to be more discreet. Even he knew that one didn't cause a scene at these things, especially if one didn't truly belong here.

The gentlemen they had been talking to moved away, not wanting to be caught up, but stayed close enough to catch the gossip. None of them were the killer Nathanial was looking for, they enjoyed taking their risqué pictures but they didn't have a darker streak. None of them carried a demon.

"How dare you turn up to ruin your sister's chances."

"I wasn't aware I had a sister. Just one or do I have brother's, too?" He had two sisters and a brother, but he had never made the effort to contact them. His father didn't want him, and he wasn't going to be part of a family that hated his existence.

"Do not play the simpleton you...you..."

Jericho leaned in close. "You are the one creating a ruckus. What lord will want you as a father-in-law? A man who cannot control his temper." He stepped back and raised his voice. "A man who cast off his eldest son as soon as he remarried?"

His father's eyes flashed. "You threw away every opportunity I gave you."

You threw me away.

"I'll have you thrown out. You don't belong here, Jericho. Go back to your bed and play with your clients."

Jericho's jaw clenched. *Let me devour him.* Eulalia's whisper was so tempting.

He'd thought about this moment more than once over the last couple of years. Wondered how he'd speak to his father or what they'd have to say to each other. Nothing. Nothing could be said that would change anything. He didn't want that man's soul passing his lips for even a second.

Nathanial put a hand on Jericho's arm, but spoke to Simon. "You are a guest here. Please treat other's with respect."

"I'll have you both thrown out for being obscene."

"Considering I am Emmaly's son and he personally invited my associate, I don't think you will get very far with your request. As for being obscene, you are the one threatening." Nathanial took Jericho by the arm.

Jericho wanted to resist, to goad his father until his heart exploded, but he let Nathanial turn him away.

Nathanial glanced back. "Tell me Mr. Fulbright, as your first wife's child, has Jericho been getting a share of the Fulbright Bird? It was his mother's design after all." He paused and sly grin lit up his face. "Oh, that's right, I already looked into that. You filed the designs yourself and haven't shared a penny. The Nobility Task Force is looking into the matter."

"What?" His father actually appeared confused.

"Did I not introduce you to Detective Bayard?" Jericho said, even as shock tumbled through him. His mother had designed the bird, not his father? He forced a smile. "On the bright side, Father, you have enough status by way of your second wife that you get investigated by the noble coppers."

This time it was him leading Nathanial away before his father could return fire.

His heart was hammering his ribs and he wanted to tear off the coat and the cravat and all the other layers that were choking him into conforming.

They passed a cluster of older married women talking about social climbers. How it ran in the family. He wanted to correct them, tell them that he didn't want to be here. That he hated these games and the fake smiles and inane chit chat and gossip. But he let it pass.

Next year it would be a memory and Nathanial could laugh it off as a youthful indiscretion. But Jericho was starting to wonder if Nathanial would get the chance to laugh. If they didn't find the man, he'd lose his job. Featherington was worried about him and what his father would do.

"Would your father really force you to go to the church?"

Nathanial nodded. "It has been his dearest wish. He thinks it will ensure his place in heaven. He already pours money into his favorite churches."

"Why would a man be so worried about heaven if he was not sinning?"

"He is devout, not a sinner." They took a turn around the ballroom, drawing stares.

Jericho wasn't so sure and Featherington's words haunted him. If Nathanial's brother-in-law thought his only way to freedom was via a marriage that would create ripples through this set, things must be worse than they appeared.

Jericho stopped as though admiring the view over the garden. "How dire is your situation?"

"I am here with you." He glanced at Jericho. "I do not mean that as an insult because I am enjoying your company. But if I have to choose between my reputation and my job, I will choose my job. I refuse to sacrifice my life at the altar." He took Jericho's hand. "I want to live my life."

He couldn't hear the music over the sound of his heart. There was no mistaking the heat in Nathanial's eyes. They were like a midsummer's day, promising everything would be fine, but it would all end in a storm.

He should let go but couldn't. "I thought you were all about waiting."

"I thought I was, too."

Jericho shook his head. "Do not rush. I do not want to be a regret." Some things couldn't be laughed away. Nor did he want to be forgotten or a memory that was cringed at the way his first time was. Nathanial's smile faded. "Do not mistake my words as disinterest."

"Then what are they?"

"Caution." There were too many things Nathanial didn't know about him and that he wasn't ready to share.

Kiss him and let me slide to him. Finding the killer will be quicker, and then you can have him. I promise not to eat you. You have been a good host.

Jericho's lips twitched. "Let's concentrate on our job tonight." They continued walking until they reached the doors leading outside. "Shall we?" If Nathanial were truly worried about his reputation he would refuse, but he stepped across the threshold without hesitation. "Are you really investigating my father?"

"Not officially. But you will have a claim when he dies."

He didn't want his father's money. What he wanted was to know his mother. How different would his life have been if she hadn't died? Would his father have wanted him and loved him? Would the scandal surrounding their marriage have faded as the money from the birds poured in?

A man and a woman hugged the shadows as they walked by. For some reason, Jericho turned to glance back. The young lady couldn't have been much more than a girl, and the man had her cornered. This was no tryst.

Nathanial's head whipped around and before Jericho could say a word Nathanial was walking toward the couple. "Can I be of any assistance, Miss?"

"She is fine. Just needed some air after the last dance," the man snapped.

"Where is her chaperone?"

"I don't know. I felt dizzy and then..." The girl was pulling away from the man.

"There was no time to find her chaperone," the man said.

"I don't believe we've met." The words rolled off Jericho's tongue without his control. He let Eulalia surge and surface. There was something about this lord…

Nathanial had the girl and was leading her inside. She would be safe and hopefully less trusting in the future.

"No…though I have heard about you. As grasping as your father. You don't belong here. You should run back to your club." The man made to sidestep him.

Jericho blocked him. "Give me your name and I'll leave it at the door so you may visit."

The man stared at him. "What is the matter with you?"

The stink of chloroform hit Jericho. The darkness in the man's soul writhed like a bagful of worms. Each one a crime against nature. Each one a victim. Jericho blinked as Eulalia howled her sudden hunger. He stumbled back and gripped rail for support. There was no demon in this man, just darkness and evil. "I feel quite ill."

He hadn't expected for the revelation to hit him so hard. Eulalia had opened him to the darkness, and he could still feel it, taste it in his mouth like rancid meat.

"What's going on out here?" Nathanial went to Jericho's side.

"Nothing." Jericho didn't want the man to think his secret was out. The man smirked and went inside. "I need a drink. Something a bit stiffer than punch."

"You don't look well."

Nathanial was seeing Eulalia on his skin and in his eyes. "Migraine." The lies kept coming, falling from his tongue like rain. He glanced at Nathanial. "Who was he?"

"Lord Foxhall. A hunting friend of father's." Nathanial frowned. "You aren't suggesting…"

Jericho nodded. He was certain. And terrified that the man had no excuse for the deaths. He did it because he enjoyed it. No demon made him. His stomach turned.

"He's not part of the photography club."

"The stink of chloroform was on him." Was he planning on taking the girl somewhere to kill and photograph?

Nathanial still looked perplexed. "You can't accuse a man like him without more proof than that."

"He'd coerced the girl out here, when clearly she didn't want to be."

"She needed air."

Jericho stared at him. "And if it had been one of the working class or middle class dragging a girl outside to get her on her own while reeking of chloroform would you be so generous with your defense?"

Nathanial opened his mouth and then closed it again. Then he spoke softly. "Foxhall is a powerful man with many connections."

Was that the reason Nathanial couldn't close cases? Was he too lenient with his suspects because he didn't want to make enemies?

"There you two are. You shouldn't be out here alone. People will talk." Margaret gave them each a pointed look.

Jericho just wanted to go home. He was done playing dress up with the nobles, but he was trapped until the Featherington's were ready to leave. He held Margaret's gaze; she seemed to know something about everyone. "You are well connected. What do you know of Foxhall?"

Her hand lifted to her throat and she blanched for a moment. "Nothing. I don't have anything to do with that man, or his poor wife."

Jericho didn't need Eulalia to see through that lie.

"Didn't Father and Foxhall have a falling out years ago?" Nathanial mused. "When did they become friends again?"

Margaret looked like she wanted to escape. Jericho was tempted to suggest they take the carriage and leave Nathanial and Featherington to it.

"I don't know when they renewed their acquaintance. I think it might have been through Mama. Lady Foxhall isn't well and she and Mama often take the waters in Bath."

"So, Bertie would know him well?" Nathanial pressed.

"Oh, heavens no. Bertie has no time for the man. Besides Foxhall is rarely with his wife; they lead quite separate lives."

Jericho's stomach settled. "You never said what the falling out was about."

She glanced at him with her lips pressed tight. "I was supposed to marry Foxhall, but I refused after I saw him hit a maid. Father was livid and declared I would marry him unless I found someone else with in the week. Bertie and I had grown close over the season and I had hoped he'd offer. When I told him, he spoke to father, again as it turned out. Naturally Foxhall was furious when I accepted Bertie's offer. He called Bertie out; the Nobility Task Force was set up soon after. But Bertie won the duel."

Nathanial's eyes widened. "Was Foxhall wounded?"

"I couldn't say." Her gaze flicked between the two of them. "You think…"

Jericho nodded.

"I think I need to look into matters more closely," Nathanial interjected. "Please don't breathe a word."

"I won't." She glanced over her shoulder. "We should go in. It looks as though they are getting ready for the gentleman's waltz."

12

Nathanial offered his arm to Jericho, and Jericho hesitated for a moment before accepting.

"We don't have to do this if really don't want to," Jericho murmured.

Nathanial wasn't sure what he wanted. People would see, and while he'd danced the gentlemen's waltz before it had never been with anyone that he liked. He'd treated it as a joke like some of the other young men. He'd wanted to fit in and be like them, but even then he'd known that he wasn't. He'd made sure never to dance with anyone he was attracted to, because he was terrified of them realizing. Already his palms were slick, and tension coiled around his heart, making it hard to breathe.

"They already think I am a climber like my father. I have withstood worse, but the gossip for you will be unbearable. They will assume the most sordid lies are true."

They already were. Margaret was defending his honor, but how many would believe her? "The gossip about you will be good for business, will it not?"

"Stop dawdling. You will create more gossip by not doing it."

Margaret smiled as though she had said something lighthearted, not bitten off orders like they were naughty children.

"Stop trying to arrange my life," Nathanial muttered.

"Well if you did a better job, I wouldn't have to." Her smile widened as they stepped inside.

Men were taking their places with their partner. Some were blowing kisses and being as silly as Nathanial expected. A couple of older men were taking it much more seriously. Perhaps they had an affection.

Jericho leaned closer. "Shall we play this for laughs?"

"I think that would be wise." He didn't want everyone to see how much he liked Jericho. Jericho was the kind of man one kept, not the kind one married; he had to remember that. But that didn't mean he couldn't have some fun. "How is your migraine?"

"Bearable."

They took their places and Jericho did a ridiculous curtsey. There was no need for it; he'd danced with Bertie and two other men, the poet from the club was here and someone else Jericho knew. But this was different. They had arrived together. People had been watching them trying to determine if there was anything unseemly going on. So, they had kept a polite distance.

One of the older men took a few steps closer and gave Jericho a withering stare. "You should respect the waltz more. Men fought for this right for decades."

Nathanial wanted to say that he knew. That he understood more than the man could ever know, but he said nothing, and the man scowled again at Jericho, then moved on to tell off another couple.

The band gave them a few warning notes and then Jericho's hand was on his waist. Nathanial made the mistake of looking up into Jericho's eyes. All ideas about keeping this dance light dissolved as he placed his hand on Jericho's upper arm. The smile on Jericho's lips softened. Then the music got properly started.

While some of the couples laughed and made fun, Nathanial couldn't find it in himself to do anything. Nor did Jericho. They turned and control of the dance flicked to him, Jericho sliding his hand into position. Somehow they'd moved a little closer together.

Not close enough.

Maybe it was because he knew he shouldn't want him, or maybe it was because Jericho was dangerous to his reputation, but Nathanial had never wanted any man as much. If he wanted to take chances and experiment, he could've visited Fleet Street where there were places to purchase sex with men. But it wasn't sex he was after as much as the need to touch another.

This wasn't enough.

Last time, Jericho had knocked him back because he was drunk and clouded by opium. Tonight, his head was clear, and he knew what he wanted.

Jericho drew scandalously close for a heartbeat, before settling at a respectable distance. The music ended too soon. They both bowed this time.

The rustling of skirts broke the moment as it appeared that every woman had taken to the floor with a female partner. Good grief, his sister had actually made it happen.

Jericho was smiling; not the forced one he'd worn for most of the night, but the one Nathanial was used to seeing him wear at the club. He half expected Jericho to undo his coat and toss it aside. Disappointingly, he didn't. "I could do with that drink now, and a moment of peace."

"You don't want to watch this?" Nathanial was tempted just to see how they would manage in the dresses. Who would lead...or would they seamlessly swap the way he and Jericho had?

"No, but everyone else will." His voice lowered in a way that implied now was the perfect time to slip away.

"Let's get a drink first." Nathanial collected two glasses of punch. They wouldn't have long before someone realized they were gone. He led Jericho down the corridor. He hadn't been to the family estate in years, but he knew where his father's study was, though it would be locked. Where else? "Library? I can show you father's book collection."

"That sounds like a good excuse."

Nathanial turned the handle and was relieved when it opened. The lights were all off, but the curtains were open and there was enough ambient light to see. However, being in the library in the dark would do them no favors, so he turned on the lights; his father had wired the estate as soon as possible. He liked to be the first to get things. The lights flared to life at the flick of the switch.

The room hadn't changed much, though the chaises appeared to be new and there were less empty shelves. He shut the door behind him and leaned against it sipping his punch. He wanted to do so much but wasn't sure where to start.

If Jericho swept him aside again, Nathanial wouldn't bother making more attempts. How could Jericho not see how he hungered? How much he wanted. Damn respectability, that had already flown out the window like one of those damn mechanical birds. "How is your head?"

"Much improved. The dance did me good." Jericho watched Nathanial closely. "We didn't laugh much."

"No." His heart hadn't settled yet. It wasn't going to until Jericho kissed him. Or should he kiss Jericho? He didn't move. The door was solid against his back. Respectability was on the other side. His sister was right. They shouldn't be alone together as that would feed the gossip. But there would be gossip regardless.

He should be thinking about the case and Foxhall, but there was the carriage ride home for that. This might be their only time alone.

Jericho was still only a few feet away. If Nathanial reached out his hand he could almost touch him. He finished his punch and then eased off the door. He went to put his glass on the table, and deliberately brushed by Jericho.

Jericho caught his arm. "This is a bad idea."

"I know." He stepped closer. "But I have no good ones. All I can think about is what I want. This burn...it's a hunger I don't want to fight."

"You have a name, and a family."

"My brother doesn't give a damn, and my father only sees me as a useful tool."

"Your sister cares."

"Yes." She did. Too much.

"She would not approve. She will think I have led you astray." Jericho's fingers smoothed over Nathanial's bicep, then up to his shoulder.

"Then I shall correct her." One more step and he'd be able to kiss Jericho. Feel his lips on his. Taste him. His prick was rigid with the anticipation. He could take his pleasure later; right now, he wanted something to feed his imaginations. He'd never handled another man's body, and he wanted to know the feel of Jericho's cock in his hand...on his lips. That pamphlet had set him aflame with possibilities.

He took that step, but before their lips could touch Jericho turned his head so all Nathanial got was warm cheek.

Nathanial swallowed his bitterness. "Would you rather be with someone else? Is there another?"

What a fool he'd been. Of course Jericho would have other lovers. He could have his pick of the men who came to his club. He was a detective, a nothing.

Jericho pulled him hard against his body. This close, there was no hiding Jericho's desire. He cupped Nathanial's head. His lips brushed Nathanial's ear. "I will not relieve you of your virginity like this." His breath was warm and sweet and sent shivers of longing deep into Nathanial's body. "Here or in such a rush."

"I did not ask you to." He wasn't ready to leap that far from safety. "But I have come to the conclusion there are other things to do." His hand slid between them, and cupped Jericho's length.

"There are." His lips brushed Nathanial's cheek. "What did *you* have in mind?"

"I want to feel you."

"You are." He rocked his hips, pressing himself into Nathanial's hand.

"Your skin."

Jericho drew in a breath and stepped away. He put his glass on the table, then scanned the room. "Anyone outside can see in." He took

Nathanial's glass and placed it on a small table covered in books. "Coming?"

"Where?"

Jericho moved into the alcove formed by two bookcases. There was a statue to share with, but she didn't take up much room. He leaned against the bookcase, his hand moving to the buttons on his pants.

"You are willing to let me touch?" He'd thought Jericho would resist or refuse, especially after the other night.

The grin was all the answer Nathanial needed. "I will let you do what you want—within reason. Though I suspect my reason and yours vary considerably."

"You have been with men."

He nodded and the first button came undone. "Did you want to help unbutton, or have you changed your mind?"

Nathanial joined him in the alcove. There wasn't much room and there was no escaping. He was not going to back away, because he'd never get this chance again if he did. He needed to taste what he was missing by waiting. Would it be worth waiting for or should he take it all and say damn to the consequences? People had affairs and did all kinds of things, and no one bothered unless it all became public.

They were alone.

He should've waited for another night, at the club, or something. But he couldn't. It was eating him up from the inside and Nathanial had no idea how to silence the awakened beast, except by giving it what it wanted.

Another buttoned opened. Nathanial brushed Jericho's hand aside and undid the last two. "What is it like, to be with someone?"

Jericho looked down. "Consuming. It's everything for that time. But afterwards there are always repercussions. There always are when people get that close."

"Others talk of it casually." Nathanial eased his hand into Jericho's trousers, and felt the heat of him through the thin fabric of his shorts. His heart stuttered.

"There is nothing casual about being with another."

Carefully, Nathanial drew aside the shorts. His knuckles grazed heated bare flesh. It was familiar yet different. The thickness was different, the head rounder. He swept his thumb over the top, already slick.

"And what now, copper?" Jericho watched him beneath lowered lashes.

Nathanial swallowed; his moth was dry. He licked his lips. His heart pounded in his ears like galloping horses. He couldn't say it, but like the man in the pamphlet, he got on his knees.

Jericho sucked in a breath but didn't move, so Nathanial took that as acquiescence. He stroked Jericho's prick more firmly the way he did his own, then as fluid beaded he leaned closer to taste.

He knew his own taste but hadn't known if it was unique or not. Mostly Jericho was the same. Nathanial glanced up.

Jericho was watching him, his eyes dark. "Do not get yourself so excited you cannot help it."

"I have control." He didn't want to be spending in his trousers. "Though I may need a moment alone later." What would it be like to have someone else's hand on him? Or even their mouth? If he did that though, he'd be crossing another line.

Jericho didn't offer to assist…Nathanial hoped he'd have been strong enough to knock him back. If another man brought him to completion, that would mean that he was no longer a virgin. That was his line. He could do what he wanted, as long as he didn't spend.

Or was that a fake line that his beast had drawn when in reality any prick entering his body took away his virginity? In which case it was too late as the head of Jericho's cock had slipped past his lips, velvety soft, salty hot.

Jericho groaned.

"Did it hurt?" Was he doing this wrong?

"No." His fingers brushed Nathanial's hair. "I never thought this would happen."

Neither had he. His life had taken a very sharp turn and he'd landed off the map and in the territory of dragons. He wasn't sure he wanted back into charted lands because all the roads were mapped out for him and it was quite dull to simply follow.

He reapplied himself more thoroughly to the task, drawing more of Jericho into his mouth while stroking. His tongue and teeth seemed to be in the way, and he wasn't sure if he was doing this right at all, but Jericho's fingers were pressed against his head and his hips were rocking.

"Christ." Jericho pulled out his handkerchief.

Nathanial tasted more thick salt on his tongue.

Jericho jerked back, his handkerchief in hand to catch his spend. Some still landed on Nathanial's lip. He wiped it away, his gaze still locked on Jericho and the way his lips were parted and his eyes half closed.

Laughter in the hallway made Nathanial's attention snap to the door. The handle turned as Nathanial stood.

"I did not expect your father to have all three volumes of Burton's Arabian Nights. I would love to borrow it as I've never heard more than a couple of the tales," Jericho said smoothly as if his trouser buttons weren't undone. He faced the bookcase as though enthralled by the volumes.

Nathanial blinked, unsure what was going on.

The couple tumbled into the room and stopped.

Jericho glanced over his shoulder. "Perhaps you would be interested in hearing some of Scheherazade's tales? Would you care to join us?"

Nathanial glanced at Jericho; he had no idea where the handkerchief had ended up or what would happen if the couple did decide to stay. From Nathanial's position it was clear Jericho was barely tucked into his pants. If they had entered the room ten seconds earlier, there would have been no hiding what was going on.

His heart gave a panicked sprint.

They had done nothing illegal. Though many men would never ask their wives to do what he had done. That was for whores and mistresses alone. Heat raced to his cheeks, his blood too hot and his skin still hard.

"Enjoy your reading." The man swept the woman out of the room. Their tryst would have to find a new location. The door closed and Jericho put the book back onto the shelves. He adjusted himself and rebuttoned his pants. His skin gleamed pale and his eyes had taken on that odd blue sheen.

There was no light that could be catching in his eyes and creating that effect. Nathanial put his hand on Jericho's cheek and turned his head. The blue faded as he watched. "What is going on?"

JERICHO DIDN'T MOVE. Perhaps Nathanial didn't mean his eyes or the demon that had surfaced to save them. He didn't even know what book he'd held in his hand. For once, Eulalia hadn't hungered for a soul. She wanted Nathanial's body to inhabit so he could go after Foxhall and she could help him with his vengeance.

The word you want is justice, Eulalia murmured like silk in his skull.

Nathanial's thumb rubbed against Jericho's cheek. Eulalia wasn't the only one who wanted Nathanial's body. He should've been the one to say no and keep this respectable. Now they had fallen over that cliff and were plummeting toward the bottom, would there be water or rocks waiting for them?

Jericho was a fool if he thought it would be water. Nathanial was not of his ilk. He had made himself an outsider to survive.

"We enjoyed a moment." One he couldn't reciprocate with the demon in him.

Kiss him and then you can.

That was another thing he couldn't do, no matter how much he wanted to. He missed what it was like to kiss a lover and feel their lust on his lips. But again, he had drawn on his demon to escape what could've been an awkward situation. He needed her. She made him better.

"No, with your eyes. There are times when you are…not yourself." Nathanial released him and looked away. "You probably think I'm quite mad for saying it."

He should have laughed and brushed it aside, but he couldn't. Not this time. "I do not think you are mad. Too observant, perhaps."

Nathanial's sharp gaze returned to him. "So, what am I seeing?"

"If I told you, you would think *me* quite mad." He'd never told anyone.

"I would rather the truth no matter how fanciful. Is it some illness you contracted while abroad with the army?"

Nathanial had done some research on Jericho's life, which shouldn't be surprising. "You could say that. Though you have nothing to fear." Which wasn't exactly the truth. Jericho fiddled with the suit that Nathanial had bought to make him appear respectable. "Unless you spend while we are touching."

There he'd said it.

He glanced at Nathanial, who was frowning as though he had no idea what Jericho meant.

"I picked up a demon in Hong Kong." The words were ridiculous when spoken aloud.

"A demon?"

"After Liang was killed, I went drinking. I wanted to kill the man who'd taken his life." The pain no longer burned, and the wound no longer bled, but it wasn't killing the man that had healed him; it was time. "I met a woman who promised revenge could be mine…I now know she lured me with the demon's voice. One kiss and the demon was transferred to me. Eulalia has lived in here," he tapped his head, "ever since."

Nathanial's eyes were wide, and his eyebrows lifted.

It did all sound rather fanciful. He was sure Nathanial was about to turn and walk away without looking back.

"Show me." Nathanial's voice was steady.

Jericho exhaled. He didn't want to, but they'd come this far. Eulalia surfaced in a rush of cold.

"You do not look demonic. Your eyes are blue, not fiery; your skin has a sheen like a pearl, though your cheekbones are as sharp as a knife. A brutal kind of beauty."

"Do not be fooled. She likes the taste of souls." The words sounded like his but there was something beneath them. A power and radiance.

"Is that your voice or hers?"

"Detective, I want to help you, be in you, but Jericho will not set me free. I can help you get Foxhall. You can make him pay for what he's done." Jericho's mouth moved, but he had no control over the words. Eulalia was promising Nathanial everything he wanted, just the way he'd been seduced half a world away.

Nathanial shook his head. "I will catch him."

"If I cannot be within you, I will consume you." Jericho's tongue traced his lip and he reached for Nathanial. He could feel the copper's lust simmering in his veins. He fisted his hand and fought for control.

Eulalia laughed. *You weaken while I grow stronger. I know your weaknesses. All of them.* But she released her hold.

Nathanial stepped back and watched until Jericho had control. "Well, at least it is easy to tell who I am speaking to."

Jericho gave him a thin-lipped smile. "Yes."

"So, what would happen if I er...spend in your presence?"

"We can be in the same room, the same bed, just not touching as that is how she takes the soul. A succubus of sorts."

"And she helped you identify Foxhall?"

"Yes. With her I can see into souls, and read the secrets that men want to keep hidden." Most of the time, he didn't want that experience.

"You see mine?"

He nodded. "Do not fear yours. It is beautiful." Nathanial's soul was a pretty thing, full of hope and longing and the desire to do right by the world.

"Even now?" Nathanial indicated to the alcove.

"Especially now."

Instead of hiding, Nathanial was letting himself be which always made a soul brighter. His club was full of bright souls and it showed. Anyone who was too dark brought the feeling down. He did his best not to make them members.

"I cannot put a demon on the stand in court."

"She would not swear on the Bible or speak the truth anyway, but she can help me talk my way out of anything."

"So, I saw." The frown returned, creasing Nathanial's forehead. "Have you used it on me?"

"I cannot make you desire me."

"That's not what I asked." The official tone that Jericho hadn't heard since that first day was back.

He could lie, call on Eulalia but the copper had him pegged. So, he told the unvarnished truth. "Yes."

"How did Doxley really die?"

Jericho couldn't remember the details of their time together, but he knew the mechanics. "I didn't feed Eulalia soon enough, and he didn't heed my warning. She took his soul. I warned you; I don't want her to have you."

But he wanted Nathanial. He wanted to be ordinary so he could fully appreciate having a lover.

EULALIA'S TALE

The world was very different, yet much the same as when I'd first touched the ground. People loved. They fought. They hungered for justice. And I helped them.

Being here is not easy; I need to survive so there was always a price for my help. A soul. It is not much, and it isn't gone forever. Nothing is forever when you have seen kingdoms come and go. Empires rise from the sand and fall into ruin. Great families have used my gift and had their revenge, only to stumble when left on their own.

For some, justice will be everything they wanted and their lives become greater. For others it changes nothing. They blame me, when I am merely the weapon they wield.

I have worn the skin of many, learned the thoughts of men who thought they were divine and deserved to rule. They knew nothing about ruling; they cared only about themselves. Their deaths were of benefit to many.

I have been a beggar who knows the ills that plague society but lacks the voice to speak until I open their mouth. I have relieved women of husbands too free with their fists and too tight with their coin. I have helped men rise above where they were born. I have no time for those who think silk swaddling makes a better man than rags. A soul can be corrupted no matter the crib.

Few can hold me for more than a year.

This host is clever. But I am a weapon, not a toy, and he has no use for me.

So, I will cut my way free the way I have so many times before.

13

There was a demon inside of Jericho, and Jericho had admitted to killing. Not just once, but many times. He'd had the demon for years. How many murders was that? Nathanial didn't even want to ask and yet he needed to. He needed to be sure, even though he'd never been less certain in his entire life.

"You killed Doxley."

Jericho nodded. "Though I don't remember doing it. The demon fever had taken hold."

"Demon fever?"

"When she gets hungry, I become sick with fever. She can take over when I get too hot." He spoke in a manner so matter of fact that there could be no doubting his words.

If Nathanial hadn't have seen it for himself, what Jericho was saying was enough to get him shut away in an asylum for the rest of his life.

How much did he trust Jericho? The taste of him was still on his tongue. A moment that he didn't want to regret, but that he was no longer sure of. Though, the attraction, and the ache to be touched, was still there.

The warning had been clear. Doxley and Jericho had clearly gotten close. Nathanial ignored the stab of jealousy that someone else got to lie in Jericho's bed and do what he wanted to. Had Doxley not cared about his family's name and standing? Or had he thought he'd not get caught?

Which he hadn't. Even in death, the secret was safe. But Jericho's was now in his hands. "Well. As I said I can't put a demon on trial, so I guess nothing changes."

Jericho shook his head. "Everything changes. You are the only person who knows. She wants to climb into your body to help you get Foxhall."

"I do not want a demon." He didn't think he'd be able to control her the way Jericho did. His will was not that strong, as they had both just witnessed in his willingness to drop to his knees like a gutter whore. Jericho was bringing out the worst in him. Making him want what he shouldn't. He stepped back, putting more space between them. "But I will still need your help."

Catching Foxhall would be like trying to catch an eel with his bare hands.

"I will help. He needs to be stopped and she loves *justice*."

"Does Foxhall have a demon?" Perhaps instead of hunting killers he should be hunting demons.

"No. I had hoped he would, and that no human could be so cruel without one. But his soul is like pitch." Jericho grimaced. "He will not stop on his own."

"Have you seen other demons?"

"I try not to look that closely at people. I don't always like what I see."

"So, no." Perhaps there were no others. Part of his mind didn't want to believe that Jericho had one. But he believed in heaven and hell and there were demons in hell so why was it not possible that Jericho was inhabited by one? Possessed. But not in the way preachers suggested possession worked.

Jericho stepped forward, but Nathanial kept the distance between them. "I could've lied, let her grace my lips, but I wanted you to know.

Maybe I needed you to know because I can't live like this. I need someone to understand."

Nathanial nodded. "I do. I see your dilemma." Jericho could never truly be with anyone. He was possessed even if he was in control most of the time. That couldn't be good for his soul. "But I don't know how to help you."

Jericho's face crumpled as he looked away. "I don't need help." He drew in a breath. "Forget about it. This never happened. You can wait for marriage, and I can long for what I can't have. A heart is just an organ. Nothing more. Nothing special. Nothing magical."

Jericho turned on his heel and strode toward the door. It swung open, almost hitting him. "You have a magnificent library, sir. I am quite in awe and most grateful that your son took the time to show me. Do you think I could borrow Arabian Nights sometime?" Jericho flashed a blue-eyed glance at Nathanial.

Then Nathanial's father came into view.

"Leave my son and I to talk alone."

"On my way out." Jericho shut the door behind him, leaving Nathanial to face his father alone.

In that heartbeat, he very much wanted a demon who could help him talk his way out of trouble.

JERICHO RETURNED TO THE PARTY, numb. He'd bared his soul, his heart, and his demon, to Nathanial and gotten a cool brush off instead. Entirely his fault.

Men like Nathanial didn't sink to his level for long. They used people like him before getting on with their lives. He was a toy, an experience to be taken before returning to the genteel gardens and dances and other useless frivolities.

He affixed a smile before entering the ballroom. He was here by invitation and he wouldn't sully Nathanial's good name, just because his was coated in mud and other dubious matter.

For several dances he ignored Margaret even though he was aware of her stalking him like a cat with its eye on a robin. He chatted with Pennyworth-Trickett and a few other men that he knew from the club —ones that didn't care if they were seen in public talking. There were others who he knew better than to approach outside of the club.

Every time he blinked, he saw the hatred seething in Lord Emmaly's soul. He shouldn't have left Nathanial in there with his father, but there was no reason for him to go back. He gave up trying to avoid Lady Featherington. She cared about her brother and she was in a position to act.

He waited by the drinks table for her.

"You led me on a merry dance. Where is my brother?"

Jericho handed her a glass, playing the gentleman. She was lady enough to take it with a smile as though they were great friends. "He is in the library with his father."

He was sure a curse word a lady would never utter aloud graced her lips. "Dare I ask why you two were alone in there?"

"I was looking at the books."

"And what was my brother doing?"

Jericho couldn't help but smile. They were so similar. So sharp. "Educating himself."

She pursed her lips and then laughed as though he'd said something hilarious. "Walk with me before I throw my drink on you for being such a fool."

How she managed to seethe while looking delighted he had no idea, but it wasn't due to a demon.

They linked arms. "Tell me everything."

"No. A gentleman doesn't reveal."

"You are no gentleman."

"So I have been reminded." He almost kept the bitterness out of his voice. Couples moved in delicate swirls. Not all wore smiles. How many were here out of duty, or hunger for gossip, or to be married off because their parents deemed it a good time to sell their children's lives on the promise of better social standing. The hypocrisy and deceit made him want to scream or raze the house. These people thought themselves so much better.

The anger wasn't all his; it was Eulalia seeking activity. Revenge or justice, neither changed anything. They couldn't bring back the dead or return lost time.

"I'm sure he didn't mean it. Nathanial can be stubborn." They were heading toward the hallway and then the library, Margaret expertly steering him.

"I can't go back."

"Do you need whalebone to shore up your spine?"

He was sure she didn't. "No. But I don't think Nathanial will want to see me so soon."

"Trust me when I say he'll be glad of rescue, regardless of who does it. I can, but then his manly pride might be dented."

"His father hates me." Nathanial didn't hate him, but what they'd had, that growing heat of attraction and the hope that it would bloom, had been poisoned. "I shouldn't have reached above my station."

"Tosh. People reach all the time. Some succeed. Your father did."

Jericho let out an impolite grunt. "I am not him."

"I didn't say you were."

"What is the problem between Bayard and Emmaly?" Why was the father so intent on making his son miserable? At least he knew his own father's reasons. Jericho had been an embarrassment and a reminder of the first wife. Now he was well and truly the bad apple in the family.

"What has he said?"

"Only that Emmaly wants him to go to the church."

"That is true. Nathanial ran off to London and got a job to spite him. He was sent to a very strict school with the intention that he would take vows. Nathanial confided that he didn't want to. Mother said he must."

"That doesn't make sense."

She leaned in a little closer. "Mother had an affair with the groomsman for many years. Father found out."

"But you and Nathanial look similar."

"Don't we? We look nothing like our older brother. By the time Emmaly found out it was too late for him to do anything but raise us as his. The groom vanished and I was all set to be married off to one of father's friends; I'm sure he did it out of spite because he knew the man was a toad. Mother opposed, but threats have kept her silent and inline. She is too ill to be without his support. Nathanial refuses to go to the church to pay for his mother's sins. And father barely gives him enough to feed a mouse each month."

"And Nathanial knows all this?"

"Yes…which is all the more reason for him to cling and cleave to the family name and money. Without it, he is nothing. He either obeys or he turns his back and lives his own life. He will not do the last." She glanced back at the ballroom. "We are pretty birds in our gilded cages, trying to prove that we are still capable of flight."

"Nathanial cannot fly." He was tamed and trapped and scared of what waited.

"Will not." She took his hands. "Open the door for him."

"Why me? I am no one."

"I have seen the way he looks at you. He will listen to you. You are free."

Jericho shook his head. He was caught in the gap between the classes, between the disreputable and illegal and respectable and legal. He wasn't free when a demon owned his soul and he killed to feed her.

"Damn you a thousand times." She released him and swept down the corridor to rescue her brother.

"THIS HAS GONE ON QUITE LONG ENOUGH. I thought you'd grow out of working for a living like a commoner." His father sneered. "But then common blood is thick in your veins."

His father hadn't had a kind word for him since he was quite small. Nathanial had thought that making his own life would prove to his father that he didn't need the church to save his soul. But it had never been about him.

Nathanial brushed an imagined piece of lint off his sleeve. At least he was too old for his father to birch him for some minor transgression. "My life is mine to live."

"It is not. I should have cast your mother and her bastards into the street."

His father had threatened to. The only thing that had stopped him was Mama's father had been even richer and even better connected. While people accused Jericho's family of social climbing, the nobility did it all the time.

"And this latest perversion! Arriving here with a man. How dare you."

"Amberton spoke to you. It is part of a case we are working on."

"Fulbright is not a policeman."

"No, he is not." Nathanial kept his voice even and cool even though sweat was racing down his back and his legs were quite shaken. "He is an informant. There is nothing untoward going on."

"I saw you dance."

"I have danced with plenty of people tonight."

His father stared at him. The vein in his temple pulsed and his nose was rather red and swollen. "When this case is over, you will go to the church or find your funds cut off."

"I will not."

"Then you will starve."

He wouldn't starve but the house would go and so would Godfrey. "I will live more modestly."

"Then I will name you as a bastard. You will have no job. Amberton will remove you. Maybe if I tell him, he will let you go without any publicity."

His gut twisted. That would be all the excuse Amberton needed.

"I never asked to be born. I didn't want any of this. But you have taken it out on me since you found out."

"Because you look like him. When I see you I feel sick."

Nathanial nodded, but didn't add that looking at the man who he called father also made him ill.

The door swung open and Margaret strode in. "Father, I have been looking everywhere. Mother is looking for you. I think she is having one of her turns."

Emmaly's eyes narrowed as he looked at his second most hated child. "At least you I was able to fob onto another man." He pointed at Nathanial. "You…your days of policing are coming to a close."

"Are you getting married, Nathanial?" Margaret tried to be bright as though the air wasn't thick with hate and poison.

"I do not want his children bearing my name. If he marries, he will be cast out. The church bell tolls for you, son." He spat the last word before leaving.

"Is Mama all right?" Nathanial asked.

"As far as I know. Are you?"

Nathanial drew in a breath. "Well, I shall either have to find a new career or get used to being on my knees."

He meant in prayer, but he knew what he'd rather be doing.

JERICHO WASN'T A COMPLETE COWARD. He located Featherington and told him there was some family drama. Featherington didn't appear at all surprised.

"I have no doubt that my wife will plead fatigue or headache and beg to be returned home as soon as she finds us."

"It might be better if we find her. She was…" How did he say it politely? "Rather cross with me. Maybe it would be better if I made my own way home."

Featherington lifted one eyebrow. "You can suggest that to her."

Jericho held the lord's gaze and decided that he wasn't that brave. "Perhaps it would create less gossip if I did as commanded and shut up."

Featherington slapped him on the shoulder. "Wise decision. Let's find my wife before the family issue becomes too public."

Margaret and Nathanial were re-entering the ballroom, Margaret looking as though she were quite faint. Featherington immediately played the doting husband and took care of ordering the carriage be brought around. They made their farewells and were on the road before Jericho could utter the question, "what in God's name is going on?".

No one seemed inclined to tell him. So, he kept his word and kept his mouth shut. Nathanial stared out the window, ignoring all. And Margaret gave up on trying to tempt conversation with tidbits of gossip.

While not a loss, the night had been a bit of a disaster in the way that Britain was a bit of an Empire.

POLLINGTON'S POPULAR NEWS

The police are supposed to uphold the moral and legal values of this fair land. Certain branches of the police force are supposed to be held to an even higher standard. And yet a Mr. B, with noble blood and a badge, was seen gallivanting at a ball with a man of questionable values and fewer morals.

Not only did the two misters dance—and appear completely entranced with each other—but there is talk they spent time in the library together…to peruse the book collection? What kind of reading could cause such a flush to the cheeks?

Mr. F is well known to the readers of this paper and has no noble lineage, though he has known plenty of noblemen. We can only wonder what his interest in Mr. B is and why Mr. B is courting certain danger.

14

Nathanial looked at the scandal sheet that someone had placed on his desk. Nothing had happened, and yet according to this piece of gossip something was happening, and Jericho was getting intimate with every man who visited his club. Which Nathanial knew wasn't anywhere close to the truth or there would be far more dead bodies.

He should've asked how often Jericho had to feed the demon and where he buried the other bodies. Or did he leave them the way he'd left Doxley? At the ball, he'd been in the arms of a murderer and he hadn't arrested him the way Amberton would expect if he knew. He'd done nothing.

Nathanial scrunched up the scandal sheet without reading the other stories and tossed it in the bin. It was impossible for him to arrest Jericho for any of the murders. For one, the demon would help him talk his way out of any charges, and two it was actually the demon's fault.

In the warmth of summer sun, the talk of demons had become some kind of fanciful dream. As had those few stolen moments in the library. He wanted to undo them and treasure them at the same time.

Jericho wound him up in knots and Nathanial didn't know if he wanted to be free, only that he shouldn't want at all.

His gaze landed on the papers pinned to the wall. Foxhall's name was on the list for all three. If he and Jericho hadn't stepped outside would that young lady have been next? Where had Foxhall been planning on taking her?

Foxhall was a friend of the family, despite the issue with Margaret, and had attended alone so there was a chance he was staying at Emmaly. Did that mean he'd had a camera set up and ready? If they hadn't been forced to leave early, Nathanial could've found a way to inspect all the guest rooms.

On a fresh sheet of paper, Nathanial began making notes about his father's party. He drew a map to place where they'd been and where the guest rooms were. Was it possible to take a semi-conscious lady that far? How long would it take? How long until her absence was noted?

At two of the other parties, many of the guests had been staying.

The third party had been at Foxhall's.

The poses were all similar though on different beds. The masked man with the scar—from where Bertie had wounded him?—and a blond woman. All of them blond.

The young lady last night had also been blond. But he couldn't put out a warning for blond ladies to avoid parties until this was solved, and he couldn't accuse Foxhall without more proof.

Amberton knocked on the door and entered before Nathanial could invite him in. He shut the door and took a seat. "It would seem you had quite the weekend."

Had it been Amberton who'd put Pollington's on his desk? Amberton believed in reading the scandal sheets because there was always a seed of truth buried it there. The trick was working out what was truth and what was manure.

"I did have a successful weekend."

Amberton considered him for several heartbeats. Nathanial's pulse had quickened the moment Amberton had walked into his office, now it was racing away like a wild horse. Had his father already told the truth about his lack of good blood?

"What did you learn, since that was the point of you attending with Fulbright?"

He was tempted to point to Foxhall's guilt, but it was too soon. "I helped rescue a young lady from a lord who was taking too much liberty."

"And that pertains to the case how? Many a lord gets too friendly after a dance riles up his blood. Young ladies need to be aware of that."

Nathanial frowned then quickly smoothed his features. Lords should learn to behave instead of expecting other people to avoid them.

"She'd been made faint with chloroform and had been taken out for air. I do wonder if that isn't what happened before. The man is married and respected." Which would give him a certain amount of standing. He wasn't known to be a rake, or even keep a mistress. His wife was sickly having born him two children over ten years.

"How well respected?"

"Very." Which would make catching him that much harder.

Amberton leaned back. "Well at least something useful came out of your jaunt. I have been asked to make sure that you are acquitting yourself as expected for a member of the Nobility Task Force."

"My sister was there as chaperone; she didn't want my good name to be covered in muck." If people started to question his parentage, they would question hers and even though she'd married well, there would be a permanent stain. His father's threat even if whispered to Amberton was enough to destroy Nathanial, and possibly his sister. The silence became a living thing. It was clear that Amberton didn't believe everything he was saying. "I did dance with Fulbright."

Amberton nodded. "That was obviously enough to give Pollington something to write about."

"Dancing isn't a crime."

"And the library?"

"Was just that. He wanted to see it and I obliged. Another couple entered the room, hoping it would be empty. Perhaps they said something to cover their own behavior."

"In my day, gentlemen could be in a room together and no one would suspect a thing. You should marry; then they would have nothing to write about."

Margaret had said something much the same. Marry to stop father from steering his life. That wasn't the right reason to marry, but many had married for less, or for worse reasons.

"I will not marry if I can't be sure of my job." He couldn't count on his allowance, that much was clear. While he didn't live extravagantly and he had some savings, it would be prudent to trim his expenses. He should start with the Jericho Rose. Returning there would be too much, and he didn't know how to face Jericho after that awful ride back to London.

The demon and his father's threats had come between them.

"Close this case, Bayard."

He was trying. He'd tried with the others, too. He'd just had a run of abysmal luck.

Hadn't he?

WHILE THE CLUB was open and everyone was having fun Jericho struggled to join their merriment. He had a Nathanial sized gap in his evening, and it was disconcerting. He'd attempted to write three different letters and each one had ended up in the fireplace because he had no idea what he really wanted to say.

He'd told Nathanial everything, and in return he'd gotten nothing. He'd thought... It didn't matter what he'd thought. He'd been a careless fool. He'd built this life and he liked it, but his business didn't warm his sheets or whisper in his ear.

For all that he was surrounded by people, men of noble blood and gutter intentions, and lesser men with noble intentions, he was alone. The men here would miss the club if it closed, but not him. He wasn't an artist or a poet or a man with money and connections; he enabled those men to meet and for friendships to form that were mutually beneficial.

If anyone noticed his detached mood, they said nothing.

He was very tempted to go upstairs and leave the club to run itself for the night. His staff would take care of it. But if he wasn't in the club, running it, who was he and where was his place?

He clearly needed another brandy because he was thinking too much.

A dark-haired man walked in and Jericho paused drink halfway to his lips. It was the man from the ball. The same man from the pamphlets? It wasn't hard to imagine men with their shirts off. Perhaps he could get this man's off and see if the scar was there. That was something Nathanial could use.

He could use me.

Jericho returned his attention to his glass. He didn't want to look in Foxhall's eyes again as there was too much darkness. And that from a man who killed to feed his demon on a regular basis.

He finished his brandy in one swallow and steeled his spine to go and greet Foxhall. It was unfortunate that he couldn't pretend not to know him.

Foxhall was still buttoned up and too respectable, his lips set in something caught between a sneer and a smile. It was painfully obvious that Foxhall didn't want to be here and worse conversation had dropped as people became more guarded. Nathanial had never silenced a room and he was a copper.

Jericho glided over with the pretense of making the newcomer welcome. "I am surprised to see you here."

"I thought I should see what the fuss was about." Foxhall's dark eyes scanned the room. If he was looking for illegal activities, he was in the wrong place. If he thought sex was for sale he was also in the wrong place. Sex was given away freely between like-minded friends. "I'm not sure it's worth the space it gets on the sheets."

"Probably not, but then people like to imagine the worst." Everyone knew this was a club for men of a certain persuasion. At first some men had wanted it to be more than what it was, but Jericho had been adamant. He was sure they were the source of those first rumors.

Foxhall's mouth turned down as though he were greatly disappointed. "Where can I get a drink?"

Jericho led him to the bar and made him pay. Foxhall would get no free drinks on his first night. It would also be his last. While it would be rude to demand why he was here, Jericho was sorely tempted.

Conversation remained muted. Someone got out the chess board but there was no gambling, nor raunchy bets made. Jericho left Foxhall standing on his own to move around the club. Someone here knew something about Foxhall and the photographs. The questions were who, and what did they know?

He scanned the room, giving Eulalia freedom to rise. The quarry was here but no trap had been set. They had to catch him, which meant they needed to know more about him, not just the history between Foxhall and Margaret.

His gaze settled on Pennyworth-Trickett. Robert knew everyone and most gossip when it came to blue bloods.

Jericho sidled over and leaned on the back of Robert's chair, well aware he was being watched by Foxhall. He pointed at something that Robert had been writing as if to make a comment on the words. With just a little of Eulalia's magic he murmured, "Tell me about our friend."

"He is the friend of no one here." Robert scribbled on the paper. *Vice and obscenity.* "A rumor as no one knows who is on the committee."

"I thought the king had done away with such things." Before King Edward had taken the throne, many of the things they enjoyed here had been illegal. Porno pamphlets were still very borderline. The Male Marriage Act had gone some ways to decriminalizing what had once been a death penalty, but those that indulged outside of marriage were still at risk and hearsay was enough to convict.

"Someone has to rat out those who take too much pleasure in life." Robert scribbled through everything he'd written. "The muse has deserted me."

"And of the man?"

"I did hear there is a reason his wife is never at home."

"She is ill."

"Sick of him according to my aunt. Horrible men make horrible husbands." Robert glanced up at him. "Where is your friend tonight? You were cozy at the ball."

"I don't know. We are acquaintances."

Robert patted him on the cheek. "You keep telling yourself that. The rest of us have got bets on."

"On what?"

"Can't say. That would spoil it." Robert stood. "I must depart."

Why would a man with such deviant tastes as Foxhall be agitating for tighter obscenity laws in parliament? Or was he merely keeping everyone busy from looking at what he was doing?

Jericho made his way around, but no one had anything else to say and people were finding reasons to leave. Foxhall hadn't moved by the time Jericho returned to his side. "What did you think?"

"It's rather dull."

"It was a quiet night. But sometimes there are poetry readings, or an artist brings a sketch pad."

Foxhall's smile had fully melted into a sneer. "I fail to see the popularity."

Jericho smiled. This wasn't a club for men like him, and Foxhall knew it. He knew he wasn't welcome in the same way Jericho wasn't welcome in some of the fine establishments that checked one's family tree before allowing membership. "I could say the same about fox hunting."

The sport of hunting animals was disgusting. At least when he hunted, he chose people like Foxhall.

Do not make me sick. I would never eat a soul like that, and you would never be able to get that close to him. Eulalia had a point.

"Perhaps this is not the club for you." The words rolled off his tongue as if oiled. The danger of having him here had sharpened as Eulalia senses picked up Foxhall's intent. He wasn't just curious; he wanted to destroy everything Jericho had because he was associated with Nathanial.

Foxhall had never forgiven Margaret for jilting him.

"I'll be the decider of that." Foxhall put his glass down and walked out.

Jericho had the feeling he'd be walking back in all too soon.

Dear Jericho Fulbright,
I misunderstood your reasons for attending the ball at Emmaly
manor. I did not realize you were assisting the police. If you are trying
to turn your life around, then I greatly approve of this choice—not
that you have listened to me in a long time. I regret my outburst but
stand by my assertion that your current profession lowers the family's
standing.

I have learned of certain events that transpired that night and it
appears that I owe you a debt of gratitude. Had you not been at the
ball the other night then your sister would have suffered greatly. I am
sure you know the incident I am talking about even if you didn't
know the young lady you assisted was your sister.

While you will not do it for me, for your sister, can you keep word of
the incident quiet?

Your father,
Simon Fulbright

15

Jericho wasn't sure what to make of the invitation to dinner from Featherington. It had arrived shortly after the letter from his father. Both were confusing. Add in Foxhall's visit last night and he wasn't sure which way was up and which way was down.

He accepted the dinner invitation from the Featherington's because refusing would be rude. Their pretty golden bird flew home with the message. Every time he held one, he now wondered why his mother had thought of it and how she'd designed it. Had they planned to come to England to make and market it and his father had done it on his own after her death?

His father's letter, he read another two times. The young woman had been his sister, and she'd almost fallen into Foxhall's depraved game. He tried not to dwell on those thoughts, because lingering on might-have-beens from the past was a sure way to miss future possibilities. The letter almost read like as apology, but not a thank you. That couldn't be right, though; his father didn't apologize. He blustered and groveled to those he thought could lift his station in life. Jericho had always been the weight around his father's ankles. Even now.

He sent the bird home to his father.

He wasn't going to close the club for a second night. He'd have to leave it in his staff's capable hands. It was only a few hours. They would be fine. Hopefully Foxhall wouldn't show up and clear out the place again.

As he dressed for dinner, in his own clothes and with only a hint of color in his dark blue cravat, he couldn't shake the feeling that this was some kind of set up. People like the Featheringtons weren't nice to people like him without good reason.

He had no idea what that reason was. He didn't have money. His reputation was so close to the ground he doubted they could raise him or drop him further—and they had seemed delightful, not the kind who would kick him for the pleasure of hearing him yelp.

Margaret loved her brother and they were determined to keep the family scandal in the family.

Oh…and he wasn't family.

Perhaps they wanted to bribe him. He wasn't sure how he felt about that either.

If they wanted to kill him, they would find that quite tricky, as Eulalia liked to keep her hosts alive. Going to dinner would at least answer his questions. Mostly he was hoping Nathanial would be there. He didn't know what he needed to do to return to Nathanial's favor.

Perhaps Nathanial had asked for this dinner. It was that thought that put a bounce in Jericho's step as he hailed a cab. While a few people had motor-carriages they were the toys of the rich. Nathanial's father had been keen to show his off; Jericho had missed seeing it which was a disappointment. Robert was trying to get one of his benefactors to purchase one for him. If he succeeded it would be quite the coup.

The Featherington's London house was not as lavish as he'd expected. While well maintained, there were bigger and fancier places around town. Usually those with position and money scrabbled for the best they could afford. Perhaps there wasn't as much money as he'd thought. Which wasn't that surprising as there were many elegantly impoverished nobles. Gambling and the division of wealth between children over many generations had that effect. If only there was away for them to get a job, and work like everyone else.

Jericho bit back a smile. Some would never do that. Others, like Nathanial, had realized that there was no security in family money and that a life had to be carved out.

He knocked on the door and waited. Jericho almost expected them to ask him to go around the back, but their butler opened the door and he was shown into the parlor. The parlor was a pretty little room that was obviously well used, instead of being strictly formal. Most of the photographs on the wall were of birds.

"Do you know much about birds?" Lord Featherington said as he entered the room.

Jericho shook his head. "They are either good to eat, pretty to watch, or mechanical."

Both men assessed each other. It was Jericho who spoke first. "I must confess to being rather confused about why I am here."

"I'm sure the invitation said dinner," Featherington said with a perfectly straight face.

"I don't receive dinner invitations."

"I cannot imagine why. You are perfectly capable of talking on a great many topics."

He was done with dancing around the issue. "I think it is because of my reputation."

"I am an oddity in that I don't care much for family history. I am more intrigued by the person."

If Featherington was hinting at something, Jericho wasn't interested. "I'm not that fascinating." And he was no one's kept man. He was his own.

Featherington's lips curved but didn't quite turn into a smile. "Nathanial seems to think you are."

Jericho turned away and feigned interest in a photograph of a garden bird on the edge of a fountain. The fountain was in several of the photographs. "I haven't spoken, or heard from him, since his father's party."

And he wasn't here. Jericho shouldn't be disappointed by that, but he was. He liked Nathanial too much.

"I'm aware. He will be here later."

"And does he know I am here?"

"No, but he wants to learn how the automatic camera works."

"That doesn't explain why I am here."

"You are assisting him, are you not?"

Was he? He didn't know anymore. What more could he do? "I'm not a copper."

"Neither will Nathanial be if his father has his way. He has threatened to expose Nathanial's true parentage."

Jericho shrugged. "He could join the regular police force. I cannot help him with his father. I cannot even do anything about my own."

That his father had written to him was something he was still grappling with. He should respond, but part of him still wanted to hit back after years of neglect. However, ignoring the letter would only make it appear that he wanted nothing to do with his father, and he wasn't sure that was true.

"My first wife and son died in childbirth; I have some sympathy for your father. Especially as it was a marriage born from love, not arrangement."

Jericho gritted his teeth. "I do not need a lecture on why my father fobbed me off to others to raise." Though grief made a man do many unwise things—like get a demon.

"If we do nothing, then Nathanial will do as his father wants."

"And why does it concern you? Many men do what their parents want and live perfectly miserable lives." Not that he wanted that for Nathanial, but he needed to stand up for himself. Jericho hadn't hated school, or the army, but he had resented that his father had a new family that he loved more.

"He will do it to protect Margaret from the shame of also being named as a bastard."

"Ah. You do not care about her actual father?"

"Love doesn't change that easily. If it does, it wasn't love."

Jericho knew what love felt like, and he had been determined not to let it happen again. If loving Liang had been dangerous, loving Nathanial was even more so. "I am not good for him. His reputation is already being tarnished." He had seen Pollington's and had expected as much.

"He has always tried to be impeccable because he knew what he had wasn't real and could be snatched away. He grew up being reminded of that at every turn. You have offered him a freedom that he is too scared to take."

Jericho laughed. Nathanial wasn't that afraid if the incident in the library was anything to go by. "What do you think I am? Some kind of savior, a way out of his father's trap? Marrying me will not help his cause."

Featherington's words had played through his mind. He'd never let himself think about things like that. Now it was all he could think about. He didn't want to be the man who ran the Rose and was nothing more. He wanted more and Nathanial deserved more.

"You need to find a lord. I'm sure many would offer."

Featherington studied Jericho for several heartbeats. "Did you see the way most treated the gentlemen's waltz? They are torn between family duty and what they want, and most will obey."

"Then they are foolish." This wasn't his problem. "If you brought me here expecting me to gladly jump at the idea of marrying up, you are mistaken."

"A lesser man would've agreed on the night of the ball."

"Then you would've been forced to find a new plan to save Nathanial from himself."

"Quite." Featherington nodded.

"Have you thought to ask Nathanial what he wants?"

Featherington was silent, his attention on the window behind Jericho. "That is what dinner is for."

As soon as Nathanial saw Jericho, he knew this was some kind of orchestration by Margaret. He cursed inwardly while presenting his best devil-may-care smile and wondering when Bertie would stand up to his sister.

"Fulbright." Nathanial managed to look Jericho in the eye. They were brown, and even though there was a distance, there was still something in them. Or maybe it was his own wishful thinking he saw reflected.

Jericho had a literal demon and still the lust for him hadn't dwindled. It was infuriating.

"Bayard." Jericho nodded, his eyebrows lifted in what could only be called polite acceptance of the situation. "Come to learn about cameras?"

"Yes. And you?"

An elegant shrug. "I am assisting you."

"Gentlemen." Margaret swept into the room with bright eyes and a smile like the sun, clearly impressed with herself. "Bertie has set up a demonstration, so I thought we'd get the work done before dinner."

"That would be grand." And then maybe he could find an excuse to leave. Or Jericho would leave. He glanced at the man in question as they followed Margaret and Bertie through the house.

"How have you been?"

"Well." Nathanial didn't know what else to say. He should say something. "I meant to write."

"I never expected you to." Jericho kept his eyes ahead.

They seem to have agreed that the event had never happened. For something that shouldn't have happened in the first place Nathanial had spent an awful lot of time thinking about it in great detail. Had it been his own desire or had the demon in Jericho compelled him somehow? But he knew Jericho's eyes had been dark; they only shimmered blue when the demon was in control.

Nathanial couldn't control himself, much less a demon. Jericho must have iron will, and a soul as black as pitch after so much killing. But not even that knowledge was enough to dampen what sparked within him when Jericho was close.

Margaret opened a door to a spare bedroom. The bed was draped in a white sheet—just as the beds had been in the photos. The sheet hid the wooden frame.

"I did my best to recreate," Margaret said as she drew the curtain.

"I voted against recreation," Bertie said as he moved to the camera. "I believe this angle gives you what you want."

Nathanial moved to stare into the view finder. It was eerily accurate. "You have a very good memory, Margaret."

"The lighting is wrong," she muttered as though that was the most troubling aspect of what they were doing.

"I don't care about the lighting. I want to know how the pictures were taken." Nathanial straightened and let Jericho look.

"We mustn't forget that there may be two people involved," Jericho said. Nathanial looked at him. He wanted to grab his collar and ask why Jericho would say that when he, or the demon more correctly, had identified Foxhall. "Someone might be behind the camera."

"But if we catch one, we can compel him to talk. This is best discussed in private." He gave Jericho a pointed look. His sister and her husband were not police no matter how helpful they were being. Nor was Jericho, but on this case that was beside the point. "How does the camera operate?"

"Fulbright, can you lie on the bed and act dead?" Bertie suggested with a smile.

Without a word, Jericho lay down. This wasn't the kind of thing a lady of Margaret's standing would want to be involved in; she edged toward the door but didn't leave the room.

Nathanial looked at the camera and the wires leading from it. One led to a large box, the other to something that looked like a small square mirror. This would take time to set up. "He has the room ready. It's all planned out. Jericho, can you put your feet on the floor?" That was more like the position the women had been in. His sister stared at him. Damn, he'd used Jericho's first name. His cheeks heated. "So how does this work?"

"The sensor," Bertie tapped the mirror like object, "is set up to take one photo every thirty seconds while it senses movement.

"Nothing has happened."

"It isn't on." Bertie pressed a button. "Now it is. As long as Fulbright is still, no pictures will be taken. It can't sense Margaret or us."

"So, I drop the body on the bed. Come here and turn it on. Disrobe. And commit the crime." Nathanial moved from behind the camera, pretending he was Foxhall. He walked toward Jericho, still prone on the bed.

Behind him something whirred and clicked. He turned, startled.

"It sees you," Bertie explained.

Nathanial moved closer. His knee bumped Jericho's.

Jericho watched him and a faint smile formed on his lips. "How far do you want to take this?" His words were meant for Nathanial only.

Nathanial bit back a smile. The camera clicked.

He leaned over the bed but put his hands on either side of Jericho's head instead of around his neck. "This should be close enough."

It was too close. He could smell Jericho's perfume and feel the heat of his body. Jericho swallowed. The camera clicked again.

Bertie coughed.

Nathanial straightened and drew in a breath before turning to address Bertie. "So, let's develop those photos."

Bertie picked up a strip of paper that now trailed out of the camera box. "No need."

"What?" He stalked over to see. Sure enough there were three photos. The pictures were good quality, and the paper wasn't ordinary writing paper. It felt like photography paper. Maybe a bit thinner. "That's amazing. How is that possible?"

"It's a French design. They created it for their...um...they have magazines." Bertie glanced at Margaret and then away.

Unlike Britain, the French didn't have obscenity laws that made producing porno pamphlets a risky occupation. While some tame pictures were allowed, many pushed the edges of decency. Usually only the publisher was prosecuted and fined, not the taker of the photographs.

"When Bertie heard about it he had to get one, because he could set it up in the garden and it would capture the birds that wouldn't come near him." Margaret smiled.

"And as much I love bird watching, sitting for eight hours isn't something I have time for. Of course, many don't like it because it removes the skill of developing photos yourself."

"But for someone who doesn't care about the art, it's perfect." Jericho sat up. "You can only get them in France?"

"As far as I know," Bertie said.

"And this is all the equipment?"

Bertie nodded. "Camera, sensor, battery."

"Can I have a moment with my assistant?" Nathanial glanced at Bertie and Margaret. Both seemed happy to leave. Nathanial shut the door after them, though he fully expected Margaret to be listening on the other side.

"He could be doing it on his own. He doesn't need an assistant or expertise."

"And he's setting it all up beforehand." Jericho looked at his hands. "That young lady at the ball, I discovered she's my half-sister. Had he set up and picked her out? Or was she the only one gullible enough to step out with him?"

"Your sister?"

"My father wrote a thank you card."

Nathanial looked at the photo in his hand. "We should burn these."

Jericho held out his hand and Nathanial passed him the photographs. He studied each one, lingering on the last where they were too close, but not close enough. "I missed you…at the club."

"I thought it best not to attend. Did you read Pollington's?"

A single nod. Of course, he did. He was in there far too frequently. "It's probably for the best that you haven't been there, as *he* showed up."

"What on Earth for?"

"I don't know, but, and you will laugh, he is apparently on the committee that wants to crack down on obscenity. It's like he was there looking for illegal activities. He cleared the place out. Maybe he's trying to put me out of business."

Nathanial sat next to him on the bed. Close enough that he could reach out a hand and place it on Jericho's thigh. He wanted to. Avoiding Jericho hadn't worked…maybe confronting him would. "Amberton read Pollington's and wanted to know what was going on. I told him nothing. Is it nothing?"

"I don't know."

"You've been in love before."

Jericho gave him a half smile. "It's not the same every time. This… You can't drag me up. I'll only drag you down."

Nathanial was going down anyway. One way or another his father would make sure he lost his job. To keep Margaret safe from his wrath, he'd need to do the right thing. Something he should've done straight away, instead of hoping that he could prove his worth and that he was no threat. He'd thought when his brother had children the danger would pass, but it wasn't about the name; it was about his father's pride. Seeing Nathanial and Margaret living good lives made him bitter.

"What does your demon say?"

"That she wants to crawl inside you." Nathanial glanced at Jericho, but he wasn't smiling. "Your sister and brother-in-law want you to marry."

"I know." That they had told Jericho only filled him with unease. Did his sister think that marrying would solve any of his problems? His father would still call out his parentage and cut his allowance, he'd still lose his job. There was no way to beat his father.

Jericho nudged him. "Maybe you could use her help."

"The demon or my sister?"

"Both."

DINNER WASN'T HALF AS AWKWARD as Jericho expected it to be. No one mentioned the camera or the case. It was as if he belonged and it was disconcerting. Finally, they were enjoying brandy in Featherington's study. No one had mentioned Nathanial's dilemma and for that he was glad.

He accepted a refill as did Nathanial who was reclining in an armchair. Jericho wanted nothing more than the night alone with him. The photos hadn't been burned. They had disappeared into Nathanial's pocket and Jericho didn't give a damn.

"Your sister dearly wants to help you, Bayard."

Nathanial blinked and he went from relaxed to almost alert. "The camera demonstration was most helpful."

Jericho looked at Featherington. He was going to ruin a perfectly good evening. He gave a slight shake of his head, but Featherington either didn't notice or didn't care.

"Not with the case, but with your father."

"I don't need help. When this case is done, I'll do as he wants."

Jericho's head whipped around so fast he almost broke his neck. "What?"

He knew Nathanial didn't want to marry, but to cave and give into a tyrant's demands? That was completely irrational.

Nathanial sipped his brandy. "I've put a lot of thought into it since the ball. And while it's not how I planned on living my life I believe it is the only way."

Featherington scowled. "It's not the only way."

"You are no better than him trying to force my hand." There was steel in Nathanial's words that Jericho hadn't heard before.

"Your sister and I are trying to set you free. It worked for her."

"I am not her."

"No, but your life is still yours to do with as you please. Going to the church is no way to live."

Jericho couldn't imagine anything worse than a life devoid of pleasure and passion. They were what made people human, what filled their souls. God knew he'd taken enough.

"Unlike you, I have faith. This way Margaret is protected from scandal and I will get a measure of peace because he will finally stop threatening me." Nathanial finished his brandy and poured another one. "I will make the most of the freedom I have left."

Anger simmered through Jericho. "You are a fool if you think your father will stop just because you meet his demands. All he will do is raise the height of the bar you must jump over, and he'll keep doing so until you break your neck." He put his glass down, the evening souring on his tongue.

How had he thought it would end up? With him back on the bed and Nathanial over him, both of them wearing less clothing?

He was the fool if he thought that was ever going to happen.

"What would you have me do? Let him out me as a bastard? Wear the shame of being a fraud? Become a social pariah even among my friends?"

"Yes. That is what I'd do. Call his bluff and see if he is willing to risk his status and life. He's the one who raised you. People will talk, and they'll talk about him. You are the innocent in his game."

"But it's not a game. And I refuse to play."

"You are afraid to play." Jericho stood. "I must return to the club."

Featherington walked him to the door. "Do not give up on him."

"He has given up. No man can be saved if he doesn't wish it."

"You wouldn't have come if you truly thought that."

Jericho sighed and looked away. He had come expecting to see Nathanial, that was his weakness. He wanted more than the life he had, but Nathanial wasn't the answer. Dinner had proven that. "I want to solve the case. There can be nothing more. I'm mistress material at best."

And he would never be happy as the kept man. He wanted all of Nathanial, but there was too much between them. While he could cast out his demon, Nathanial would never cast off his family loyalty. Loyalty that Jericho had never had when growing up. It was that loyalty that made Nathanial the man he was. The man Jericho could never have.

Dearest Margaret,
Thank you for dinner the other night. The lesson in photography was
most informative.

With regards to the other issue, I beg of you not to make what I must
do any harder. I know you would like things to work out differently—
and it is plain that you have plans for me and my associate. But it is
not to be. Though I will confide I wish it were otherwise.

I will see you again before I am done with London. Can you recom-
mend a maid for a few weeks? Mine has had to leave to take care of
her mother.

Your loving brother,
Nathanial

16

The raid on the town house at the address Jericho had given Nathanial had amounted to nothing. The regular police had watched it, waiting for activity but no one was ever there. Finally, a man turned up. The police had taken him into custody immediately. It was clear he was no noble and shouldn't even have had a key to the house.

He didn't know the man who rented it. Only that he would get a message when there were photos for him to collect and deliver. But there were no photographs in the house. It was completely empty. The man seemed perplexed as to why he'd even been sent to the house if there were no photographs.

At that point, Nathanial had walked away from the interview. He knew why the man had been called to the house. Foxhall had somehow discovered that the house was being watched and had made the police spring the trap too soon. They'd never be able to get him now. The owner of the house had sent a message that the tenant no longer wanted it and that it would be re-let if they were done.

Which they were.

He was back to having nothing. Like so many of his other cases, this one was falling apart at the seams like a poorly stitched garment.

He ran his fingers through his hair. What did it matter? Too soon he'd be surrendering the life he wanted to the one his father wanted him to have. There'd be no more allowance, and his father could finally wash his hands of him. He pressed his lips together knowing there was no way he could argue with his father and win.

Not unless he had Jericho's demon. The idea tempted him more than it should. He tried to imagine sharing his body and mind with another but couldn't. The idea was too strange. And he was too weak. The demon would rule him, and he'd do all manner of things—and no doubt enjoy them all. And then what? Once he'd talked himself free, what then? He couldn't keep the demon forever and his father would make new threats and he'd still be a terrible policeman.

It was better that he not see Jericho again. He'd written to his sister to tell her no more schemes. She hadn't replied. Not even his sister thought his wishes mattered.

Nothing he wanted mattered. And when he took church vows, none of this would matter.

The three dead ladies would beg to differ. Their need for justice mattered, and he didn't want to leave the Nobility Task Force as a total failure. He shut the case file and stared at the wall with his papers pinned to it, but he didn't see only this case.

What had gone wrong all those other times? How had he always stumbled at the last hurdle? He didn't believe it was because he was bad at his job. And after a couple of hours of reading through old files, he didn't believe it was a run of bad luck either. It wasn't possible.

It was only now with the contents of all his years' work strewn across his desk that he was able to see that. In one, the suspect fled to France the night before, as if he knew they were closing in on him. In another, a witness suddenly changed their mind just before the trial— that witness then went on a holiday to the continent.

The list went on. There was always something.

Sometimes the victim decided not to go through with a trial, and if the victim would no longer speak up, then there was nothing the police could do. It was like someone was playing against him. Always one move ahead.

Impossible. Wasn't it? Surely no one here would speak about the investigation to the people they were investigating? Like Nathanial, the other two men were nobles, they all had ties to the various families, and at some point had been too close to an investigation. But to undermine it would mean breaking the oath they swore to the king.

Even the common policemen swore that oath.

Nathanial didn't like the idea that anyone was whispering details about his cases. Especially not to bring them to a halt. Where was the concern for the victims of crime if the police were tipping off criminals? He didn't like where his thoughts were taking him.

He looked at the papers stuck to his wall. Then he got up and crossed out Foxhall's name to make it look as though he'd been discounted when he was indeed the only suspect.

THE BIRD WAS WAITING for Jericho on the kitchen table when he finally dragged himself out of bed. Jericho sipped his tea and tried to work out who the bird was from. Would it be his father? Unlikely. But a letter from Nathanial was even more unlikely. It had been three days since dinner, and he'd heard nothing.

The only thing that had gone right since that night was that Foxhall hadn't visited again.

He toyed with the metal bird. Some people put their mark on them or had them personalized. Many didn't because they didn't want their mail intercepted. The police used birds that needed a code to be opened.

This wasn't a secure bird.

He pressed the button and the bird opened. He caught a glimpse of a photograph and his heart leaped. Had Nathanial sent him a picture from the other night? A smile formed as he unfolded the paper. His lips froze as his delight turned to horror.

It was another bloody porno pamphlet. A bedroom, a dark-haired woman—which was different—and the man with the scar and mask. Foxhall had clearly been too busy to visit.

His stomach turned. He needed to get this to Nathanial before it went public.

"Jeremy get me a bird," Jericho called as he tore off to his study for paper and ink. He scrawled a hasty letter. It was late in the morning, so Nathanial would already be at work.

When he came back downstairs Jeremy had a bird in his hand. Jericho folded the message and keyed in the address before sending it out the nearest window. Its wings gleamed in the sunlight before it vanished into the sky, lost in a flock of glittering birds.

He'd better dress; he didn't want to be caught in his pajamas by the police again. He'd much rather see Nathanial in his pajamas. Or did the copper wear a night-robe?

Would there be any harm in asking?

Less than an hour later Nathanial was at his door and being shown in by Jeremy. Jeremy brought the copper up to the study. This was not the kind of conversation one had where the staff could hear.

Nathanial stood in the doorway. "Fulbright."

The use of his surname stung, but he ignored it. This was bigger than the two of them. They had to stop Foxhall before they could solve any of their other problems. "Shut the door and have a seat."

Nathanial lifted one blond eyebrow at Jericho's sharp tone but obeyed. "This had better be good. This is not a social call."

"I do not need to write to invite you over; my door will always be open to you." He meant every word. He pushed the folded paper across the desk. "When I woke there was a bird waiting for me. This was inside of it."

Nathanial's finger brushed over the paper, but he didn't open it. "It's another one isn't it?"

Jericho nodded. "I don't know why it came here."

"He knows you're helping me."

"He knows we can't catch him."

How could they? Men like Foxhall didn't fall. They could literally get away with murder and people would assume him of good character because of his birth, when in fact it was his birth and wealth and title that had corrupted his character and made him untouchable.

Foxhall was the very reason the Nobility Task Force had been set up, but even they weren't up to the job.

Nathanial grimaced. "We raided the address you gave us when a man showed up there. It was a set up."

"When was that?"

"Two days ago."

Nathanial opened up the paper. He stared at the picture. There was no story. Not yet. That would be added later. Jericho watched as his face paled and his lips moved as though he had forgotten how to form words, or he was gasping for air.

"Are you all right?"

Nathanial still couldn't speak. So, Jericho got up and poured him a brandy. He put his hand on Nathanial's shoulder and stared at the photograph. It was no more shocking than the others, though the woman's face was clearly visible. She seemed to be looking at the camera. And, though he couldn't be sure from the angle, it looked suspiciously like the masked man was not using her quim.

"This…" Nathanial picked up the brandy and drank it in one swallow. "This is my maid. This is her room in my house."

17

Nathanial's hand shook as he held the photograph. How had it happened? When had it happened? He closed his eyes and sighed. When he'd returned from Margaret's the morning after dinner, with a very sore head and a queasy stomach, he'd been handed the letter by his butler, informing him that the maid had already gone. He'd quizzed his butler, but the man had gone to sleep and not woken until morning.

"I stayed the night at Margaret's. After you left, Bertie and I got into the brandy." They'd also argued about everything. Given that Margaret hadn't replied to his letter yet, she probably had nothing to say to him either.

Jericho didn't say anything.

"When I went home the next day, my maid was gone. I didn't think anything of it." How could he have been so stupid?

"You couldn't have known."

"He was in my house." His voice was too loud, but he couldn't hush. "He killed my maid."

"And he sent *me* the photograph."

"How long until it goes public?" Nathanial glanced up at Jericho who still had his hand on his shoulder.

"I'll speak to the printer. Pay him off if needed."

He placed his hand over Jericho's. "I'll have to take this to my boss." Amberton would be furious. Not only was he failing to catch the killer, but the killer was now openly taunting him. "Thank you for sending for me."

"Of course."

"After that dinner…"

The silence thickened and Jericho pulled away. "It's your life and your choice. But you have barely lived."

"I have lived more than some." But not enough. He wanted to drink it all in before his life became dull and gray. Jericho was the colors he'd never see again. He concentrated on folding up the paper. "Let me know what happens with the printer. Or do you want me to speak with him, officially?"

"I'll go and if I have no luck, you can have a turn."

Nathanial pocketed the paper and stood. Jericho was too close to be polite, but too far away for him to reach for. His fingers curled. How much life could he fit in his remaining weeks – or was it days— of freedom?

Or would it be better to not know what he was missing?

"Thank you for your help." He offered his hand, but Jericho drew him into an embrace, and Nathanial let himself be held. Then he put his arms around Jericho. This wasn't a formal dance with people watching. Nor was it a stolen moment. He wanted more of those moments before his time was taken forever.

But he didn't know how to say it, and he knew that Jericho's demon was a danger. Although at this point in his life, being consumed by a demon instead of obeying his father's wishes was not a bad option. He bit back a laugh.

"What is amusing?" Jericho studied him as though he'd lost his mind. Maybe he had.

"I was thinking about your demon." He released Jericho and found some space even though he wanted the opposite.

"Do you want her? She still wants you."

But did Jericho? The words didn't form.

While Jericho had housed the demon for years, Nathanial knew he wouldn't be able to; he'd need to pass her on and then where would he be? He shook his head. He didn't want the demon. "I need to sort this on my own."

"But you aren't on your own." Jericho closed his eyes. "If you want Eulalia, I will give her to you." Jericho's eyes were blue when he opened them. His skin gleamed as though he were no longer human. "Everything you want, Nathanial. I can get you the justice you crave."

One kiss and the demon could be his. His words would be like magic and he could have what he wanted. Foxhall would go to prison, and Nathanial could outsmart his father.

He took a step closer. It wasn't only justice that he wanted.

"I have lived too long in this body. I have helped make Jericho who he is. I can help you." The words fell from Jericho's lips, but his voice had changed, and the magic wrapped around Nathanial and drew him closer.

He touched Jericho's cheek. "You have made him a killer." He was talking to the demon. "I cannot kill to feed you."

The price of her help was too high.

THE DOOR to Jericho's study closed. He didn't follow Nathanial or call out for him to stay. He'd offered Eulalia to him, and the copper had turned the demon down. He was too good for this world, but no one else saw it. Eulalia was oddly mellow, too.

He resisted me.

Jericho nodded. No one resisted her. And he'd never offered to give up her power to anyone. He'd been knocked back. Nathanial had other things to worry about—like solving the case before Foxhall got completely out of hand, or worse, got Nathanial implicated.

Jericho stood there for a few minutes longer, sharing in Eulalia's shock. He had to go see the printer and stop that pamphlet from being made.

At least the printer will not be able to resist me.

Which was true. Where once he'd worried that he'd become too dependent on Eulalia, now he was sure of it. He couldn't make it through a day without letting her voice color his. It was one of the reasons he had to feed her so often. He should do that soon; if not today then tomorrow.

He wasn't in the mood for death, and he had no fever. Nor was she clamoring for a soul. Perhaps today they would just drown in rejection. He could have any man he wanted…but the one he wanted had walked away.

Even the few moments they'd been together hadn't been about Nathanial's pleasure—couldn't have been given that Eulalia would've swallowed Nathanial whole. Jericho shook his head. He truly had nothing to offer a man like Nathanial.

He caught a cab to the printers, determined to see this through regardless.

The man was easily dazzled by Eulalia and she was equally happy to dazzle.

"The pamphlet has already been printed."

"Printed? When?" Eulalia purred while Jericho reeled in horror, he was unable to voice while she was in control.

"Last night. It's been sent out already." The man fidgeted, clearly worried this time. "Is there a problem?"

"I want to see it."

"I don't keep copies."

The lie smelled like rotten meat. "You do. Show me." The compulsion rattled in Jericho's bones. Eulalia was not holding back, and he wasn't trying to restrain her. The power rushing through him was like that golden moment of completion. His head would hurt later, the fever would start soon after, and he'd have to kill. But for the moment it was a sharp-edged pleasure.

The man blinked and stuttered then went out the back to retrieve the pamphlet. He handed it over with a trembling hand. While he didn't want to obey, he had to, and he knew something wasn't right.

Jericho scanned the page. The picture was the same as the one he'd been sent. The story was appalling. Detective with a dark desire. The stories usually had some secretive aspect as though the writer and the reader knew what they were doing was wrong, yet at the same time every detail of the act was there. "Who wrote this?"

"It came with the photograph."

And it was too late to stop what was happening. Jericho screwed up the paper. "When the police come, you will get out all of your proofs and tell them what you do. You will assist them in anyway way you can."

He turned and stalked out, anger flooding him. Eulalia was just as angry. She was invested in this case and her need for justice. Had he misjudged her this entire time? Her dark laughter echoed in Jericho's head as he made his way home. He couldn't go to the police station with this.

But he could send a message.

He wrote the address on a slip of paper. With the message, 'It's too late. Shut the printer down.' He put a tag around its neck with Bayard written on it, and sent the bird to the police station, where it would hopefully land on Nathanial's desk.

Now there was nothing he could do but wait and see what happened. He hated waiting, so he changed into rough work clothes and slipped out into the city to feed his demon before she could give him a fever.

AMBERTON WAS INCREDULOUS. Nathanial sat as his boss's face alternated between rage and disgust and incomprehension. "Did you not think it odd that your maid just up and left?"

"Yes, but what am I to do? Go chasing after her?" Servants left; that wasn't uncommon. His biological father had fled when the affair had been discovered. "I could not compel her to stay even if I had found her."

"And you are absolutely sure it is her and that it was taken in your house?"

Nathanial nodded, his finger's curling into a fist the only show of anger he could allow himself. If he wasn't going to be leaving London, he'd be needing to find new accommodation. "Yes. That man has been in my house."

"And your butler let him in?"

"I haven't been home to talk to him. I was given this and came straight here. I thought it best that someone else interview him."

"And Fulbright gave you this." Amberton put the paper down. "Is it possible he is involved? Throwing you off the trail, but appearing to be helpful? He does have dark hair."

"It's not him. He's gone to speak to the printer, to try and halt the printing."

A wrap on the door startled them both.

"Come in." Amberton shouted.

The secretary stood there holding a bird in his hand. "This just arrived. It's addressed to Bayard. I thought it might be urgent." His gaze darted about the room. How often had Nottwood been in here?

The secretary's suit and cravat were well tailored. He wasn't from a wealthy family and yet lately his clothing had taken on a quality that couldn't be denied. Nathanial held out his hand and was given the bird.

It wasn't secure so anyone could've opened it and read the message. The secretary moved freely between the offices and between the regular police and the Nobility Task Force. Nottwood left the office, but Nathanial's gaze remained fixed on the door even after it had closed.

"Bayard?"

"I was thinking, Sir. Nottwood is dressing rather well, isn't he?"

"I hadn't noticed. I do not see what that has to do with anything, though. What is the damn message that was so important?"

Nathanial turned to face Amberton. He didn't want to suggest there was a breach, and yet it was the only reason that could explain all his cases that had fallen apart. He opened the bird at he played for time. A few lines in familiar handwriting. He gritted his teeth and drew in a breath. "There is the printer's address. I suggest you sent some police there urgently, as that photograph is about to go public."

Amberton took the slip of paper, swore, and got up. "You wait here."

He left the office, barking orders.

Nathanial leaned back in his chair. He'd crossed Foxhall's name off the list. Yet the man had made his crimes more personal. What false information could he give the informant? Something that would prove beyond doubt that his work had been sabotaged. Nothing came to mind before Amberton was storming back to his office to finish their meeting.

Amberton shut the door with too much force. "This is beyond the pale."

Nathanial could only nod in agreement. "Someone will interview my butler?"

"Yes. You are to go on leave."

"I can't. I have to finish this case. Whoever is doing this has to be caught."

"And he will be, but not by you. Too many have slipped through your fingers. I have given you too many chances."

"Someone has leaked information about every case. I went through them all."

Amberton just stared at him, like he'd claimed he could fly. "Do not blame others for your own failings."

"I'm not. Do you not think it is suspicious that only I have such a high failure rate, that my first few cases were trouble free before..." Before Nottwood had started. That was the change.

"I've heard enough. You are on leave. I will let you officially resign out of friendship with your father."

Nathanial couldn't breathe. "My father never wanted to me to have this job in the first place."

"I find that hard to believe given how proud he always said he was. I had to hide how many times you'd failed to close."

"And I failed because something always happened at the last moment. The death of a witness or the change in testimony. Evidence going missing."

"Carelessness on your part." Amberton opened the door. "Take two weeks, but I want your letter on my desk by the end or I will have no choice but to fire you."

Nathanial wished he'd kissed Jericho and taken the demon.

He lifted his chin and held Amberton's gaze. "This isn't over."

"It is. We will catch whoever killed your maid, but you are too close to the case and too unreliable."

Featherington,

I am attempting to catch a spy and have used your name as the lure. Should a man approach you, warning of your impending arrest and his ability to make evidence vanish or turn in your favor, you must play along, yet inform Amberton. My very job depends on it.

Bayard

18

____

*N*athanial didn't go directly home from work. Instead he went via the printers mentioned in Jericho's note, but he couldn't even get close to the building as it was on fire. He stared at the flames. It wasn't an accident.

The driver asked him where to next. He didn't want to go home, not while his butler was being interviewed and the police were there. He couldn't face Margaret and Bertie in person after what he'd done. What had he been thinking of putting Featherington in danger like that? All to save his job. A job that no longer even mattered. But there'd been no time to make other plans; he'd needed to set up a false lead.

While he'd already written to his father to say he would be leaving the Nobility Task Force to join the church as he wished, it was another matter to have Amberton effectively dismiss him. The case would move on without him. No doubt the spy would pass that on and trip himself in the process.

He gave the driver the name of one of his clubs. Not the Rose; that wouldn't open until after supper, and he didn't want to see Jericho either. If he did, he might kiss him just to get the demon and get his job back. It was still far too tempting, but in the end, it would be for nothing. He would obey his father, so maybe Amberton had done him a favor. He would resign tomorrow. Pack up his house and it would be done.

No more lingering and dwelling and fretting. No more choices to be made.

No more threats.

He would have an utterly peaceful and dull life.

At the club, he ate well and ordered the best wine to go with it. Then followed up with brandy. He played cards and lost some money, though not a great deal, then won it back and half again. What need was there for restraint when restraint was all he'd have for the rest of his life? Better to revel in luxury now.

He poured himself into a cab while he could still walk in a moderately straight line. The sky was dark and dotted with stars, the scent of smoke lingered. From the printer or some other fire? He leaned back and let his body bounce with the jolt of the carriage. He was twenty-five and his life was shuttering around him.

He'd never asked for any of this. But who did? No one was born with a grand plan in mind.

Nathanial closed his eyes and imagined running away to the continent. He'd have no funds, but there were ways to overcome that. He could become a thief, a soldier, or a whore. At least whores had sex. He'd never even done that. So proper, waiting to ensure he never sullied the family name, never caused a scandal the way Margaret had done by jilting Foxhall.

Yet it still wasn't enough.

The cab stopped and Nathanial paid and tipped generously; why shouldn't he spend his father's money while he still had it? Perhaps he'd make some generous bequests, too.

The light out the front of the house was on, but there was no other indication that anyone was awake. He gripped the handrail and dragged himself up the stairs, stumbling only once.

Godfrey opened the door. "Sir."

"Butler." He rolled past him, keeping a hand on the wall. Sure, the night air had added fuel to the liquor in his blood. His head was heavy, and his body was light; he really should get drunk more often. "I trust you gave a good account of the night I was at my sister's to the police."

"Yes, Sir. I am sorry I did not hear or see anything. I would've stopped him if I had."

"Why the bloody hell didn't you hear anything? What were you doing?" he yelled, as he leaned against the wall. The house spun around him like he was at the center of a merry go round.

"I did hear something, I went to the front door, but no one was there. So, I went back to my tea. Sarah was with me. Then we both went to our rooms. I slept like the dead. Copper thinks I was drugged."

Nathanial closed his eyes and the wall slid from beneath him.

Godfrey caught him. "Let me help you up stairs, Sir."

Nathanial fought him off and fell to the ground. "I'm fine." He clambered back up. "I'm fine." He stumbled to the stairs. "The house will be packed up tomorrow. I'll give you a reference." He couldn't look at Godfrey as he spoke. He had to concentrate on the tricky stairs.

"Sir?"

"I'm leaving London." He stumbled and caught himself on the step. His shin would be bruised tomorrow. He kept climbing, determined to make it to his room on his own.

He scrabbled at the handle, got the door open, and tumbled inside before collapsing on the bed. He lay there, feet on the floor, trying to understand why his life was in ruins. He'd done everything right. Nathanial had followed all the rules society had set down and still there was nothing left but ashes in his mouth. Even if his father suddenly decided to love the children from his wife's affair, he still wouldn't have a job. Even if he had a job, his father would still tear him down, and Margaret too, because of his own shattered pride.

No one would miss him when he left. Godfrey would find a new job.

That wasn't true.

Jericho would miss him. And he'd miss Jericho.

All he could think about was Jericho's blue eyes when the demon was in control. He'd been offered the demon and had turned it down. If Jericho were here right now, he'd…still turn it down. The idea of sharing his already muddled head with another… He shuddered. He didn't know how Jericho did it.

Maybe he should ask him, gather the facts.

Yes. That was a good idea. Then he could say goodbye and do this right. He levered himself upright and found paper and pen. He hesitated for a moment then wrote,

Meet me at home. -N

The message was in a bird and on its way before he could question the wisdom of the idea. He sat on the edge of his bed.

It wasn't the demon that Nathanial wanted from Jericho. It was something much more intimate. To Hell with waiting for marriage.

JERICHO WAS HALF LISTENING to a discussion on politics that was almost putting him to sleep. While not full, people had returned to the club after Foxhall had scared them off.

That man was up to something. He could feel it and Eulalia knew it. If he could get Foxhall against the wall he might be able to dig into his brain and find out what. To kill Nathanial's maid in his house and with that story…it was despicable. It was also highly personal.

Jeremy came over and handed him a bird. Jericho took it and opened it, glad to have an excuse to stop pretending to care about the situation in Germany. He was sure the Germans would sort it out. There was always bickering along the European borders and he'd spent enough time in the army to know that it didn't make a jot of difference what men like him thought about anything. The lords in parliament or the kings and queens would solve it with money or marriage.

Those two things seemed to solve everything.

They also created most of the problems in the first place.

He unfolded the note and read it twice. It was Nathanial's handwriting, but what was the meaning of the note? It was close to midnight. From another man he might have thought it an invitation to bed. From Nathanial…he couldn't be sure. Probably not. He was not going to be in the least bit hopeful. Although maybe he'd decided to ruin himself before obeying his father. As amusing as that idea was, it was also unlikely.

Which left the alternative two options. The first being there'd been some break-through on the case, or Foxhall was there and Nathanial was in trouble. Which meant he had to go. But that didn't mean he couldn't be prepared for all three possibilities.

"Gentleman, I must depart."

Robert glanced up at him. "You have a better offer? Do we know the gentleman?"

"No."

"Liar. If I were to guess, he is blond and pretty and buttoned up too tight. Perhaps I should come and help you." Robert's grin widened.

Jericho doubted very much that Nathanial would want to even dabble in the joys of ménage. Robert's benefactors, from all accounts, had conspired to skewer him on occasions. "I shall keep your generous offer in mind."

He did up his waistcoat and redid his cravat while Robert fetched his coat from where it had been flung earlier in the night. As Robert did up the buttons, he leaned in. "Don't let him slip away. If you do, I will have to box your ears."

Jericho doubted Robert could even throw a punch. "That is not for me to decide."

"Convince him. You have a way with words and people." He patted the collar. "There you go, respectable enough for a late-night visit."

It wasn't him who had the magic touch with people. That was Eulalia and he would not use the demon to convince Nathanial to marry him and ignore all the reasons why they shouldn't. Aside from that it would be morally wrong to coerce someone to be with him, Jericho would forever know that it wasn't him Nathanial truly wanted. Better to be alone than unwanted.

Jericho gave Robert a weak smile.

Robert put his hands on Jericho's shoulders. "I mean it. We want a wedding." His smile faltered. "Some of us will never get the respectability that would grant."

"Except I am not respectable."

"I never said you were." Robert stepped back. "Go. We will be sure to misbehave."

There was never any doubt that he wouldn't go. He gave Robert a nod, picked up his hat, and left the house—after telling Jeremy not to wait up for him. He walked down the street to the corner to hail a cab, then tried to relax for the relatively short trip.

While he'd never been to Nathanial's house, he knew where he lived. It was a pretty building, though one that could be walked past without ever looking twice. He paid and got out, half expecting to be turned away by the butler. He hesitated on the bottom step. And if he was not allowed in?

He glanced up at the dark windows. He would cut ties, he decided.

Jericho would not be jerked around like a puppet on a string, just because Nathanial didn't know what he wanted. Or rather wouldn't commit to taking what he wanted. Jericho climbed the steps and knocked as loudly as he dared. The street was so quiet, completely different to where he lived where there was a bar down one end of the street, his club, and then a house a little further down that had a very steady stream of gentlemen to visit the ladies. It wasn't the best street, but he liked it. It was alive. This street wasn't.

Maybe the houses were all locked up for summer so the owners could go to the country for fresh air instead of enjoying the summer stink of the Thames. The door creaked open. Nathanial stood there in his suit yet still managing to look disheveled. A cloud of brandy hung around him.

Ah. The good detective was drunk, and his moral guard had slipped.

Jericho should leave. His feet remained stuck in place.

Nathanial stepped back to allow him entrance. "I didn't think you'd come."

"Why wouldn't I?" He wasn't going to admit to thinking Nathanial was in danger.

Nathanial shut the door behind them and then started walking upstairs. The house was silent. The servants must be in bed. This did not feel right. It was as though they were sneaking around. Which they were to a degree.

"Why did you invite me over?"

Halfway up the stairs Nathanial turned. "If you need to ask, perhaps you should leave."

"I know the reason. Why the change of heart?" His feet were already following. The heat in his blood had nothing to do with Eulalia's hunger and everything to do with his. Already he was rising.

"Amberton requested my resignation. I'm going to give it to him and go."

"Go? Why did Amberton do that?"

Nathanial stared at him. "Something to do with not solving the case before my maid got killed in my house."

All he needed were five minutes with Foxhall and the man would never trouble anyone again. Eulalia may not want Foxhall's soul, but Jericho had learned other ways to kill while in the army. "I am sorry."

"Don't be sorry. I didn't ask you here to wallow with me. I've already done that." Nathanial fingered his cravat and then undid it. "I want to live what's left of my life." He unbuttoned his coat then hung it over the rail. It slid down to Jericho's hand. The fabric was still warm from Nathanial's body.

"You're going to the church, not dying."

"Near enough. I won't be able to do what I want. What a waste of time waiting for marriage was. I should have been out there every night not caring who talked." He flung off the cravat.

Jericho went up the stairs to stand level with him. He took Nathanial's hand and kissed his fingers. "You are drunk. I don't want to be a regret come morning."

"What I regret is not acting sooner. Pretending to be oh so noble when I'm not. I'm common. As common as you. So why do I care what all the toffs think?"

That was much harder to answer. When Jericho didn't speak, Nathanial clumsily unbuttoned his coat. Jericho didn't resist. This is what he'd wanted since first meeting Nathanial. It still didn't feel right.

But for Nathanial there was no more waiting. He didn't have time.

Jericho pulled him close and kissed his cheek. "I cannot kiss you on the lips unless you want Eulalia."

Did he?

Nathanial shook his head. "I do not want the burden of the demon."

Jericho understood that. He hadn't realized at the time what the weight would be, but he'd been so consumed by anger that he probably wouldn't have cared.

He needs me, now more than ever.

While that was true, Jericho wouldn't pass Eulalia on to someone who didn't want her. "And you cannot spend while touching me. Unless you wish to die." He put a finger under Nathanial's chin, so the detective had to meet his gaze. "I will not be responsible for your death."

"I do not want to die." He tugged loose Jericho's hastily, and poorly, tied cravat and let it slip to the floor. "Nor can we stay here."

Nathanial led him the rest of the way up the stairs and to the bedroom. A small light was on, casting deep shadows. The pale sheets on the bed were most inviting, but this wasn't right and Jericho shouldn't be here doing this no matter how much he wanted to.

It would go nowhere. Couldn't.

Robert's words about marriage echoed in his ears. He did want to get married. He didn't want to be alone, running the club until he died.

Nathanial stripped off his waistcoat. "So how do we do this?"

Jericho lifted an eyebrow. "Not so fast."

He closed the distance and put a hand on Nathanial's chest. His heart was beating fast, from lust or nerves or both? "It's like a dance." He let his hand slide lower, then up to undo one button on the collar. "The fun is in the footwork, not the last beat and the bow," he murmured in Nathanial's ear. His lips brushed the shell, then his tongue flicked against it.

Nathanial flinched. He clearly wasn't used to anyone being so close.

Jericho put a hand on Nathanial's hip to draw him in tight. The hard length of the detective's prick pressed against him. *Do not take his soul if he messes up, Eulalia, I beg you. I will find you another host. Just let Nathanial live.*

I want him as a host. But I cannot help what happens.

Nathanial's hands found their way to him, cupping his hip, tracing his arm, his shoulder and jaw. His fingers traced Jericho's lip and Jericho drew one into his mouth and sucked. The detective drew in a breath. Jericho had never wanted to kiss someone so much. Was that his desire or Eulalia's need to swap host? He didn't know, but he wasn't going to slip and saddle Nathanial with a demon he didn't want no matter how much he needed her.

He settled for kissing along Nathanial's jaw, then down his throat as he undid more buttons and revealed more skin. He could be doing this faster. It didn't have to be slow, but he wanted to give Nathanial time to change his mind. He wanted Nathanial to never forget him. His hand brushed over the front of Nathanial's trousers and all he could think about was the way Nathanial had knelt before him in the library. The buttons popped open and he kissed his way lower before tugging Nathanial's shorts down enough that the ruddy head of his prick was revealed. He licked the swollen plum but was also well aware how quickly things could unravel like this.

He glanced up and growled, "remember my warning."

Nathanial nodded and pushed down his trousers and shorts so his shaft jutted forward, eager to be sucked and swallowed. Jericho happily obliged, teasing the heated skin and taking as much of the length as he could. The moment he tasted the first formation of the salty spend he drew away.

Nathanial's chest lifted with each breath. "I'm...I'm all right."

Jericho narrowed his eyes. Maybe Nathanial was. But he still wasn't going to continue. He stood up and shed his shirt. Nathanial hands were on him, worshiping him. He experimented with different with licks and kisses and little bites. Jericho closed his eyes and let the other man take his fill.

For him, sex was too often about death. This was all pleasure.

A hand stroked his prick and he rolled his hips. He cracked his eyes open. Nathanial was watching him.

"I want you to mount me," Nathanial whispered. "I want to know what that's like." His lips were dangerously close, so Jericho turned his head.

"I cannot kiss."

"I know."

But did he understand? Would he remember in the throes of passion not to surrender?

Jericho cupped Nathanial's face. "I do not want to damage you."

Nathanial mimicked the gesture. "I want that damage. I will not spend; I am not so drunk to forget how to live." He grinned, wide and untroubled. So unlike the reserved expression Jericho was used to seeing. "That is what tonight in about. Living. Doing all the things I haven't done. I brought oil up from the kitchen."

Jericho groaned. There when his next excuse; he didn't want to be breeching a virgin arse without oil. "You aren't that innocent, are you?"

"I read...someone gave me a porno pamphlet that was most informative." Nathanial's hands pushed down Jericho's pants and they tangled around his ankles.

"Not everything you read in them is true or possible."

"So, you do not need it?"

He did not, but it was infinitely more pleasurable for both if there was some kind of lubrication. "We do. Where is it?"

Nathanial motioned to the small desk. Two mechanical birds sat near a small sheaf of paper. A small white milk jug was also there. He was guessing it no longer contained milk. His lips curved. "Let's shed our shoes and this mess of clothing and I'll join you on the bed."

19

Nathanial was sure his face was crimson as he bent to undo his laces so he could remove the rest of his clothing. Even though Jericho wasn't looking at him, he was close. His heart was beating so fast it was sure to stop.

He was doing this. Part of him was still screaming that it wasn't too late to send Jericho home. The rest of him wanted to feel Jericho's prick inside of him.

Jericho didn't fumble as he undressed. He even tossed his trousers over the back of the chair as he collected the oil. Nathanial couldn't help but watch the way his buttocks moved, the shape of his legs and the dark hair that covered them. His skin was golden from head to toe, his shaft darker than the rest and rising out of a tangle of black hair.

Even though he'd had it in his mouth and tasted him, Nathanial hadn't really seen him. Hadn't had the chance to admire Jericho. This was a man who hadn't accepted what fate had handed him; instead he'd refashioned what he'd been given into something he was comfortable wearing.

Or not wearing at the moment.

Jericho dipped his fingers into the oil. He rubbed it between his palms then stroked himself, until his prick glistened.

Nathanial could barely swallow. His ass clenched, but his balls tingled.

This was illegal.

No one would know. He was stealing this night for himself. And Jericho? Nathanial didn't want Jericho to think that he was using him, and yet he'd offered his body for experimentation in the library. There was a look in his eyes, when they were brown, that couldn't be written off as simply lust.

Or was that his imagination because he didn't know any better?

Nathanial stepped out of his clothing, naked with another man for the first time in his life. If it weren't for nerves winding his stomach tight, he was sure he would've already melted.

Jericho turned, his hand still on his prick. "Lie on the bed."

Nathanial nodded. But how did he lie? He considered for a moment before opting to lie on his back because he wanted to see what Jericho did next. Jericho approached the bed, jug in hand, and put it on the bedside table, then lay next to him. His oiled hand stroked Nathanial's nerve wilted length. "It doesn't hurt. Or at least not in a bad way and not for long."

Wasn't all pain bad?

And then Jericho's lips were on his throat, sucking and biting, and his fingers were dipping lower, caressing a tender piece of skin that Nathanial never gave much thought to. Then a finger swept over the tight pucker. He gasped, but Jericho didn't pull away. He slid one leg over Nathanial's as if to keep him there and bit near his collarbone. God, he didn't want to move.

That finger never strayed as it circled. With the shock gone, it started to feel good. When the pressure increased, he wanted more. He rocked his hips, and one of Jericho's fingers pressed into him. He stilled

"How does that feel?" Jericho whispered near his ear.

He had no idea. Different...good...his prick had never been harder. He nodded.

"I could finger fuck you all night, just so I can watch your facial expressions." Jericho propped himself up on his elbow and proceeded to make good on his words.

The finger moved within his channel. As he got used to that and rocked his hips, Jericho added another. The stretch was so much more. The good hurt built as those fingers twisted and pumped…oh God, yes. Nathanial drew one leg up, his hips turning toward Jericho as though silently pleading for more.

But he pulled his fingers free. Nathanial groaned.

"Settle, love," Jericho murmured.

Cool oil spilled over his balls and trickled between his buttocks. The sheets would be ruined but he didn't care. Then Jericho's fingers were back, rubbing the oil in, massaging that tight muscle and delving deeper. Three fingers and Nathanial bit his lip to keep from crying out.

"Perhaps that is enough." Jericho's fingers moved inside of Nathanial's arse.

"No. I want you."

A flicker of something crossed his face and was gone. "You haven't broken your promise yet. You could still wait for marriage."

"I won't be marrying."

"We could. We could flit to France until the fuss died down." He kissed Nathanial's throat.

It was so tempting. If not for his sister, he would. But Margaret had protected him from their father as a child and he owed her. "You have a demon and I have family duty."

"Neither of which precludes marriage." Jericho moved to lie over him. His oiled shaft rubbed against his a very tempting manner.

"I cannot ever kiss you or spend in your presence. I am risking death being in bed with you." And also a prison sentence.

Jericho glanced down. "That is true. But you aren't tossing me out."

"Because I want you. I have since I first saw you despite the thousand reasons why I shouldn't." He traced along Jericho's jaw to the fullness of his lips. It would be nice to kiss him.

Jericho leaned close and pressed his lips to Nathanial's cheek. "I didn't think I'd ever get you naked and in bed."

"I believe it was I who invited you over." Nothing had ever felt so right. There was nothing between them, skin to skin. He'd knocked back Jericho's marriage proposal; he wasn't some maid needing a ring. He wasn't risking pregnancy, and no one would know.

But he would forever be able to hold onto this night.

"And I accepted, even though I know the danger better than you."

Maybe that was part of the thrill. Too much pleasure and his life would be over. Enjoy, but not too much. Don't kiss and make this intimate.

But he wanted Jericho's kiss. He already wanted more than what was possible.

"Don't make me wait longer."

"You must tell me to stop before you succumb."

"I will." Though there were worse fates than dying in such a handsome man's arms.

Jericho drew back; the heat that had been between them dissipated leaving Nathanial's chest cold. Jericho's fingers slid over him and pressed in deep and hard. He didn't know how many it was, only that it left him breathless. His body responded before he'd even caught his breath, hips bucking with some wild need. Jericho's lips curved as he freed his fingers. "Push back. It will make it easier for me to enter."

Nathanial had no idea what Jericho meant until the blunt head of his shaft was pressed to the tight ring as though to force its way in. Jericho's grip on Nathanial's hips tightened, and the pressure increased, then Nathanial pushed back, opening and Jericho thrust into him.

Jericho stilled. "All right?"

Nathanial nodded. He wasn't sure he could breathe. He wasn't sure if it hurt or felt good and he knew that was exactly what Jericho had meant. Then Jericho started to move, slowly at first a gentle rocking motion as though to accustom Nathanial to the rod in his channel.

He closed his eyes to enjoy the sensation, the pleasure growing with each heartbeat.

"Stay alert. I would touch you...but I do not want to risk an accident."

Nathanial nodded and ran a hand over his aching prick. He already knew if he wrapped his hand around it would be too much. Jericho lifted one of Nathanial's legs and pressed in deeper. A moan slid into the air and he wasn't sure if it was his or Jericho's. He moved his hand away, unable to touch himself just in case.

Jericho leaned forward. "Still good?"

"Yes. Finish...then I will." He could wait. He had to wait.

Jericho held his gaze as he rolled his hips, thrusting deep and hard. Nathanial's fingers clamped around Jericho's arm as his hole started to sting; he wasn't going to ask Jericho to stop. Semen leaked onto his belly. It was getting harder to resist. This change in position made every stroke that much sweeter. Jericho's face became a mask of concentration, then his lips parted with a groan and a shudder raced through his body. The heat of him flooded Nathanial.

As much as he wanted to lie there, he couldn't. "You have to move."

Jericho drew back and away as though Nathanial's touch was poison. Nathanial stroked his prick just once and his completion tore through him, leaving him gasping for breath, and sticky with sweat and other. Jericho watched from the far corner of the bed. Given that he was still very much alive—though limp from the little death—there didn't need to be much distance between them.

"That was rather too close."

"That was perfect." Nathanial smiled. Truly, he didn't know why he'd waited so long.

THE ROOM WAS FLOODED with predawn light when Jericho woke. A warm body was pressed to him and it took several panicked moments for him to work out where he was, and for him to be certain the man next to him was alive.

I didn't kill him.

Jericho had never been more grateful in his entire life.

He pressed a kiss to Nathanial's cheek and slid out of bed. He didn't want to be caught here by the servants; that would create gossip. Gossip he didn't need.

Nathanial stirred and watched him through squinted eyes. "Why are you up so early?"

"I should leave." The happiness he should feel having found someone who could work around his demon, someone he was beginning to love, was tinged with bitterness.

Nathanial hadn't taken his offer of marriage seriously. He'd rather go to the church than marry him. While he knew it wasn't because of him, it didn't hurt any less. Maybe it hurt more. There was nothing he could do to change Nathanial's mind.

"Stay. I have nothing planned for the day." Nathanial sat up, his golden hair a mess. He put a hand to his temple. "I think I shall stay in bed."

Jericho still hadn't discovered if Nathanial wore pajamas or a night-robe; both of them had slept naked. He shook his head. "Fresh air will do you good." His gaze skimmed down Nathanial's chest. It was tempting to linger. "Aside from your head, you are…well?"

Nathanial frowned for a moment. He glanced down as his cheeked reddened. "Yes. Perhaps you could stay and make sure."

Jericho walked over, wearing only his trousers. He sat on the edge of the bed and held Nathanial's hand. "For what reason? Your mind is made up and nothing I say will change it, no matter how much I wish I could."

Nathanial's fingers tightened around his. "But we have this time."

It wasn't nearly long enough, and Jericho didn't want to tumble more deeply into love while knowing he'd have to cut it off and live with the wound. "The more time we spend together, the more scandal will find you. It may ruin your chances with the church."

And how unfortunate that would be. But Jericho was well aware that they had crossed the line last night. Nathanial had a reputation to maintain. He was a detective; he couldn't be seen to be breaking the law.

Nathanial's fingers went limp. "You plan on walking out and not coming back."

Jericho closed his eyes, fighting for control. And lost.

Eulalia took over. She used Jericho's body to pin Nathanial to the bed. "You will not let me help. What would you have him do?"

Nathanial's eyes were wide. Jericho saw the fear through the haze, and he wrestled to regain control. She'd been in him so long and knew him so well that it was getting harder.

"He has done everything to help you." She moved closer, her lips only a whisper away. "I do not want to, but I will respect his wishes."

She subsided, leaving Jericho over Nathanial, so close to kissing him. He could get rid of his demon and help Nathanial with one kiss.

Nathanial turned his head.

"Damn you. You will not help yourself." He gathered up his clothes and dressed fast, not caring if his shirt was rumpled and his cravat was folded all wrong.

"And be beholden to the devil?"

"It's better that being beholden to your father."

"No. Then I would have to answer to two demons, and one is bad enough."

He shoved his feet into his shoes and stared at Nathanial. "Do you not care for me at all? Or was I simply a way for you to have some fun?"

"Of course I care."

"But I am not the kind of man you would wed."

"You have a demon and a club and I have…"

Jericho put on his coat. "You have what?"

"Responsibilities."

"Well, I hope they keep you warm. I can tell you, mine have only ever been cold and unforgiving." He put his hat on and turned to go.

"Wait." Nathanial got out of bed, sheet gathered around him even though Jericho had seen it all last night. He shuffled across the floor so as not to trip on the edges. "Why did you ask last night?"

"To do right by you. I may not have your bloodlines and class, but that doesn't mean I have no care or consideration." His eyes were burning. God damn.

Nathanial gave him a weak smile. "If I thought it would help, I would."

Jericho shook his head. That wasn't what he wanted. "Either you do want me, or you don't. I don't care about the other rubbish. Your father, or work, or whatever."

"Then yes. If I were free, I would say yes."

"Then find a way to be free. It's not that hard to open a door and walk out of the cage you have made." But few did. Especially those in the peerage. The outside world was a terrifying place without all the rules on manner and clothing and behavior. He saw it every night. Men would come to his club to pretend they were free. "You know where to find me."

"You aren't any freer. You are a slave to your demon. You kill for her."

Jericho pressed his lips together. "Yes, but that didn't stop you last night."

"I was overcome with…"

"Drunk is the word you are looking for." And he should've known better, but he'd wanted to believe that maybe if Nathanial knew what he could have, he'd change his mind.

"I wasn't that drunk."

Jericho snorted. Even now Nathanial smelled of liquor. Jericho didn't care; he still wanted him. Eulalia squirmed inside of him, just as unsettled as he was. He had wounds he didn't know how to heal. "I'm going to leave. Please don't contact me unless you have changed your mind."

Nathanial didn't try to stop him.

He paused for a moment before shutting the front door. With the soft click, the heart he'd pieced together after Liang's murder fragmented. It would take more than a demon to put it back together.

Dear Lord Amberton,

Please consider this my resignation letter. I have greatly enjoyed my time on the Nobility Task Force, but I have discovered I am not suited to the job.

It has recently come to my attention that I am not the youngest son of Lord Emmaly as thought, but the product of an affair between Lady Emmaly and the groom. Given the delicate nature of my mother and the potential to cause embarrassment to my father, I would appreciate if this information were not spread. I'm sure my father will be happy to confirm the details with you should you require.

On another matter, you should investigate Nottwood, as he lives well above his means and I believe he is tipping some of the nobles off so they may get away with their crimes. I haven't been able to conclude my investigation, though you will note that I have laid a false trail implicating Featherington in the photography case.

Your faithful servant,
Mr. Nathanial Bayard

2 0

athanial bathed, dressed, and managed to eat a piece of toast. He felt like his head had been run over by a carriage, and that wasn't the only place that was feeling a little tender. He drafted a letter to his father but didn't send it. He wasn't ready for that.

It had taken him three attempts to write his resignation letter. In the end, he'd decided to put everything in the letter. Someone should know about his father, and Amberton was a good man. Not being noble was a good reason to resign, an honorable one in that he couldn't pretend to be what he wasn't. That would look good on his record; maybe Amberton would think that was why he had failed so often. At least until he read the last paragraph.

Bertie hadn't replied. Either he was aghast at being implicated or nothing had happened because the spy didn't believe the trail. Nathanial hoped his suspicions weren't wrong. He hoped there was a spy and he wasn't useless. With a melancholy heart, he folded the letter and sent it to Amberton in a secure bird.

He'd have to return those birds to the task force.

He needed to do a lot of things and had the will to do none.

Godfrey hadn't mentioned last night's outburst and if he'd heard anything after midnight, he said nothing about that either. Perhaps it would be best to hide in his study all day and venture out to eat that evening, thus avoiding Godfrey all together.

His head pounded despite the laudanum and there was an ache within him that had nothing to do with the physicality of last night. He had lost Jericho. Tossed aside a perfectly shiny penny. No, not a penny, Jericho was some rare gem that he'd held for a moment before letting it fall from his hand.

He'd turned down marriage.

His sister would tear strips off him.

He was going to have to face her at some point. But not today. He drew JF on the paper on his desk in a scrolling flourish, then added his initials. All he'd had to do was say yes.

Yes, and he could be telling his father to go to Hell. Yes, and he could be seizing his life with both hands. They could wed and leave for France…a few months on the continent did sound nice. And then what would they do?

He had no job and no skills.

He had nothing.

Nothing except his name and even that wasn't really his.

So, he had less than nothing. He was a no one, while Jericho was his own man. With no title and no family money to rely on, he'd created himself. Nathanial had never even had to try; he'd held onto all the things that weren't his because he was afraid of who he'd be without them.

Perhaps he should take a walk and see what he could be since he was nothing. Something would inspire him or give him purpose. Anything to avoid the fate his father had planned.

He gathered his coat and hat and went out. The dull day did nothing to lift his mood. Even though it had been a cool summer, his skin still grew sticky. He walked through the gardens where at night one could buy all kinds of delights but in daylight it was respectable. Further down the road he stopped to admire an ancient little church. It wasn't fancy like some of them and was never used for society weddings because it didn't hold enough people. But it was pretty.

He'd never much fancied the idea of wedding that was more of a performance for the right people. Margaret's had been small, but then she was Featherington's second wife.

What would it be like walking up its path and through the doors to wed?

He let his imagination lead his feet into the shade of the doorway. He could send a bird saying yes. Or turn up at Jericho's door and tell him that he'd been an idiot. That he very much wanted to marry him. They could stand up and make those vows in front of a few friends and it would all be done. His father would run out of steam and bluster.

Nathanial breathed in the cool stone and the scent of the flowers.

There was only one reason he wanted to be in church.

"Can I help you?" the priest came around the corner, almost knocking Nathanial out of his daydream.

"I was wondering if you hold male marriage services." He should be asking what it was like to live such a cloistered life. Did the priest never want more than the distant love of God? He'd told Jericho he believed, but now he wasn't sure. Surely God wouldn't want someone like him in his service, a man whose heart was elsewhere.

"Yes. All unions are catered for here because there is nothing greater than sharing God's love. Did you have a date in mind? I could check the calendar." The priest stepped deeper into the church.

Nathanial's heart bounced and he followed. This was wrong. He was lying to a priest. His list of sins was growing longer by the day, but he couldn't stop himself. He was still caught up in the fantasy of what his life could be if there were no scandal sheets waiting for gossip and if his sister's, and her children's, respectability wouldn't be affected.

"If you do not mind a weekday, I could fit you in in two weeks." The priest pointed to Thursday.

"That soon? Um…I'll have to consult with my fiancé and family."

"Of course. Can I get a name?"

Nathanial swallowed. He couldn't say Bayard. "Fulbright."

The priest penciled Fulbright into Thursday, then handed over a slip of paper. "The deposit would need to be paid by the weekend. And this is the bird address."

Nathanial nodded. He was going to Hell for this. He would have to cancel, but he could do it by bird. His stomach rolled and he was sure he was about to lose his breakfast. But he managed to smile and walk out into the sun that had now broken through the clouds.

Maybe he could do it. If he spoke to Margaret. If he took the demon and caught Foxhall. If he could face down his father for the final time.

If. If. If.

He wasn't a detective anymore, and Foxhall wasn't his problem.

His father simply wanted him out of sight and no longer receiving an allowance. And Margaret...he knew she wanted them to marry. He would send her a note telling her that he'd call on her that evening. Hopefully she was still in town.

He caught a cab home, his spirits high. He'd also write a note to Jericho, though he had no idea what it would say.

Godfrey was waiting for him when he got home. "The man about the faulty lights came back to finish. He left you this."

Nathanial took the thick envelope, dread embracing him. "There was nothing wrong with the lights. I never called anyone to look at them." Who had been in his house? His stomach bucked but *that* thought was too awful to even consider.

"Sir?"

He tore open the envelope and pulled out what was inside. "Christ."

His blood ran hot then cold and the ground raced toward him. He put his hand on the wall, the photograph crumpling in his hand. "Who was this man? What did he look like? Where did he go?"

But Nathanial already knew. The photograph in the envelope had been taken last night by an automatic camera. His face was clear and there was no doubt at all about what was being done to him. He crushed the paper. He was ruined.

He shoved the photograph into the envelope, hoping Godfrey hadn't seen the details.

"The lights upstairs needed fixing."

"No, they didn't."

"Sarah said they did, and that you had arranged it." Sarah…dead Sarah. How much had she been paid to say that? "She let him in the first day and he returned today. Obviously I had to let him in."

"Which rooms was he in?"

"I don't know. He went up into the attic."

Nathanial raced up the stairs and pulled down the ladder. He scrambled up, the envelope still in his hand. A shaft of light pierced the dark. There were marks on the dusty floor as though something with three legs had stood there. Worm trails from cables tracked through the dust. He put his eye to the hole and saw his bed. Nathanial closed his eyes and rested his forehead on the wood while heat of the attic and dust invaded his lungs.

If the camera had been set up to take photos every thirty seconds while there was movement, there must be tens of photos. Godfrey called up the ladder, but Nathanial was tempted to never come down. Being possessed by a demon was suddenly seeming like a really good idea, which only exemplified how desperate he was.

How long did he have before these most private photographs were made public?

THE CLUB HAD ONLY JUST OPENED, but Jericho was already in the smoking room. He didn't usually indulge but he didn't want to think tonight. He didn't want to play the host and act as though everything was all right. It was all wrong. A second chance at happiness had slid through his fingers like smoke from his mouth. He exhaled, knowing he should stop, or he'd be completely useless all night.

Robert tapped him on the shoulder. "Did you want to talk about it or sulk?"

"Sulk." He didn't want to talk about it ever again. He didn't want to hear Robert talk about love or imagine happiness with another. That was clearly not for him.

That's what he got for housing a demon in his heart and soul for so long. He was too corrupted for anyone to want him.

"Come and do it in the other room."

Jericho let Robert lead him out, glad that he had at least one friend who wouldn't desert him. But then Nathanial and he had never been friends. He'd been helping Nathanial with a case, and somehow more had happened even though it shouldn't have. He'd known that and had still rolled the dice hoping for something other than abject failure.

He slumped into a chair, glad that not many were here yet. Robert handed him a scotch. "You need something stronger."

"I need…" He had no idea. Nathanial. But he couldn't have him.

What a waste of a man; the church didn't know what they would be getting. At least Nathanial would know what he was missing. A hard smile formed, and he downed the scotch, enjoying the burn. It was tempting to drink himself to death, but Eulalia wouldn't let that happen. She'd take over and make a bigger mess. He ignored her hiss of displeasure.

"You need some entertainment."

"No, I need to be alone."

"I think that is the problem. You never let anyone close." Robert's fingers brushed Jericho's forehead.

There was a good reason for that. He had a demon, a club, and a certain reputation. Could he clean up his life? Why should he? Maybe he only wanted Nathanial because he couldn't have him. Which didn't explain why he'd proposed and been shot down like a dirigible in enemy territory—which was terribly messy and fatal.

That summed up how he felt. His life was a wreck of twisted metal and useless flesh.

"I proposed. Do not breathe a word or I'll kill you." He was only half joking. Eulalia fancied Robert's soul, so bright and full of life.

"From your mood, I'm guessing he didn't accept."

"He'd rather become a priest or a monk or something…" Whatever one did when giving their life to the church and God.

"Oh. I did not take him for that type of man."

"He isn't but his father has him all tied up in knots and knows what strings to pull." And it wasn't his place to reveal what those strings were. Jericho let his head fall back. "I am an idiot."

"You're in love."

"Same thing." It hurt. He hated that it hurt, and that Nathanial had the power to make him hurt. That he'd stayed the night even though Nathanial didn't want him for anything more than a casual experiment. He closed his eyes, the opium and the liquor swirling around within him but not stealing any of the ache.

Even now he still wanted.

Robert sat on the arm of the chair. "He liked you."

"Don't. I don't want you to try and make me feel better. Maybe if I remember how much it hurts; I won't do it again. Perhaps the nobility have it right. They don't marry for love, but duty and name and lineage."

"Their affairs are for love."

"But they don't expect them to last. Their hearts are forever safe."

"Unused." Robert plucked a piece of lint off Jericho's sleeve. "To fall in love would be a glorious thing."

"I thought you loved me?"

Robert laughed. "Like a brother. I would not trade our friendship for all the rubies...well, maybe..."

Jericho smiled and his face didn't crack.

"Sir. You need to come to the door." Jeremy had appeared next to him. "Foxhall has returned."

"It's a little early for him to be making trouble isn't it?" But Jericho hauled himself out of the chair. The room wobbled and his legs felt... he wasn't even sure he could feel them.

Robert followed and Jeremy led. Foxhall was on the step, smirking like he knew some secret Jericho should be aware of. He didn't fight as Eulalia shimmered closer to the surface. She hated Foxhall but was too disgusted to devour him. In that they agreed; Jericho didn't want to get that close to the man.

"I thought we had agreed you weren't welcome here, Foxhall?" Jericho leaned against the door frame, blocking it, but also needing the wood to stay upright.

"I'm not here to dabble in your club of vice and filth."

"There is no vice or filth, just art and conversation. Vice is up the road to your left, not too expensive either." He winked. Or rather Eulalia did, her voice on his lips. He shouldn't have drunk that scotch. Foxhall was dangerous and Jericho was relying on a demon.

If he couldn't get the man he loved to say yes, how was he going to get rid of the man he hated?

Foxhall thrust an envelope at him. "The obscenity committee has been watching you. You're done, Fulbright."

Jericho took the envelope and tore it open with clumsy fingers. Eulalia's curiosity burned as bright as his. He stumbled back, and Robert caught him. "Where did you get these?" Though the where was clear. It was Nathanial's bed. "How?"

"That is not your concern." Foxhall stepped back and that was when Jericho saw the two regular coppers on the street.

"You invaded his house. His privacy? What does it matter what a man does in his own house?"

"You're under arrest for sodomy out of wedlock, you perverted creature. You'll never last the two years of hard labor. You've never worked a day in your life." Foxhall stepped onto the sidewalk.

"I served in his Majesty's Army. I have worked far harder that you have ever done." But that wasn't what this was about. "I know about you. Your dark desires. Do you like it as they choke out their last breath? Is that what it takes to get you off? You call me unnatural, yet your desires are perverse, created out of pain and fear, not love."

Foxhall blanched and the coppers glanced at him.

"Arrest him," Foxhall screeched

Robert tugged on his arm as if to get him to run. He could flee out the back and into the night, but there was no point. He couldn't talk himself out of these charges. Not when the photographs were so clear. He thrust them at Robert and shook his head. "Clear out the club. Get everyone away."

He didn't know if there would be a raid once he was gone or not, but Robert knew where to hide things and what to burn. He'd also make sure Jericho's servants were taken care of. With Jeremy protesting, Robert shut the door, leaving Jericho on the step.

Eulalia was silent as Jericho let himself be dragged away to the waiting carriage. The metal bars gleamed in the streetlights. Even she knew there was no dodging this one. Her magic only went so far.

He vowed to let her go free the first time she found someone she could help. She didn't purr happily at the thought. Her presence was a cold weight in his heart.

NATHANIAL RODE his automatic bike to the Jericho Rose. It wasn't respectable to be riding in the dark with his hat barely staying put, but he didn't care. He no longer cared about such frivolous matters. He parked out front, but he'd never seen the house so dark and quiet. The knot in his stomach and the panic in his heart swelled. He was too late.

He put his hand to his throat and blinked rapidly. No. He couldn't be too late. Perhaps Jericho had closed for the night and that was all. He'd asked Godfrey to buy all the new scandal sheets. His name hadn't been on them. Not yet, though he knew it was only a matter of time. Jericho's name hadn't been there either. Maybe they wouldn't end up in Pollington's. Instead the photographs could be used for blackmail for the rest of their lives. Absconding to the continent was a very real possibility.

He swung off the bike, determined to tell Jericho that he was as idiot and that France sounded delightful. But he didn't make it to the door.

Pennyworth-Trickett opened it and stood on the step. The young poet stared him down. "You are too late."

Nathanial stared up at him. He didn't want to believe that Jericho wasn't here. "What do you mean?"

"He was arrested nearly two hours ago. You know what for."

Nathanial put his hand on the railing. He wanted to sink to his knees.

"How come you are still walking around? Oh, that's right, you have the right breeding."

A manic laugh slipped free. The right breeding? That was the source of all his problems. He didn't have the right breeding, but everyone thought he did so he was forever trying to live up to the expectation so no one would find out and tear him down. That would have been preferable to this mess.

"How can you laugh when you wounded him so greatly? How can you even dare to show your face here? Do you know what you have done?"

Nathanial hadn't known that he'd hurt Jericho. Did Jericho care that greatly about him? "I didn't mean to. I was set up."

"You invited him to your house. And he was more than happy to fall into your bed...and you."

"And I would do anything to change that. This isn't what should have happened." He studied the step in front of him as though the crack was suddenly interesting. "I should've said yes. Then at least we'd have been engaged."

"That wouldn't have changed the photographs. Aren't you for the church?"

Nathanial shook his head. "Not by choice."

But the church might save him from prison. However, marrying Jericho might save them both. He lifted his gaze and looked at Pennyworth-Trickett. "I need to get him to the altar."

It wasn't too late to arrange a wedding. Was it?

Pennyworth-Trickett considered him for a moment. "Come in. I have an idea...if you meant what you said about doing anything." He stepped aside to let Nathanial in.

"I did." He didn't want Jericho in jail. He didn't want any of this. He wished the booking he'd made at the church was real and going to be used. For that to happen, Jericho needed to be let out of prison. The house was quiet and dark with only one light on in the dining room. "Why are you here?"

"Jericho trusted me to tidy affairs should something like this happen."

"He planned on getting arrested?"

"It was inevitable at some point, but sodomy out of wedlock is rather more dramatic than he ever planned for. That's two years of hard labor. Do you know what that will do to him?"

The poor conditions and food broke many, or illness claimed them. If the other inmates discovered what he was doing time for, they would make sure he suffered extra. Nathanial nodded. He was facing the same charge himself. If it came out he wasn't his father's son, there would be no lenient sentence for him. He doubted they'd end up in the same prison.

The two men sat opposite each other in the dining room. A fire full of disintegrating papers crackled in the corner, making the room unbearably hot. For while Nathanial was properly dressed, Pennyworth-Trickett had no coat or waistcoat on.

"Why didn't you say yes?"

"Because I'm an idiot." He'd tossed aside Jericho's love, his proposal, and his demon's help because he was so caught up in doing the right thing no matter what. Doing the right thing had brought no rewards. Neither had breaking the law. "I shouldn't have asked him to visit."

"It is too late to re-write the past. But we can change the present and the future."

"What do you mean?"

"Well clearly *you* proposed, because you have the higher status and him doing the asking wouldn't be appropriate?" Pennyworth-Trickett smiled.

Nathanial gave a tentative nod.

"Good. Then you both got caught up in the moment."

"There is no ring. Given that he's already been arrested, it will be hard to slip on his finger." Then there was also the problem of acquiring the ring without it leaking that it had been bought after the event.

"Silly, he was showing us all when he was arrested. It was left here in my possession."

"Right...so where is the ring?"

"I have a friend who owes me a favor. Now, blue topaz is very popular at the moment as is red carnelian." Pennyworth-Trickett frowned for a moment. "You could go for onyx but that's very last year."

"Red—"

"Carnelian," Pennyworth-Trickett said. He smiled. "Exactly. I'll make that happen.

"You don't know his ring size."

"He has artist's hands." Pennyworth-Trickett wriggled his fingers.

That was true; Jericho's fingers were long and thin. Nathanial tugged at his cravat, not wanting to think too much about those fingers. He needed to tell Pennyworth-Trickett about his visit to the church. If they could make it look like they were preparing to wed then maybe…no, his father would never let it happen. It would all get called off at the last moment and Jericho would never be his. But the fierce look of determination on Pennyworth-Trickett's face gave Nathanial hope. "I made a booking at a church today."

"Why?"

"Because I was imagining what it would be like if I'd said yes. Then the priest was asking me questions, and now I have booked a wedding for next Thursday."

Pennyworth-Trickett started laughing. "That is too perfect. Now all we need is suits and invitations. I'll arrange the suits. Give me your tailor's name." He slid a piece of paper across the table and Nathanial obliged.

"My tailor has Jericho's measurements already."

"Another point in your favor. We'll have him sprung in no time."

"I'll get my sister to draw up the invitations and get them out by bird in the morning." This was going to happen. He should be more excited about his upcoming wedding, instead panic was still racing through his system and he was too aware of how fragile this chance was.

"Yes. We shall treat this as a huge misunderstanding."

Jericho's arrest was exactly that. It should never have happened because no one should've known. "The real crime is who was in my house and taking the photographs."

"You are the detective; I suggest you act on with that while I, as best man, sort out your wedding." Pennyworth-Trickett stood and walked around the table. He put a hand on Nathanial's shoulder. "I swear if you hurt him again, I have the connections to make sure you will never be able to show your face in polite society again." He gave Nathanial a pat. "Best get on your way, we have a lot of work to do before they bring you in for questioning."

He wasn't going to wait for them to drag him in. He was going to go to Amberton, who now knew the truth about his parentage. Would that make his boss an ally or an enemy?

And he still needed to find a way to see Jericho. With a demon, he could talk his boss around, but there was no way for him to get into the prison tonight.

POLLINGTON'S POPULAR NEWS

A notorious Mr. F has been arrested for something so unmentionable it can't be printed. Suffice it to say if he'd had a wedding band on his finger the crime would never have been committed. This sordid affair has tarnished the reputation of the upstanding detective Mr. B and everyone is wondering what will become of him.

While we cannot print the evidence, there are photographs of the crime in progress so the verdict will be guilty for Mr. F. He was the active participant, his lecherous intent quite clear.

The trial is set to happen in a few days and will be covered in detail as it will be sure to scandalize and tantalize. What can be known is that Mr. F's establishment is closed. There will be some sighs of relief from those who didn't like its corrupting influence. If even a detective can be dragged down, what hope is there for some of the weaker willed young men who are daring enough to risk everything?

2 1

*N*athanial had no idea what he was going to say to Margaret. He half expected her to turn him away. It was late, but she must have heard the news or at least heard a rumor about the photos. Things like that did not stay quiet once made public. If she were wise, she'd have nothing to do with her scoundrel brother.

He was counting on their affection and the way they had helped each other as children. He was praying for her support as he knocked on her door. If he had family support, even if it wasn't his father, things would go better. Dealing with his father was a worry for another day. Hopefully he hadn't heard the news yet. Though Nathanial was almost certain photographs would've been sent to others.

Foxhall wasn't the kind of man who left things to chance.

A sleepy butler opened the door and stared at him. "Lord and Lady Featherington are in bed, Mr. Bayard."

"I do apologize, but this is an emergency. And no, I haven't been drinking." Perhaps if he hadn't have gotten so drunk previously events would never have gotten to this dire stage.

The butler blinked, then swung the door open. "Have a seat in the parlor. I will arrange for some tea."

Nathanial nodded and went through, turning on the light as he went. But he couldn't sit and make himself comfortable. He paced and fiddled with the ornaments and wished his sister would hurry up. Maybe she was telling the butler to toss him out.

He pulled off his hat and ran his fingers through his hair, then dropped the hat on the chair.

Margaret swept into the room with her robe fluttering behind her. "Bertie will join us in a moment. I had to make him promise not to throw you out as he is rather livid that you suggested he was responsible for those porno pamphlets."

"I had to."

"No, you didn't."

"There is a spy in the office, and I need to know who is tipping off my suspects and ruining my cases."

"This isn't just about your work. This is about Bertie and me. He could go to prison if enough people think him guilty."

"No one thinks he's guilty. There's no evidence." Nothing he had pointed to Bertie. All he'd needed was a distraction. If he hadn't been so rushed, and if he hadn't been thrown off the case…

"If the spy is smart enough to ruin cases, then he can leave alternate trails. This could all come unstuck."

"It has. You didn't see this evening's Pollington's?"

"We stayed in." Her hand brushed her stomach. "I wasn't feeling well."

His sister was pregnant, and he was asking her for help. "I should go. You don't need my mess."

"Sit," Bertie said in a tone that reminded Nathanial of the cranky teacher who'd sought any excuse to birch a student. Nathanial sat, perched on the edge of the sofa. They hadn't heard and he didn't want to tell them. But someone would tell them tomorrow and it was better they hear it from him. "You have already disturbed our rest so what new drama has occurred?"

Margaret and Bertie sat opposite him.

Nathanial laced his fingers to keep them from betraying his nerves. He cleared his throat as their stares intensified. He decided that a very brief summary would be best. "The man responsible for the photographs killed my maid, and while in my house set up an automated camera in my bedroom, in the hope of catching me doing something, um…untoward."

Margaret put a hand to her temple. Bertie appeared to have turned to stone, his expression thunderous. Nathanial's hope for help was dwindling.

"That same day, I was told to resign and I went out and was a little merry when I did get home. I had planned to follow father's request but thought it would be wise to see what I was missing out on."

"What is in the photos?" Margaret asked. She didn't appear to be annoyed, more disappointed.

"I don't think I need to divulge the details." Sweat tricked down his sides and he wanted to loosen his cravat.

"Divulge," Bertie commanded.

"I invited Jericho around." He closed his eyes. He was going to have to tell them what had happened. "He did the right thing and proposed beforehand, but I said no because of father and…well, you can imagine the details. Suffice to say it was illegal. The upshot being Jericho has been arrested, and I'm sure I will be joining him swiftly."

There was absolute silence for several minutes. The butler brought in tea and left. Still neither Bertie nor Margaret spoke. They glanced at each other in a kind of horrified manner that conveyed more than what Nathanial could interpret.

Finally, Margaret broke the silence. "We will get you a lawyer. Father will not pay for one."

"Why the blazers did you not say yes? I thought for sure you weren't that stupid, and you'd take any option to escape your father's noose." Bertie dumped sugar into his tea and leaned back. "Fulbright may not have status but in your situation that hardly matters."

"It wasn't about that. If I don't obey father, he could out Margaret."

"You think we care about that? The children have my name. We have settled that issue a long time ago. Your father would just appear petty to take aim at Margaret."

"You don't have to protect me, Nathanial. I am safe. Or I was. Who will take over your case now? Will they still think it's Bertie?"

Bertie made a sound like a growl.

Nathanial knuckles whitened. "I'm going to see Amberton tomorrow morning. I've already handed in my resignation, and I told him the truth about my birth; I didn't want to give father the pleasure. I also told him there was a spy in the office."

"Who is the spy?" Bertie stirred his tea.

"Edward Nottwood, the secretary. He has access to all the offices and the files. He could tip off the people involved. He seems to live above his means, not that I've had a chance to do a full investigation."

Bertie's eyes narrowed. "I know the family."

"Can I stay here tonight, and can you have the lawyer meet me here in the morning?" He didn't want to go home in case the police were waiting for him. And it wouldn't be wise for him to go to the office without a lawyer. But he put more faith in Jericho's demon and the magic of her tongue.

Margaret nodded. "It's still a crime and they have been throwing the book at people since the Male Marriage Act."

"I know. But I do have something that may help." He told her about his wandering and the church booking, then his visit to the club and what Robert Pennyworth-Trickett suggested. "Aside from my illegal activity, what about the implications of setting the camera up to watch me? That's why I was caught."

"That is no defense," Bertie said, shaking his head.

"But it is a separate crime. One that is in danger of being over-looked because of the scandal," Nathanial pressed.

"Give me the list of names Pennyworth-Trickett gave you." Margaret held out her hand and Nathanial handed her the piece of paper that listed a dozen of Jericho's friends. "Assuming this engage-ment and wedding is enough to keep you out of prison, you realize that you will have to go through with it?"

"I am aware. I do love him, but I was trying to do the right thing." He should've ignored his father from the start. "Father will be furious. With no job and no allowance, I am going to be in a delicate situation."

"Fortunately, your fiancé has a successful business and if Amberton is as smart as he thinks he is—which he usually is—he will take you back. After all, you used yourself as bait to catch the pornographer. Well done." Bertie smiled but it was more of a grimace.

"I'm going to write these invitations and get them in the birds." Margaret got up and came around to kiss him on the forehead. "If your gamble brings Bertie down, I swear I will cut you off."

He gripped her hand. "I will not let that happen."

Then she left him alone with Bertie.

"Who is the man you are after?"

This time Nathanial couldn't dither. "Foxhall. But I don't have enough to arrest him yet."

"How do you know it's him?"

He couldn't tell Bertie it was because Jericho had a demon who'd seen the corruption in Foxhall's soul. "He had the opportunity at each party. It was also pretty damning that I caught him outside with a young lady who was woozy from chloroform."

"And you think he set up the camera."

"I'm sure of it. I also think he's behind the bribing of Nottwood. By killing my maid in my house, he made it personal, then he came after me."

Bertie was quiet for a moment. "He never got over Margaret jilting him. He would seethe in public and make it quite clear there was bad blood between us. He blamed me, even suggested that your sister and I had were intimate beforehand. I called him out for that."

"And you wounded him."

"A graze on his side. Nothing serious."

A scar on the man's side in the photograph. And all of the women were blond like Margaret.

"For a while your father and Foxhall weren't quite as friendly. I've long suspected that one knows something about the other."

"I'll unearth it. I never meant for you to take the blame."

"That may not have been your intention, but these are powerful men. They don't like to hear no." Bertie put his teacup down. "Nottwood's family is quite destitute due to gambling debts. His older brother recently got a commission in the Aerial Army if I'm not mistaken, and they aren't cheap. There was talk about how it had come about. Now it makes sense. But again, proof will be hard to find."

"I don't intend to get proof. I will get him to confess and turn on Foxhall." All he was going to need were a few minutes with Nottwood and Jericho's demon smoothing his words.

"How will you do that when you have nothing to bribe him with? And you aren't half as frightening as Foxhall."

"I have a plan." And it was as flimsy as gauze spun from moonlight, dependent on so many wishes and prayers he didn't know if it would hold together in daylight.

***

THE CELL WAS OVERCROWDED. Eight men crammed into what was meant for six. Jericho claimed a place against the back wall where he could see anyone who was approaching. But he hadn't slept, and his eyes were gritty, and his back was aching. He'd had to fend of two fellows who wanted to relieve him of his coat and any valuables in his pockets. He had nothing of importance as he'd been at home.

The stink of piss and sweat was something almost solid that clung to the back of his throat. Eulalia had shrunk to almost nothing within him. Perhaps she thought he deserved this. Maybe he did. He had danced with the law for years; it was only right that he should stumble. He'd thought it would be a murder charge laid at his feet. That he could've owned. But to be here because he had fallen into bed with the man he loved—and who didn't love him enough to disobey his father and marry him—was a bit too much.

It was wrong. The law was wrong. When men could visit a brothel and break their wedding vows every day of the week, as long as the whore was female, and the police did nothing, something was broken. When the male brothels were raided and the nobles walked away, but the men making a living were punished, something was damaged. The law wasn't about morality, it was about control and those with money had the control.

A chorus of shouts went up. Someone of standing was walking

through. Cries for money to pay for a lawyer, money for their wives. Just for money. He had money and it still wouldn't save him. Not with all the evidence so artfully captured.

Three men stopped at the cell.

Jericho lifted his chin. His gaze locked with Nathanial's. *Shit.* Was he joining him in prison?

"Fulbright. On yer feet you have a fancy visitor," the jailor said.

Jericho got up, feeling every minute of sitting on that filthy floor. He probably stank like the rest of them. As walked toward the bars, Eulalia woke with a rush of heat.

I need to be in him.

Jericho ignored her pleading. She wanted out, but Nathanial didn't want her.

I don't care. I can help you from within him.

Even that wasn't enticement enough for him to force a demon onto an unwilling man.

He stood near the bars, but not close enough to reach out and touch Nathanial.

"I had to bring my lawyer with me," Nathanial said, indicating the gray-haired man with the curl of disgust to his upper lip.

"I don't have one. But then—"

Nathanial reached out his hand. "You need to listen." Jericho hesitated then took the offered hand. Nathanial pulled him close. "The wedding is on Thursday week."

"I don't think I'll be able to make it." What wedding? He'd be serving time.

"Pennyworth-Trickett says your engagement ring is safe with him and that your house is tended."

Jericho nodded even though he had no idea what Nathanial was talking about. He was the one who had proposed, not Nathanial. Not that he'd bought Nathanial a ring. It had all just happened. And Nathanial had turned him down.

"I'm sorry that this happened. I am searching for the person who invaded my house and exposed what should've been private." He squeezed Jericho's fingers. "I will make this right."

How could Nathanial do that when he was supposed to be taking vows of celibacy? The confusion must have shown on his face because Nathanial stepped closer. "Trust me to get you out of here."

"So we can marry on Thursday week."

"I found the most perfect little place. My sister is sorting out the invitations."

Had he fallen asleep and was dreaming an escape? Jericho nodded again.

The lawyer cleared his throat and the jailor jangled his keys. They didn't want to be here, and they didn't care.

"One more minute." Nathanial turned back to him. "Give me a kiss for luck."

Yes. Let me into him.

"With everyone watching?"

"I don't care about them. I need...*luck* to make this right." His grip was tight on Jericho's fingers.

"Are you sure?"

"I have never been more sure of anything. Except for when I asked you to marry me."

Which had never happened. But Jericho wasn't going to let a small detail like that get in the way of freedom. He held Nathanial's hand tighter. If he gave up Eulalia, he would truly be on his own if Nathanial abandoned him.

"You truly love me?" The words were barely a whisper. "Even though it has brought us to this?" Many men would have walked away. "Even though your reputation and status are now in doubt?"

How can you not see it?

"Yes. I don't care about any of that, only getting you to church."

Jericho's lips curved, and Nathanial returned his smile. They both knew that was not how it was supposed to be. He leaned against the bars, the metal cool on his cheek. Eulalia surged like a fire within him. That pure rage and energy he'd felt when first flooded with her was a burn he would miss.

Nathanial pressed his lips to Jericho's. He opened his mouth for the demon to slip free. Nathanial's lips were warm and soft. God, what would it be like to be able to kiss his lover, his husband, if all of this fell into place?

It will. Have faith, Jericho. Eulalia's voice echoed in his skull.

He was going to miss her presence, but it would be nice to no longer be possessed by a demon.

I was never a demon. You thought I was because you were so angry at the world. I came to earth to help the wronged get justice. I am an angel. A fragment of divine. Bringing out the best in you. Showing you who you could be.

For a heartbeat he was filled with radiance and the knowledge that the words had been his, and she had only made him bold enough to speak.

Then she was gone. He gasped at the loss. The hollowness swelled, wanting to suck him in until he crumpled like a piece of paper.

Nathanial stepped back. His eyes blazing blue, his skin luminescent, and his features harsher, sharper. Jericho saw the angel that had lived within him. When he wore her face, he'd seen only the need to feed her and kill, not the beauty or the gifts she had given him. Nathanial wore her righteousness well. He blinked and his eyes softened to their more usual blue. He stared at Jericho for several heartbeats, then released his hand.

"We will be wed. I swear." Then he was gone, taking his lawyer and the angel of justice with him.

Jericho had either just made the biggest mistake of his life or the best decision. He wasn't sure which and wouldn't know until he stood in the courtroom to hear the verdict.

2 2

The world was brighter and sharper with Eulalia in his body. She moved within him as though trying to get comfortable in Nathanial's skin. He couldn't help but fidget on the cab ride to the office of the Nobility Task Force. The lawyer seated next to him barely moved. He probably thought he had a losing case, and was only here because Bertie was paying him.

Bertie and Margaret had begged him not to see Jericho in prison, but what kind of man abandoned his fiancé? To that they had no argument. But seeing him there had turned the knife in his heart a little deeper. The need to bring down Foxhall burned a little hotter.

Eulalia promised him justice. She was the answer to his prayers, God's justice for those who needed it. No demon could blaze so brightly or fill him with such drive.

The need to act and remove those who had corrupted the system of law radiated through him; how no one could see it amazed him. When the cab stopped at the office it was all he could do not to rush out the door and up the stairs. Instead he followed the lawyer sedately as if he didn't have a care in the world.

If the common police officers knew the unfolding scandal, they didn't show it. Upstairs the reaction was very different.

Nottwood paled when he saw Nathanial. Nathanial had no doubt that Nottwood had read his resignation letter. He probably read everything that came into the office.

"You can't be here. You don't work here." Nottwood stood as though ready to bar Nathanial from entering Amberton's office.

He had no control over Eulalia, but he felt the way she burst to the surface and his mouth felt alien as the words formed on his tongue. He was awake but trapped in a dream he had no control of as she used him to get what she wanted. The odd sensation caused panic in his brain, but at the same time he knew she wouldn't bring him to harm. No being so completely made of light would do him harm.

Nathanial stepped closer to Nottwood. "I know all about the bribes you've been taking and the games you've been playing." The greed was written in his eyes and discolored his soul. Like a grass stain on a white shirt it would never come off. How had he failed to see that before? How many people did he walk past without really seeing them? What had Jericho seen in him?

Nottwood's eyes widened. "I don't know what you're talking about."

The lie had a certain texture, a sour resonance. "All those cases had a common link. It was you. It took me a while, but now I know. But aiding a murderer, that is a step too far. You will go down with him."

Nottwood shook his head but couldn't form a word.

"You want to tell the truth before it is too late. Before he casts you aside and leaves you to rot. Then where will your family be?" It was Nathanial's voice, but he barely recognized himself. He'd heard the change in Jericho's voice, but never had he fallen under his spell.

I never tried to lull you. I had no need and neither did he. Her voice rung in his head like a bell. Too loud, too clear. It hurt. How had Jericho lived like this for years?

"I can't. I'll be arrested," Nottwood whined. "He said he'd kill me."

Nathanial leaned on the desk. "He threatened an officer? That is a crime in itself. Confess."

The resistance went out of Nottwood's eyes as he slipped

completely into Eulalia's thrall. Nottwood knocked on Amberton's door and went in.

Nathanial glanced at the lawyer who was staring at him. Did he see Eulalia and recognize possession?

The lawyer cleared his throat. "I thought we were here to ask for house arrest before the trial?"

"We are. But my crime is tied to these other cases. Nottwood has been perverting justice."

"And he decided to confess today when he saw you?" The lawyer's eyebrows drew close like thunder clouds.

"I don't think he expected to see me, or for me to figure it out."

But you did and now they will all tumble.

Nathanial winced and tried to shake off the ringing in his ears.

"Are you all right, Sir?"

"Yes. The stress is giving me a headache, that's all." He'd get used to it. Jericho had.

The lawyer held out a handkerchief. Nathanial wondered why for a moment, then he felt the hot trickle of blood from his nose. "Thank you."

"Amberton will see you now," Nottwood said from the door. His eyes were reddened.

Nathanial wanted to feel some sympathy for him—a young man with a destitute family to support and two more sisters to find husbands for, he'd done what he needed to—but there was no sympathy to be found at all. He'd taken money from the guilty to mask their crimes and had somehow ended up in Foxhall's pocket.

As Nathanial walked past him, he saw that confession had happened, but darker things were moving on the young man's soul. He stopped and put a hand on Nottwood's arm. "Do not do anything rash. Testify against him. We can protect you and your family."

"You couldn't protect your own maid."

"Did he threaten your sisters, too?"

Nottwood turned away. "Worry about yourself, Bayard. I should've known that it wouldn't last, but he wanted you out."

"And I am." Too many failed cases. So many guilty had walked away because one man had sought to ruin him. In the process another man had been destroyed. To Foxhall Nottwood was nothing but a cheap tool. "When did Foxhall become involved?"

He shrugged. "I'd fiddled with a couple of cases, not just yours, before he approached me. I know it wasn't right, but I needed the money." He lifted his gaze. "I'm sorry."

His words were true. The ability to tell a lie from heartfelt truth was a treasure. Nathanial dabbed at his nose again. No blessing came freely.

Leave him be.

Nottwood would be dead by nightfall. He could see the man's thoughts as clearly as his own.

You cannot save everyone. Justice takes a toll.

Nathanial hesitated. The lawyer coughed, wanting to get this meeting done. Nathanial wasn't his only client. He glanced at the old man. His disgust that he was having to represent a sodomite, and a passive one at that, glittered in his eyes. He was only doing it for the money. What fool paid for legal defense when there was no chance of success?

Nathanial blinked and tried to clear his vision of the angel's sight but couldn't. While she wasn't in full control, she was seeking to unravel all the knots that bound him. Every lie would be dissolved.

He wasn't sure he wanted to look at Amberton.

But you will because you want to know.

He stepped into the office of his former boss, the lawyer on his heels.

The lawyer started talking as though he knew exactly how to play this. A guilty plea, no other way given the evidence. House arrest is requested given the accused's standing and position he rattled on. He didn't mention the engagement or the wedding the way they had discussed with Featherington.

Nathanial sat staring at his hands. He needed to look up. Eulalia's voice slid off his lips like honey. "I'm getting married next Thursday."

The lawyer's mouth was open.

Amberton frowned. "That is relevant to the case?"

The lawyer stammered. "Yes, I suppose, but you weren't married at the time of the event."

"But I was engaged and got carried away." That is what the lawyer had been ordered to say. Nathanial had been in Featherington's parlor as the instructions had been given to this man.

"I know your brother-in-law thinks that is an acceptable defense, but it will carry no weight in the eyes of the law." What the lawyer meant was it carried no weight with him.

Amberton lifted his hand. "What are you talking about, Bayard? First, I get your resignation letter—which I find quite frankly absurd —now you are engaged and there were revealing photographs left on my desk. What exactly is going on?"

There has no hatred in Amberton's eyes. He was perplexed. Despite what it had felt like to Nathanial, he'd never wanted him to fail. That bolstered Nathanial's courage as much as having the angel on his tongue.

"It would appear that when the murderer was in my house with my maid, he was doing some other work setting up an automatic camera. I had proposed to Fulbright the evening the photos were taken." The lie sat easily and was spoken as though it was the truth, the angel's spell making all who heard believe. "And we went too far. I regret that. I should've known better. As for the resignation letter, it contains the truth."

"Nottwood and the suspect both know your truth."

Nathanial nodded.

The lawyer glanced between the two of them. "What does this have to do with my client's charges?"

"He hasn't been charged yet," Amberton snapped.

"But Fulbright has been. My fiancé is in prison with drunkards, thieves, and murderers." Nathanial didn't want Jericho languishing there for another minute. "Then there is the issue that a camera was set up in my ceiling, above my bed for the sole purpose of catching something that should've been private. If not for that camera, we wouldn't be sitting here."

Silence filled the office. The lawyer coughed again, and Nathanial wanted to reach out and clip the man over the ear. The cough was an affectation whenever he felt uncomfortable. Was this lawyer the best Bertie could do? He breathed out slowly he should be grateful he had any lawyer; it was a losing case.

"You cannot argue that," Amberton said slowly. "The activity remains illegal."

How many crimes happened behind closed doors? Too many. The men usually arrested were skulking around public pissoirs or shadowed nooks of parks.

"The circumstances are unusual though," the lawyer eventually said. "An invasion of privacy with intent to catch someone out is most underhanded. Though the invader must have suspected something."

And that would be enough to convict him. No one would believe he was innocent until that night. "It is a personal vendetta linked to another case." He remembered, or Eulalia found, the conversation he'd had with Bertie. "Perhaps I was bait."

"It was still illegal, and he would've sent photos to too many people. I will have to charge you," Amberton said, regret coloring his words.

Nathanial nodded, his heart sinking. The chance that he would be able to wriggle out of this was becoming slimmer. If he couldn't, then Jericho had no chance.

Eulalia hissed.

"And we would like house arrest until the trial," the lawyer spoke up as if remembering he had a role.

"Agreed. Fulbright will have to sit tight, though. His reputation is too well known. I don't know if your name and ring will be able to save him."

Eulalia's growl reverberated through him. But like him, she would have to wait for the trial.

23

The trial was set for Tuesday. Two days before what was supposed to be his wedding. Nathanial wanted to throw up from the nerves. It would also be the first time he'd seen Jericho since the visit to the prison.

Each day Godfrey had bought the latest Pollington's so Nathanial could monitor the growing scandal. Someone had leaked information about the personal grudge and the murder of his maid. Someone else had let slip about the upcoming wedding.

Nathanial didn't know if any of this would help or hinder.

No one from his family had contacted him. Had his sister even sent out the invitations? He had to trust her with that matter.

He was given a police escort to the courthouse like any criminal. He sat on the accused side. His lawyer barely looked at him. This was going to go badly. Eulalia hadn't even surfaced. Since his visit to the office she'd barely whispered in his ear. His skin was hot, and he vaguely remembered Jericho saying how he needed to feed her. He hadn't had a chance and who was he supposed to kill?

Would she not wake to help him?

Do not fret. Justice will be served.

219

Nathanial was sure that the people in the court were hoping for just that, but they were hoping to see Jericho and he sentenced.

That is not justice. That is entertainment in the guise of moral superiority.

Jericho entered, looking worse for wear. His face was ashen, and he had dark circles beneath his eyes. He was well on the way to having a beard after over a week without a razor. He sat on the chair near Nathanial, but it was a moment before Jericho looked at him. Was he afraid of what he'd see?

Here he was all clean and bathed, and in possession of the angel. Jericho needed her more than him.

No. I can only do this through you.

Nathanial smiled. And after another heartbeat lifted his gaze to meet Jericho's. Jericho was the fragments of a man held together by only the finest strands of hope. All the pretty clothes and the laughter...they had been armor he could hide behind. Eulalia had been his sword. Without her or his club or suits, he was broken.

He wanted to reach out, but Eulalia curled his fingers so he couldn't.

A smile curved the corner of Jericho's lips. There was no malice, only understanding that Nathanial saw it all. Nathanial gave him a small nod. Jericho had put all his faith and hope in him. If not for him, they wouldn't be here.

Do not take the blame. It is not yours. It is his.

Nathanial found himself looking at Foxhall. He had a seat near the back with a fragile woman that could only be his wife. The way she glanced at him with barely restrained hostility told the truth about their marriage. Nathanial saw everything.

The hunger of the crowd who wanted details.

Foxhall's glee that he had done this.

Lady Foxhall's disgust at the monster that was her husband.

The prosecutor's distaste. He didn't want to do these cases, especially not one where there was so much wrong—not with the evidence, but with the situation.

His lawyer who thought he might use this case to make a name for himself.

The room filled to capacity, and people still tried to stand around the edges. Nathanial tugged at his cravat as sweat trickled down his spine. The room was quite airless.

The swirling emotions were going to drown him.

"Breathe. It takes a while to get used to," Jericho murmured without looking at him.

He didn't want to get used to it.

You won't. I want to go to her.

Nathanial's gaze was forced to land on Foxhall's wife. Her need for justice shimmered through her hate and fear of her husband. He saw the bruises on her soul, not the ones on her flesh, and he understood why she spent so much time at sanitariums. He also knew that once filled with the angel; she'd kill her husband the next time he forced himself on her.

Eulalia purred, a tone that set his teeth on edge. *I can think of no better way. He will hate that his wife got the better of him in the end. And I will make sure he knows.*

Usually, Nathanial would want to stop a murder. Not this time. But he wanted Foxhall to know the shame of being charged for murder. He wanted him to go to prison and suffer even though it wouldn't bring back the dead. Nor would it change the damage that had been done to his career and Jericho's business.

What exactly was justice?

The judge entered and they all stood. The charges were read out and he wanted to slide under the chair. Jericho sat proud next to him. He nodded at someone in the crowd.

Pennyworth-Trickett was here, confidence radiating off him.

He scanned the crowd again, hoping to see Bertie or Margaret, but no one was there to support him. That was to be expected, but the strike still stung.

Jericho pled guilty. There was nothing else he could do. His only excuse was that he was overcome with passion after accepting the proposal. The lack of ring was noted by the prosecutor.

Jericho pointed to Pennyworth-Trickett. "I was showing it to my friends the night of my arrest. I never got a chance to put it back on."

The ring has handed over for the judge to inspect. "Let the records state the ring is engraved with JF and NB."

"That ring could've been acquired later," the prosecutor said.

The judge peered at Jericho. "Put the ring on, Fulbright."

Nathanial held his breath, but the ring slid on perfectly.

Jericho smiled as he looked at it; he lifted his gaze and his smile widened at Nathanial. Hope glittered around him, and love made him shine. He couldn't be the only one who saw it. Doubt and fear lurked not far below.

Whispers filled the court.

Nathanial's lawyer stood. "Of the act, there is no doubt. The ring is on his finger and the ceremony is supposed to be in two days. They would not be the first couple to take liberties before marriage." He sat again and the whispers became wild speculation.

The judge called for silence. "I want to hear from the co-accused before I make any decision."

Then Nathanial was in the box, swearing on a bible to tell the truth. Eulalia was on each word. He gave his account of that night, including why he'd been out drinking—the loss of his job for too many unsolved cases and the suspected leak. The story thickened and with Eulalia's magic, no one interrupted him. He was able to spin the whole thing in a way that on his own could never have happened.

"I am still reeling from discovering that someone set up a camera in my house, to watch me with the sole intend of destroying me." He kept his focus on Foxhall. "The same man who has been named the porno killer in the scandal sheets. Now I sit here, charged with loving my fiancé too much, while he sits free."

His mouth closed. No more words spilled forth.

The crowd erupted. They knew the man was in the room. Heads turned trying to pinpoint him, and Foxhall turned a furious shade of white. His anger a living beast.

"Order!" the judge shouted.

It still took several minutes for the court to calm down.

"Why was the wedding booked under Fulbright if you made it?"

"Because I knew my father would be furious."

"Because you are marrying a man?"

"Because he wants me to become a priest even though it is not my calling. I feel it would a greater sin to give my life to God while feeling nothing in my heart than it is to disobey my father."

Witnesses were called. The priest from the church who confirmed Nathanial had made the booking. His tailor who had made the wedding suits. The jeweler who remembered him buying the ring. It was a lie, but people were invested in the story now. They cared about what happened. They worried about what might happen if an automatic camera were set up in their bedroom.

The mood shifted from one of scandalized outrage seeking entertainment to one of compassion. They'd had their feed, now they wanted more.

"Let them marry!" someone shouted.

The judge beckoned the prosecutor and his lawyer forward.

Nathanial couldn't hear what was said. He glanced at Jericho and reached out his hand. Jericho's fingers wrapped around his.

JERICHO HAD NEVER HAD SO many people lie to save him. The angel shimmered in Nathanial's eyes, making them bluer. His skin was pearly. The shame that he had doubted Nathanial lingered. Nathanial could have pleaded that he was a victim. He could've tried to save himself. Instead they were in this together.

Of course, if the judge resented the way the case had twisted around to be about something more, he could still send them both to prison. Different prisons.

While the lawyers and judges talked, the crowd also talked. They argued about what should happen. They hated the man who'd done this. He should be the pervert standing trial.

But men like Foxhall never got to trial.

The stink of prison was ingrained in Jericho's skin. He didn't know if he would be able to do two years. That fear had kept him up at night. That and the knowledge than some knew what he was on trial for and they had tried their luck. Without Eulalia, he'd had to break a few fingers and ribs. Skills he hadn't used since leaving Hong Kong.

He'd survived, though he didn't want to go back. Couldn't.

Yet even as he lay awake listening to the groans of the sick and injured, he couldn't wish away that night in Nathanial's bedroom.

"Order." The judge drew all attention back to him. "This case is both clear and muddied. The evidence has been spread all over London with clear intent to smear Detective Bayard's name. While Mr. Fulbright's reputation has preceded him, until now he has never appeared in court, so his character has been called into question. His business closed. The invasion of privacy was malicious, and if I were to ignore that it could set a precedent for future cases. In my mind it is clear that Bayard and Fulbright were honest with their intentions to wed. If they were not, then that will be punishment enough.

"However, to be clear, this wedding defense will not be applicable to most cases. One does not find a husband in a back alley in the same way that one does not have their private life displayed for all to see. That is a penalty no one should have to pay, and I fear those photographs will linger." He cast his gaze across the room. "My sentence is that Bayard and Fulbright are to marry on Thursday as arranged. Let it be noted that no divorce shall be considered for two years—the same as the prison sentence they would've faced." He gave Jericho a cool smile. "Surety against a sham."

Jericho had been holding his breath waiting for the waffle to end and the sentence to be announced. The punishment was to marry. He wasn't sure he'd heard correctly.

"We did it," Nathanial breathed.

"You did it." Without Nathanial creating a wedding he'd have most likely died in prison. Or at least wished to be dead. "We're getting married."

"Yes, we are." Nathanial grinned. Then pulled him into an awkward embrace that nearly tumbled him out of the chair.

"This is preposterous. There was clearly a crime." Foxhall was standing.

The crowd turned on him, booing him until he sat, still livid that his plan had failed.

The judge banged his gavel and they drew apart. "You are not to see each other before the wedding to avoid another incident. I will release you both into the custody of your family." Jericho had no family who would come for him, but it would be better to be locked up here for one night than in prison for years. "Is there family here?"

Lord Featherington raised a hand. "Brother-in-law to Bayard."

There was silence as the judge looked for someone else. Jericho studied the dirt under his nails.

"Simon Fulbright, father to Jericho Fulbright."

Jericho looked up, sure it must be another of Robert's schemes. But it wasn't. His father was here and had heard the whole trial.

"Very well. Speak to the bailiff."

The crowd dispersed, satisfied with the gossip they'd gathered. Nathanial's lawyer shook his hand, but Jericho noticed Nathanial was much less thrilled than the lawyer was. Had this been a sham for him?

Surely not? Though Nathanial had been the one to knock back his proposal—a rebuff that still burned. So how had a wedding been arranged so fast?

Without Eulalia he couldn't tell. He wasn't used to being so blind to what people were thinking or feeling. When their eyes met, he wanted to believe it was real.

With no chance to talk before the wedding, he would have to wait for answers.

24

$\mathcal{N}$athanial wanted to stay and talk to Jericho, but they were quickly separated. Bertie signed whatever the bailiff put in front of him and was ready to manhandle him out of the door when Lord Emmaly, the man he'd once thought of as his father, appeared.

Had he been there the whole time?

His cheeks were blotchy red. "You disgust me. I will speak to the bank and ensure you get nothing."

"What is it that disgusts you father? That I am marrying the man I love, or that I didn't follow the plans you had for me?" He stepped close. "You cannot make the children pay for the sins of the father."

They were not his words. He saw why his father hated him so much. It wasn't the affair, but the rage that had followed. The groom hadn't fled, he'd been hunted down, and used for sport. There, poking at his father's rage, was Foxhall.

The tangled web went beyond Margaret's jilting. Perhaps her hand in marriage had been part of the price of keeping silent about the murder.

Nathanial stepped up to his father as if to embrace him. "Where did you bury the body of my real father?"

"I don't know what you are talking about." But fear widened his eyes.

"Then I suggest you do all you can to quash the rumors that I am not your son, so people don't start asking questions." Nathanial released him and smiled. "Be happy, Father. I shall not trouble you for a penny either way."

His father's face was still white with shock. He turned and walked straight into Foxhall, brushing him off as though he had no time for a man who was a friend and the keeper of his darkest secrets.

"Let's go." Bertie nodded toward Foxhall but kept his voice low. "We don't need more trouble."

Eulalia clamored to get to Lady Foxhall. *Let me finish. Foxhall will trouble you no more.*

He couldn't walk up and kiss Lady Foxhall. Eulalia's laughter echoed in his skull.

"Entertain Foxhall for a moment."

"What? Why?" Bertie looked as though Nathanial had just asked him to swim to France.

"I need to ask his wife a few questions about the case." Before Bertie could argue that Nathanial was no longer a detective he'd broken away.

Bertie greeted Foxhall and Nathanial closed in on Lady Foxhall.

She startled like a bird suddenly realizing the cat is too close. "Please forgive my husband."

Nathanial smile. "If you have a moment, please come to my office."

Her eyes went wide. "I don't think I can help."

"But I can help you." Before she could react, he kissed her. It wasn't the lingering kiss Jericho had given him, his lips barely touched hers, but it was enough. Eulalia's heat and grace left him, and he staggered. Lady Foxhall put her hand out. "Are you all right?"

Eulalia shimmered in her eyes and danced on her lips before sinking down. Foxhall would be dead by dawn. He would join his victims and suffer in hell. His wife would be free.

It wasn't justice by the law, but Nathanial didn't care. "I'm fine. Just overwhelmed." Which was only partially a lie.

He cast his gaze around for Jericho but didn't see him. Bertie got him out the door before he could beg for a few moments with him. No doubt Bertie was taking the judge's proclamation seriously.

"Christ, you were lucky today. I thought you were gone."

"Your lawyer thought I deserved prison." Nathanial stared out the window of Bertie's carriage. "However, he performed well in the end."

"He did the best that anyone could with the evidence."

"Can we not talk about it anymore?" Those photographs were going to haunt him forever. "I'd much rather know who Margaret has invited to my wedding."

<hr>

JERICHO WAITED for his father to sign the paperwork. He had no idea why his father was here but was grateful none the less that he wasn't having to spend another night in prison. He kept his mouth shut until they were in the cab. Without Eulalia, he didn't trust his voice so easily. The emptiness of her leaving hadn't been filled. He expected to hear her hiss of displeasure or mocking laughter, but there was nothing except his own thoughts.

The silence in the cab was a prickly thing. Jericho didn't know how to speak to the man opposite him. They were strangers tied together by blood and tragedy.

He fiddled with the ring on his finger. It felt odd. Heavy. Not like a dress ring, or some trinket. This had weight and meaning even though Nathanial had never actually proposed. Perhaps this was all an elaborate lie so Nathanial didn't face any penalty. He certainly hadn't wanted marriage before; he'd made that quite clear.

His father cleared his throat. "I wanted to thank you again for helping your sister."

Jericho had never replied to the note. He knew he should've, but he hadn't gotten around to it. "I didn't know she was my sister."

"Yet you stepped in anyway. Plenty of people wouldn't have. They'd have looked away instead of risking displeasing Foxhall."

Jericho gave a narrow smile. "People with power don't scare me.

They are usually trying so hard to keep that power that they spend their time worrying about everything that could undo them. Those people always come unstuck." That Foxhall was still walking around rankled. How could a man like that be free, while Jericho had spent over a week in prison awaiting trial for something that should never have seen daylight?

Of course, if there had been no photographs, then he wouldn't be getting married. Nathanial would be committing himself to God instead. Perhaps Jericho should write Foxhall a thank you note. Maybe after the wedding, after he'd had a chance to confirm Nathanial's true intentions. While he didn't doubt Nathanial's happiness at walking free, or even his desire, he harbored doubts about everything else. Mostly that a man with standing would actually want to shackle himself to a man like him.

Even his father had put distance between them.

"Your bravery was commended in the Army. You could've had a stellar career."

Jericho nodded. He'd like the Army well enough. Not everyone had liked him. "I don't think it was a good fit given my…proclivities." He risked a glance at his father, not sure how he felt, and not really caring that much. He had his own life. His own funds. He didn't need his father's approval. "Why were you there?"

"It may be hard for you to believe, but I do care. I didn't want you to go to prison."

"Because it would make you look bad?"

"Because you'd most likely die in there. And you are all that I have left of her."

Eulalia would be able to see straight into his father's soul and determine the truth, but Jericho was blind. He had no cleaver remark or insightful comment. "You treasured that part so much."

His father grimaced. "You're right. For the longest time I couldn't look at you. I couldn't be your father when I was so lost in grief."

"You managed to remarry."

"Eventually I had to move on. You were at school and doing well and I didn't want to disturb that."

"I felt like I wasn't welcome when I was home for the holidays." He hated it. His father had been cool, his stepmother didn't know what to do with him, and when the first baby came along all the attention went there. Jericho wasn't needed or wanted. At boarding school he'd had a place. While he wasn't popular, he generally wasn't tormented. He had also been adept at selling favors, so he always had money and secrets.

"I know I have failed you as a father, and it is too late for me to try. But I would like to get to know you." He watched Jericho, hope lifting his eyebrows.

Jericho considered him for several heartbeats, then mimicked his posture. "Why now? You could've spoken civilly to me at the ball. You could've written and invited me over for tea."

"I misunderstood your presence at the ball, and I was worried about your sister's reputation being sullied by yours."

"My reputation is mostly lies and half-truths wrapped up in smoke and silk ribbon."

"But your club?"

"Is just a club." Did everyone think him a prostitute? He'd never considered himself that, though truthfully for his senior years at school he had been taking money and selling pleasure...which probably explained where some of the rumors came from. Some men wouldn't want their wives and friends knowing what had gone on in the dorm rooms. "Nothing happens there that is different to any other club."

"Except that the men are like you."

He gave a careful nod. "We share a common interest. But is that not the foundation of most clubs and friendships?"

"And this wedding? For how long was that planned? Or was it a scheme that you are now trapped in?"

If it was just a scheme, then he'd have two years of marital hell to endure. Robert would get no thanks for his troubles. And Nathanial... God, Jericho was going to have to get used to living with him and not hurting if it was all a lie. He rubbed his forehead. "Truthfully I have no idea. Marriage was discussed, but that was as far as it got."

That was as much of the truth as his father was going to get.

"Marriages have been made on less. You are going to shut down the club?"

"I haven't given it much thought. But why would I when it is a profitable venture?" Was that the cost of his father's friendship? If so, it was too steep. "I appreciate you stepping in like this." God knew the smell alone would make most people reconsider. He didn't even want to be sitting with himself. "But you cannot tell me how to run my affairs."

"And Lord Emmaly?"

"Has no say in Nathanial's life." Nathanial had no job and no funds —unless his father suddenly changed his mind. They were going to need the club or starve. "If we are to be friends, then the boundaries must be that of friends, not parent and child."

His father leaned back. "That is true. I have to accept you as you are."

The silence returned. Jericho closed his eyes, feigning tiredness. He didn't need a father and he didn't need new friends.

Well, depending on the wedding that had been arranged, he might be seeking new friends. When he finally got his hands on Robert he didn't know if he was going to kiss him or slap him. The same went for Nathanial.

No matter the reason behind the wedding, at least he wasn't going to prison. For that he would thank them both.

He opened his eyes as the cab rolled to a stop. "Thank you for coming to the trial. It couldn't have been easy."

25

Nathanial paced the parlor. He was dressed and ready to go even though there still an hour before they had to leave. Margaret had given up on getting him to settle.

Jericho's suit would've been delivered, and he'd be getting ready.

This should be exciting and wonderful; instead, he was turning himself into knots because it wasn't actually real. It had been pulled together on the hope that it would save them both from a much worse fate. It was the wrong reason to get married. He wished he could've proposed properly.

Or at the very least said yes the first time.

He wished he'd been able to plan today with Jericho.

And he really wasn't sure about the fine red stripe on the white cravat. It seemed a bit too much. Why hadn't his tailor put a stop to Pennyworth-Trickett's plans? A carriage stopped out the front and a man got out. Nathanial peered past the curtains.

Amberton.

That was the second last person he wanted to see. His father was the last person.

What he wanted was five minutes with Jericho to settle his nerves and make sure that everything was all right between them. No doubt this was part of the judge's punishment. Nothing to be said, or written, before the wedding. Then two years together. The judge hadn't been entirely convinced.

Amberton wasn't alone. Bertie was with him and they were deep in conversation. While he was aware Bertie had gone out, he hadn't known why. Nathanial forced himself to sit and pretend he was fine as the butler opened the door and showed them in. They came directly to the parlor, but only Amberton sat. Bertie left and closed the door.

He was sure Bertie would be glad to get him out of the house.

"While I will be attending the wedding, I wanted to speak with you beforehand." Amberton leaned forward. His suit was impeccable and his cravat and shirt snowy white.

Could he switch his cravat for white? It wasn't too late. But he was loath to change when this is what he'd been given.

"About what, Lord Amberton?" He was careful to use his previous boss's title.

"Nottwood gave a full written confession the day you came to see me. That evening he was run down by a carriage. This morning it has come to light that Foxhall suffered a heart attack."

Not a heart attack. Eulalia had devoured him. Horror and relief that it was over washed through him, but Nathanial arranged his face into polite surprise. "That is awful." While he'd seen what Nottwood planned to do, he hadn't fully expected the young man to do it. Had he felt the shame would ruin his family further? Aside from the ruining of Nathanial's career, he had been a good secretary. "On both accounts."

Amberton grunted. "Foxhall died in bed. Gave his wife quite the turn."

"Is she all right?" Did she still have the angel?

"She's coping and helping with the investigation." Amberton fixed him with a stare. "I want you to come back."

"But my letter...?" He'd told Amberton that he wasn't his father's son.

"I checked with your father. He denied any such thing and

suggested that it was the stress you were under. I am inclined to agree. I am also not inclined to dig into family history because there would be a great many discrepancies. The job is yours. You can even have a week off after the wedding to sort your affairs."

"Thank you, Sir." Truthfully that solved one of his very great problems which was what he was going to do next. He didn't want to live off Jericho. Eulalia's threat to his father had worked; that meant he was safe from scandal and so was Margaret. A little of the tension eased as his future became more stable.

"Excellent." Amberton stood. "I won't keep you any longer. You need to get to the church, so the judge doesn't change his mind."

Nathanial winced. Would his wedding be forever marred by the trial and photographs? Too many people would think it a lie and a lucky escape. He wanted so much more than that.

Jericho deserved more than that.

He wouldn't change his cravat. Jericho's friend had planned the wedding and he wasn't going to ruin it. It would be perfect.

As soon as he stepped outside, it started raining and showed no sign of letting up as the sky was gray and low. So much for summer. Though rain was meant to be lucky, wasn't it?

26

Rain drummed on the roof of the church and the smell of damp clothes filled the air. Robert had managed to pack the church with friends and family. As more people came into to take their seats, Jericho struggled to hide his shock.

Robert stood next to him, waiting for the ceremony to start.

Jericho fiddled with the ring. "How did you do all of this?"

"Connections and money. I plan on sending Lord Emmaly the bill. Do you think he'll pay? I hear he's very determined to make sure people know how proud he is of his youngest son."

"I feel like the whole world has changed and I have missed out on all the gossip."

"You have. I'll catch you up when you reopen. You will be reopening, yes? Tell me the date and I'll make sure everyone knows."

"I will." He wanted to. But would Nathanial want to be wed to a notorious club owner?

"Try and sound more convincing."

"I need to sort some things out first." He didn't know how to live without Eulalia in his head.

"You mean you want to spend three days in bed with your husband." Robert grinned and Jericho couldn't help but respond.

"That, too." Though where would that bed be? They hadn't had a chance to plan their life. He was tumbling into this unprepared. Even though he'd been the one to suggest it, he hadn't actually thought it through. It had been more of a do-the-right-thing-in-the-moment occurrence. "Not that he is here yet."

If Nathanial didn't attend…Jericho didn't want to think about where he'd end up, but it wouldn't be good.

Robert pulled out a rose gold pocket watch. "There's still five minutes to go. You were early because you didn't want to be late."

There was a rustle in the crowd as Lord Emmaly and wife walked in and took their seats. She looked happy; he looked like he'd bitten an apple and found half a worm after swallowing the first bite.

"So how long do I wait?" He didn't want to wait a minute longer than he had to. The humiliation of it all…

"I will drag him here if I have to."

"If he doesn't want to be here, I will not force him."

"Stop it. I told you, this was his idea. Besides, I don't think he wants to go to prison."

"That's a very uplifting speech."

Robert stared at him. "There is something different about you…"

Did he realize Eulalia was gone without knowing what was missing? Jericho knew he was going to have to find a way to go on without the angel. He wanted to apologize for calling her a demon. He wanted her back.

He fixed Robert with a look. "How many nights have you spent in a squalid cell keeping fingers out of your pockets and pants?"

Robert looked away. "Here he is."

Jericho couldn't help but look across the aisle to where Nathanial now stood. There was no walking up the aisle to be handed over; they would simply meet in the middle in front of the altar. While Jericho's cravat was red, to match his engagement ring, Nathanial's had only the finest stripe. Next to Nathanial was his brother-in-law.

Robert put his hand on Jericho's back. "You can calm down now."

Seeing Nathanial had done nothing to calm him. If anything, his heart was now squeezing so hard it hurt. He could barely breathe or swallow as Nathanial took his place. Nathanial glanced over and smiled. There was no shimmer in his eyes. No sign of the angel. Had he passed her on already?

This was the first time neither of them had been possessed.

The priest started proceedings and it was all Jericho could do to follow the service and do his part. His voice wasn't nearly as steady as he'd have liked. But Nathanial's hand was warm and when the gold ring was slipped onto his finger, a lump the size of an orange formed in Jericho's throat.

When it was his turn to put the ring on Nathanial's finger, he had never felt less capable. His fingers were too clumsy, and he stumbled over his words. Without Eulalia he was terrible. But Nathanial simply smiled as though he couldn't change his expression for all the royal jewels in the Tower. Then it was finally over.

He'd thought he'd enjoy it more.

That it would mean more.

"You may kiss your husband," the priest said.

Jericho hesitated.

Nathanial stepped closer. "We need to talk later," he murmured before his lips brushed Jericho's in a perfectly chaste kiss. No angel or demon slipped between them.

He could actually kiss without concern.

He put his hand around Nathanial's waist and kissed him harder—though he was still mindful of the audience. With no angel in either of them, there was something else he could do without fear. Though that would have to wait until later. Much later.

NATHANIAL HELD Jericho's hand in the carriage to the club and didn't want to release it at all. Today it wasn't open as the Jericho Rose but as the venue to celebrate. The effort that had been put in was extraordinary.

He had to release Jericho of course because there was family to talk to and friends to see. And Jericho had just as many or more. Not everyone who'd been at the church had followed but enough had that the rooms felt crowded and the noise was too much.

All he wanted was five minutes alone with Jericho.

Even in the carriage they had been accompanied, though the wedding was done. The judge would be satisfied, and they didn't need to be chaperoned anywhere. He sat on the stairs that lead up to Jericho's private rooms, needing a moment before diving back into the maelstrom of guests.

He ran his fingers over the gold band. His wasn't plain; it had three small red carnelians in the design, to match with Jericho's ring. Pennyworth-Trickett had done an excellent job on making the wedding look real.

It was up to him to make sure that it was.

Feet came into view. Nathanial glanced up.

"Want to make room?" Jericho asked as though he needed permission to sit on his own stairs.

Nathanial slid over as Jericho sat next to him. "I thought you loved a party."

"I do, but not today." He laced his fingers over his knees. "Why are you hiding?"

"I needed a moment alone." He put his hand on Jericho's knee before he could think about getting up and leaving. "But I am glad to share it with you."

"You thought of this?" Jericho touched the engagement ring.

Nathanial was sure that Jericho must have quizzed Pennyworth-Trickett. "Not entirely. I could never have done this on my own." He put his hand over Jericho's. "I know this isn't how it is supposed to be, but I do not regret it. I regret not saying yes, for hurting you. I hope you forgive me for that."

Jericho nodded. "I do."

"You've already said that today." That won him a smile. Even without Eulalia, Jericho's smile was dazzling, then it faded just as fast as it had appeared.

"I did a terrible job. You were much more composed."

"I felt like a wooden doll going through the motions. You looked like you were genuinely happy and nervous and everything you should've been."

"Do you think it would've been different if we'd planned it and done it in six months' time?"

Nathanial swallowed and studied his shoes. "Without those photographs, we both know I would've made a terrible mistake. That's awful. God, forget I said it."

"It's true, though." Jericho turned and put his back against the wall. "Does that mean you actually wanted to marry me, and you weren't doing it just to please the judge?"

"Of course I did." If not for his father's threats, he'd have said yes that night.

"I thought because I didn't have her anymore…" Jericho glanced away. "I'm a commoner who runs a club that even my father thinks is a front for a brothel. Now you're stuck with me."

"I don't want to be stuck with anyone else. Besides, I'll keep you honest and out of trouble. I got my job back." He moved closer and put a hand on the wall by Jericho's head. "I don't think I've said it before." His lips were almost close enough for it to be a kiss. "I love you."

He didn't need to hear the words echoed back, the heat in Jericho's eyes was enough. The feel of his lips and the way his tongue sought his own said even more. The hunger that they'd each been holding back unfurled. Every other kiss had been with a purpose, passing the angel or for show. This one was for them. Jericho's hands were cupping his jaw and on his waist. The step bit into his leg in this most awkward of positions but he didn't want to pull away.

"I love you, too," Jericho whispered before stealing his breath again.

JERICHO SHUT the door at the bottom of the stairs. Their guests could continue to celebrate without them. He offered his hand to Nathanial who accepted without hesitation and led his husband to his room. It was as he'd left it, in what seemed another lifetime ago.

He'd been a different man then. He hadn't realized how broken his heart had been until Nathanial had come into his life and started fiddling with the pieces like it was some kind of puzzle.

Slowly he undid the buttons on Nathanial's coat and then waistcoat. There was a tremor in his fingers had never been there before. It was nerves. He hadn't been able to be with someone completely in years, and suddenly he wasn't sure what to do. He glanced at Nathanial.

Nathanial put his hands on Jericho's cheeks. "We don't have to go slow tonight. We have the rest of our lives." He kissed Jericho hard, tugging at his cravat and opening the collar of his shirt as though hungry to feel his skin.

Jericho followed Nathanial's lead. He pushed off Nathanial's clothing as Nathanial tugged at his. Naked they tumbled to the bed. There was no need to hold back. No fear of accidental death from too much pleasure. As he kissed his way down Nathanial's body, he had no intention of stopping until he tasted every drop.

He licked along Nathanial's length and took him in his mouth. Nothing could go wrong this time. It was legal and there was no angel between them. Nathanial's fingers tunneled into Jericho's hair.

"I will not last." Nathanial's words were soft, each breath fast.

"That is the idea." He teased the head with his tongue, watching Nathanial as Nathanial watched him. His hand worked over the shaft. He wanted to see his husband spill. That wasn't a pleasure he'd had in so long. To touch another as they spent.

Salty fluid beaded and Jericho lapped it up. Nathanial bucked his hips as though unable to stop. He bit his lip as his body shuddered and he came over Jericho's hand.

Jericho licked his finger before reaching for the oil.

"I would like to try that sometime…if you do not mind."

Jericho teased Nathanial's hole with one slick finger. "I look forward to it." Then he pressed into Nathanial's channel. A shudder of pleasure raced through him.

Nathanial groaned, his legs hooked over Jericho's hips, and Jericho moved closer to kiss his lover on the lips. He'd never get tired of that. He tried to make their wedding night last, but Nathanial was right. It didn't need to be perfect tonight; they could work on that together. So, he let himself tumble over the edge as Nathanial stole his breath.

They curled together in a tangle of limbs. He should go downstairs and make sure that everyone left, but Robert could take care of that tonight. Jericho didn't want to move. He kissed Nathanial again before finally falling asleep.

Jericho was woken by sunlight sliding through a gap in the curtains. He threw his arm over his eyes and rolled over not ready to face the day. The blond-haired man next to him moved closer. Jericho softly kissed Nathanial's forehead, careful not to wake him, content to linger in bed and bask in the warmth of his husband's body. He didn't need an angel of justice when he had Detective Nathanial Bayard by his side.

EXCERPT: WARLOCK IN TRAINING

*I*T WASN'T that Angus Donohue couldn't summon a demon; it was that he didn't want to. He didn't even want to be here. A cool breeze brushed against his skin, and the trees around him rattled like a closet full of old bones. Maybe if he didn't put enough will into the spell the whole thing would fall apart.

If he couldn't summon a demon, he'd fail the class and get kicked out of the exclusive Warlock College his father had forced him to attend. While there was a certain prestige in being a warlock, it wasn't what Angus wanted to do with his life. He certainly didn't want a demon to draw magic from. He had to fail this class. His father would be horrified, but Angus would be free from all things magical.

"*Widdershins*, three times," the lecturer commanded.

All the college students of Demonology 102 started walking anti-clockwise around the circles they had carefully constructed out of will. Angus suppressed the shiver. He wasn't afraid of demons. Okay, maybe just a little. What if his demon was something truly monstrous?

Last semester they'd been learning about the different types of demons and the theory behind drawing magic from one. This semester was about putting that knowledge into practice. Those people with magic who didn't draw on demons were called wizards and usually sold their services cheaply in the local paper. Angus didn't want to be a practicing wizard either. Just because he had magic didn't mean he needed to make a career out of it, and telling his father that hadn't been a wise move. His father had spent three hours railing about why wizards were dangerous and should be banned from practicing magic.

So here he was, trying to summon a demon that he didn't want, to give himself more of the magic that he didn't want either. He let his circle weaken and his attention drift. He would not summon a demon.

He'd have rather been a vet.

Maybe studied medicine.

Although the rich, these days, saw specialist warlock healers who had demons. Though his father sneered at them too. He sneered at anything that didn't increase his power and standing. That he was on the board of the East Vinland Warlock College did not make life easier for Angus.

Angus tried not to focus on the spell, but it was hard not to think about the demons on the other side of the void. Whatever demon popped into the circle would be his personal demon to summon at will. He'd be able to control it. And when it was no longer of use, or drained of magic, kill it and move on to another demon. It all sounded perfectly safe as long as he followed the rules.

Still, none of the rules he'd learned about dealing with demons had worked to assuage Angus's fears or doubts. It was safer not to summon one.

After all, if humans could summon demons across the void, what was to stop demons from summoning humans across the void? No one ever talked about that. Not in public anyway, though wizards and warlocks occasionally went missing. Those who had been found and brought back from Demonside never spoke publically. What had happened to them in Demonside?

There were groups, websites that suggested that demons were no different than humans. They looked nothing like humans. The college reminded students at every opportunity that demons were lesser beings.

Cold balled in Angus's gut as he made his third turn around the circle. He cleared his mind of demons and did everything short of dropping his carefully made circle.

His skin prickled as the circle went pop. The power was there, a breach in the void between the worlds now existed in his circle. *Damn it.* He hadn't even meant to get that far. The lecturer looked at him, his face fixed in a mask of expectation. They all knew who he was. His father was too well known, and his family had attended this college for generations.

Angus couldn't shut the tear in the void without the lecturer noticing. Maybe he could avoid calling a demon through. If he didn't call, surely there would be no answer. Maybe he didn't have a demon waiting for him.

Around him other students held their circles, the forest now full of little tears in the void. What if they ripped and joined up…?

"Now call your demon to you. Feel the energy. There is a link between the worlds, a demon that wants to rush to your side and act as a magical conduit for you." The lecturer's voice rung out, bouncing off the trees. "Your demon that will give you the power you need. This is a very important moment. The kind of demon you call will say a lot about your magical skills and your warlock potential."

Angus wished that his parents hadn't insisted on him going to Warlock College. He really just wanted to be a normal nineteen-year-old guy who was nothing like his father. Not everyone who could control magic should.

The air in his circle shimmered as something came across the void. *Oh, crap.*

This wasn't supposed to happen. He was supposed to fail and be kicked out of college. Failing demonology was an automatic out. There was nothing his father could do. Angus would've been free.

He risked a glance around. Demons were popping into existence in the circles of the other students. A cat-like thing with a scorpion-like tail, that was a scarlips. A hulking purple saber-toothed gorilla. A white-skinned woman with blood red lips and talons to match—a vampry—powerful and dangerous.

Angus snapped his attention back to his circle. A tall mannish creature with elegant black horns and a tail stood there. His demon. He was now officially a warlock. All his hopes of failing and leaving the college fell apart. He closed his eyes for a moment. He needed a new plan. He didn't have one. He'd pinned all of his hopes on not getting a demon.

Now that he had one, he was going to have to deal with it. He opened his eyes to study what he had summoned.

In his circle was a typical black-horn demon. A garden-variety demon, nothing too horrendous or dangerous, nothing his father could boast about. While its chest was bare, the demon was wearing black pants and carrying a rather ferocious looking machete. It was also smiling.

That was disconcerting, as though the demon wanted to be there. Maybe his lecturer hadn't lied about demons wanting to serve. The longer Angus looked at the demon, the broader its—his—smile became.

The demon was supposed to be anathema to him. He wasn't. Intrigue fluttered in Angus's chest. Then he remembered that he was in class, and he was supposed to be exerting control over his demon.

"I am your earthbound master," Angus said, echoing several other students.

The demon laughed, dark and rich. "And I am your Demonside master."

No one else's demon was answering back. They were all waiting for orders.

"That's not the way this works." Why did he have to get the smartass demon? Why did he have to get one that could talk?

The one that looked almost friendly in a dangerous kind of way.

The lecturer was still speaking. Angus struggled to tear his gaze away from the demon. A warm breeze brushed against his skin. Summer had just finished, not that it had ever really begun. There was talk they were heading for an ice age. No one could agree on why, but the top warlocks were working on it. The heat was tempting, and he took a step closer to the circle and the demon. Until one of them died, he was stuck with this demon.

"Right, now everyone has their demon, let's try a simple gathering of energy before we send them home." The lecturer sounded pleased with his class. That everyone had a demon meant that he'd got a 100 percent pass rate. No doubt he'd won a bet or would get a bonus. Not every student was successful.

Angus had screwed up failing the class.

He returned his attention to his demon. The demon stared at him. Angus was sure the demon was creating the warm air but he didn't know how. He had a bad feeling about drawing some power from the demon since his demon was smiling and looking entirely too comfortable. In the fading light, his skin had lost its reddish gleam. For a demon he was attractive in a dangerous kind of way.

Angus pushed aside the thought. He should not be admiring the creature in the circle. Or the way it was so calm. Other demons were obviously agitated, thrashing their tails and snarling. The vampry was picking her at her nails as though bored. Angus shuddered; she was creepy. At least his wasn't creepy.

All he had to do was draw some magic, and then he could get rid of the demon that he hadn't wanted to summon in the first place, until the next class when he'd have to see him again. Now whenever Angus needed power, all he had to do was summon him and tap into his demon. He'd spend the rest of the semester, his life, being entirely too close to the horned creature.

Angus closed his eyes and tried to feel the magic flowing from Demonside. It was soft and spicy like a freshly baked treat that was begging to be eaten. He wanted to reach for the magic and sample its delights.

His demon laughed.

Magic swelled, but it wasn't Angus's doing.

"I want to see what lies within your heart." The demon broke the circle. Before Angus could protect himself—the first thing every warlock learned—the demon grabbed Angus by the wrist and pulled him through the void.

Heat slammed into Angus and then sank into his skin. He stumbled on the uneven ground, the demon's grip on his wrist tightened to prevent him from falling. The air was hot and thick and heavily scented. He wasn't in the cold forest of Vinland anymore. He knew where he was, but he hoped he was wrong.

Angus squinted and blinked against the bright sun. Around him the conversation quieted and then became appreciative murmurs. Someone clapped and a few others joined in.

"Thank you. I was prepared. If a mage of my level cannot snare a young warlock, then something is amiss," the demon Angus had summoned said.

Angus looked around, his eyes dazzled by the glare coming off the sand. Everything was too bright. He blinked a few times. He seemed to be in some kind of market.

In a shimmery blue circle with his demon.

With a small gesture, the circle shattered like crystal, leaving a sharp tang on the air.

Wait…. Magic was visible here? He had seen the circle. Had anyone else?

"Don't try to run, there is no settlement for several days and the scarlips will find you most tasty… assuming another demon doesn't get hold of you first." His demon's voice was smooth and too close. He was still holding Angus's wrist as though he expected him to flee.

Angus lifted a hand to shield his eyes. Beyond the mats of wares, there were colorful tents, beyond them miles and miles of red sand. Red, not yellow. He glanced up. Above him in a slightly more purple sky than he was used to was a fat orange sun that seemed too big and too close.

He knew the answer, but he still had to ask. "Where am I?"

"What you call Demonside. We call it Arlyxia. It is one of the dimensions closest to yours, thus the bleed through."

"What?" Only the first part of that sentence made sense. He knew where Demonside was, and he hoped that he wasn't there. All the talk about demons summoning their warlocks had suddenly become truth. Some of those missing warlocks were never heard from again.

Angus felt that he should be panicking or crying or begging or something, but all he could muster was a kind of numb shock.

The demon stared at him. His skin was a dark reddish brown and glittered as though covered in metallic dust. His eyes were black, as black as his horns. The typical black-horn demon was considered relatively harmless. They had no sharp teeth, or claws. If anything, aside from the horns and tail, they looked fairly human. There was no glory in having a common black-horn demon. His father would be disappointed. No, his father was going to be infuriated that a demon had dragged him across the void to Demonside.

"Aren't you supposed to be an all-knowledgeable warlock? Hmm?" The demon lifted a brow ridge. He had no eyebrows or any hair on his head. "Did your classes not give you the whole truth?"

"Um… no?" None of his teachers had ever mentioned what to do if taken. Not in ethics, spell casting or the theory of summoning, or even the history of demons and their use throughout ancient and classical history. Modern history and the demon wars of the early twentieth century were well known.

Had he read something about horned demons being tricky and debauched? Gaining mastery over your demon was so important so they didn't act up. *Oops.* He obviously hadn't succeeded, that or his demon was trickier than usual.

Nice work, Angus. He could hear his father's disappointment already. Did this count as a fail? He hoped so.

"I should be getting home. My parents will be worried." How hard could it be? Make a circle and open up the void. Easy. Demons crossed the void all the time and ran wild through cities until the college stopped them. He started to imagine a circle. It formed, and shimmered around him, then shattered.

Angus gasped. That was twice in one day this demon had brought down his circle. Had the demon called himself a mage? What was that exactly? Was it like a warlock? If it was, he was in trouble. More trouble.

The demon shook his head. "I don't think you understand your situation. I told you I am your Demonside master and I meant it."

Angus blinked at the shimmery, handsome demon. "You can't be my master. That's not the way it works." He needed to get home. "I am going home."

He cast another circle only to have it pulled apart again.

The demon laughed. "Humans. You have such a limited understanding of magic. You think you can pull us through the void and tap us for power whenever you want. Where do you think that magic comes from?" The demon stalked closer.

"Here." Everyone knew that magic flowed cross the void from Demonside, but only some humans could use it.

"We call it alchemy; I believe you call it physics. Energy cannot be created or destroyed, yes?"

Angus nodded, suddenly aware that there were still people, demons, watching them.

"So where do you think the magic comes from, and where do you think it goes?" The demon crossed his arms over his bare chest. "What happens when the two worlds become unbalanced?"

"I haven't studied that yet."

"I don't think you will. It isn't in the syllabus." He turned away. "Follow." Then he glanced over his shoulder with a grin, his teeth were a little too pointy for it to be reassuring. "Or not."

Angus did a quick assessment of the market full of demons and decided that, in this situation, it was most definitely better to go with the demon he knew if he wanted to get home.

OTHER BOOKS BY TJ NICHOLS

Studies in Demonology trilogy

Warlock in Training

Rogue in the Making

Blood for the Spilling

Mytho series

Lust and other Drugs

Greed and other Dangers

Familiar Mates

The Witch's Familiar

The Vampire's Familiar

The Rock Star's Familiar

Holiday novellas

Elf on the Beach

The Vampire's Dinner

Poison Marked

The Legend of Gentleman John

Silver and Solstice

A Summer of Smoke and Sin

A Wolf's Resistance

Olivier (an Order of the Black Knights novel)

Hood and the Highwaymen

Writing as Toby J Nichols

Ice Cave

ABOUT THE AUTHOR

Urban fantasy where the hero always gets his man

TJ Nichols is an avid runner and martial arts enthusiast who first started writing as child. Many years later while working as a civil designer, TJ decided to pick up a pen and start writing again. Having grown up reading thrillers and fantasy novels, it's no surprise that mixing danger and magic comes so easily. Writing urban fantasy allows TJ to bring magic to the every day. TJ is the author of the Studies in Demonology trilogy and the Mytho urban fantasy series.

TJ has gone from designing roads to building worlds and wouldn't have it any other way. After traveling all over the world TJ now lives in Perth, Western Australia.

TJ also writes gay action/horror as Toby J Nichols.

You can connect with TJ at:

Newsletter

Patreon

9 780648 722809